THE CORPSE WITH
THE SILVER TONGUE

THE
Corpse
WITH THE
Silver
Tongue

CATHY ACE

TouchWood
Editions

TouchWood Editions
touchwoodeditions.com

LIBRARY AND ARCHIVES CANADA CATALOGUING IN PUBLICATION
Ace, Cathy, 1960–
The corpse with the silver tongue / Cathy Ace.

Issued also in electronic formats.
ISBN 978-1-927129-09-8

I. Title.

PS8601.C41C67 2012   C813'.6   C2011-907341-2

Editor: Frances Thorsen
Proofreader: Lenore Hietkamp
Design: Pete Kohut
Cover image: stocknshares, istockphoto.com
Author photo: Jeremy Wilson Photography (www.jeremywilsonphotography.com)

We gratefully acknowledge the financial support for our publishing activities
from the Government of Canada through the Canada Book Fund, Canada
Council for the Arts, and the province of British Columbia through the
British Columbia Arts Council and the Book Publishing Tax Credit.

MIX
Paper from
responsible sources
FSC® C103214

The interior pages of this book have been printed on 100% post-consumer
recycled paper, processed chlorine free, and printed with vegetable-based inks.

1 2 3 4 5 16 15 14 13 12

PRINTED IN CANADA

This book is dedicated to:

My Mum and Dad—who taught me that giving one hundred per cent was all that mattered, whatever the outcome.

My Sister—who loves and always supports me in spite of all my faults.

My Husband—the love of my life, and a man with a good deal more patience than his Wife.

Friday Evening

THE CHATTER AMONG THE DINNER guests was bubbling along nicely, when Alistair Townsend suddenly clutched at his chest, made gurgling sounds and slumped into his bowl of escargots. Reactions around the table varied: his wife told him to stop messing about, one of his guests looked surprised, one a little concerned and a couple were quite cross. All of which led me to suspect that "How to react when one's host drops dead at the dinner table" is *not* tackled in any modern etiquette books.

I was the only one who leapt up, rushed to Alistair's side, and shouted that someone should call an ambulance. Silly of me, really. Any fool could have seen that he was dead before his face hit the garlic butter. I felt I had to do *something*, because everyone else was glued to their seats, agreeing with Tamsin Townsend that her husband was putting on some sort of attention-seeking show for us all.

Gerard Fontainbleu was the first to pick up on my concerns, and he moved to the telephone as quickly as his bowed octogenarian legs would carry him. He barked instructions into the instrument "requesting" that action be taken. The seriousness of the situation only gradually dawned upon the rest of the group.

Admittedly, *my* first thought upon seeing Alistair's rather alarming face-plant into the snails was "heart attack." Alistair was over sixty, overweight and overindulgent. He smoked several fat cigars each day and apparently thought that exercise consisted of meandering from one bar on Nice's famous Promenade des Anglais to another. He was the personification of "a heart attack waiting to happen." Now, it seemed, the waiting was over.

When Alistair's ethereally blond, twenty-eight-year-old trophy wife, Tamsin, finally realized that her husband wasn't "messing about," and was in fact dead, she began to act very oddly. Trust me, I'm a criminology professor, so I have a pretty good idea of what constitutes "odd" under these circumstances. Everyone acts and reacts differently to a sudden death, of course, but what *she* did took even *me* by surprise—which takes some doing. She rushed from the table and returned moments later with a bunch of smoldering twigs in her hand, which she proceeded to waggle around her late husband's body. To "ease the path for his departing soul," she said. She chanted to some ancient gods with guttural names as she brushed "evil spirits" toward the open windows with the smoking twigs. See what I mean?

Understandably, my fellow guests removed themselves, rapidly, from their seats and scuttled away from the table. Before dinner we'd all gathered on the large balcony that led off the apartment to admire the view of red-roofed Old Nice below us and the glittering Mediterranean beyond. Now the balcony offered an attractive alternative to sitting in a room with a corpse. Not a difficult choice, I suppose. Given that the only person I'd known at the table before the party was now slumped dead in his chair, I hesitated before making any suggestions about what we should do while waiting for the sadly unnecessary attendance of the paramedics. But I know from experience that at such a time *someone* has to take charge.

"Does anyone know if we're supposed to call the police, too?" I thought I'd better check. I know only too well what happens in the event of an unexpected death in Britain, my old home, *and* in Canada, my new one. As a visitor to Nice, I wasn't sure if we needed to make an extra call, of if the French police would automatically show up along with the ambulance.

"We will not require the police, Professor Morgan," replied Madelaine Schiafino in her delightfully formal English. I'd gathered from the introductions over pre-dinner drinks that Madame Schiafino had been a lawyer in Cannes for decades, and that one pronounced her name "Sha-feeno." Now over ninety, she was a frail, bent woman, but she managed to maintain a dignified air, despite the unnatural darkness of her hair.

"Please, it's Cait." Away from my academic life at the University of

Vancouver, I don't care much for "Professor." It makes me feel like some crusty old has-been who decorates her office walls with diplomas and degrees. I'm not crusty; I don't think that forty-eight is old, and I like to think that my best is yet to come. However, I *do* have my degrees hanging on my walls—in my defense, it's the sort of thing that students expect.

"We will not require the police, *Cait*," said Madelaine Schiafino, smiling and nodding: her dark, intelligent eyes twinkled quite cheerfully, given the morbid circumstances.

"I 'ave tell them to send the police," announced Gerard Fontainbleu gravely as he joined us on the balcony. His weathered complexion and gnarled hands bore testament to his almost seventy years of tending the gardens that surrounded the Palais du Belle France, where we were all gathered.

Madelaine "tutted" and rolled her eyes, as Chuck Damcott snapped, "Madelaine says we don't *need* the police, Gerard!" He sounded cross, impatient with the old gardener, unfairly, I thought. A tall, slim, sandy-haired American in his late forties, Chuck Damcott had been living in Nice for ten years. Our host had seated him next to me at dinner. After all, why *wouldn't* an American spy novelist, now living in France, and a Welsh criminology professor, now living in Canada, get along? To be fair we hadn't had a bad evening, until Alistair had dropped dead, of course. Chuck had been attempting to "entertain" me with stories about how the Palais du Belle France had been Gestapo headquarters for the area during the Vichy years. He'd apparently been delighted to be able to buy an apartment there, it being so well known among World War Two espionage aficionados. Odd though the topic had been, he'd been engaging and almost charming in his childlike enthusiasm. His rather acid rebuff of the aged gardener was, therefore, all the more unexpected.

By way of a reply, Gerard Fontainbleu shrugged slowly. When he spoke, it was disdainfully.

"*Whatever* Madame Schiafino might say, it is better to 'ave the police. Otherwise they think we do something wrong. Monsieur Townsend, he is English *and* he is rich. There will be an investigation." Gerard spoke with all the authority that his presence at the Palais allowed.

"If *you* think so, Gerard," was Madelaine Schiafino's polite yet curt reply. All through drinks and dinner I had noticed the body language between these two: they didn't like each other, and they weren't new to the emotion.

Doctor Benigno Brunetti was the next to offer an opinion. His rich, Italian baritone made Chuck Damcott's high register sound positively nasal. "I, too, think it is better to call the police. Alistair's death is a shock, but we have our reputations to consider."

Beni, as he'd jovially insisted we call him, was the head of the nearby Cimiez Museum of Roman Antiquities. Somewhere in his mid-fifties, he possessed perfect English, perfect white teeth, perfect olive skin, and probably, knowing my luck, a perfect wife. He was obviously well educated as well as charming, witty, and heart-achingly good-looking, with dark eyes that bored into your very soul. Well, they bored into mine, anyway.

"But Beni," cooed Madelaine, "it is clear that Monsieur Townsend has suffered a heart attack. It was not unexpected. He was an unhealthy man." Madame Schiafino was echoing my own initial thoughts, but she was doing so with all the coquettish charm that a woman in her nineties could muster. Beni Brunetti smiled graciously: I suspected he must have grown accustomed to women of all ages batting their eyelashes at him.

"What do you mean, Madelaine? Alistair was hale and hearty," Chuck Damcott whined, as though he had suffered a personal slight. "He loved his life here in France and took an interest in everything around him. Why, he initiated the whole idea of the swimming pool just so he and Tamsin could exercise right here at the Palais without having to go to one of the local hotels."

"Tsst! The swimming pool . . ." Madelaine hissed angrily at the American.

I'd caught something earlier on about a swimming pool that was about to be dug into Gerard Fontainbleu's beloved gardens, but the topic had been abandoned at Tamsin Townsend's request. She'd said that it was too "divisive" for her birthday dinner. Frankly, I'd been surprised at the time that she'd even known that the word existed. Alistair hadn't dropped the subject without making a final snide remark about "good things coming to those who won't wait."

Typical of Alistair, of course. Selfish bugger. He always *had* to have the last word. As I looked out again over the city beneath me and the sea beyond, I wondered whether I was even sorry that he'd died. I know they say you shouldn't speak ill of the dead, but I'd never had a good word to say about Alistair when he'd been alive, so it would have been hypocritical of me to start now that he was gone. It was best to say nothing.

You see, before I'd gone off to get my master's degree in criminal psychology, I'd worked at the London advertising agency that Alistair had owned. He'd certainly earned his industry-wide reputation as a pompous bombast who specialised in finding timid clients with huge budgets—clients who could be talked into spending more than was really needed on a campaign. Somehow, he'd also managed to coax great work out of several of the most famous creative prima-donnas in the business, so his agency didn't just have huge billings, it also had an awe-inspiring array of creative awards from around the world. I'd worked there for a few years, but, honestly, I'd hated the man (no one says you actually have to *like* the person who pays your salary, do they?) and I could quite happily have lived the rest of my life without seeing his florid face ever again.

Which was why I'd been so dismayed when he'd unexpectedly accosted me as I was relaxing outside a bar in Nice's beautiful Cours Saleya earlier that very day.

"Good heavens, it's Cait. Cait Morgan!" He'd cried out so loudly that everyone relaxing at the bar had turned to look at us. "What brings *you* here? I expect you're surprised to see me! What? What?"

Surprised? I was speechless. A condition which, for me, might last a whole second. I'd closed my eyes, hoping I was imagining the whole thing. But when I opened them again, he was still there. Beaming. Effervescing with fake bonhomie.

"Hello, Alistair." I sighed, resigned to his unwanted presence. "How are you?" Like I cared.

"Top hole. Top hole."

I'd forgotten he did that—talked like some Hollywood version of an Olde English Squire.

"What brings you to our fair Cote d'Azur? Eh? Eh?" he quipped, with a wink. Ugh!

"I've been presenting a paper on the psychology of internet fraud to an international symposium here. I'm a criminologist now." I must have sounded as though I was apologizing—which was annoying, because presenting a paper at an international symposium is a Big Deal.

"How jolly nice. Jolly nice," had been his irritatingly patronizing reply. I'd felt my shoulders hunch with annoyance and I slurped at my rosé wine, which no longer seemed refreshing but necessary.

"Will you be with us for long?" Alistair seemed to imply that my visit to Nice was all about him. Again, typical.

"I leave on Tuesday," I said before I could stop myself.

"Ah, so you'll have the whole weekend with us ... Marvellous! Marvellous."

Not if I can help it, I thought.

"Oh *sweet, sweet* Cait," he cooed, as he insinuated his flabby body, uninvited, into the chair next to mine. "You were *always* one of my most *valued* employees, *most* valued," he'd lied. "I was bereft when you departed for pastures new—I could never imagine *why* ... And then there was all that *terrible* trouble you had in Cambridge ... Oh dear me, yes, Cambridge ..."

There it was! *That* was why he remembered me. He couldn't remember a thing about all the hours I'd put in for our clients, all the boring press stories I'd written, all the successful campaigns I'd managed ... all the money I'd made for him. Oh no, if my face hadn't been plastered on the front page of every British tabloid, accused of "viciously slaying" my boyfriend, he'd never have remembered me at all. Of course, I'd been *completely* cleared. I was never even charged. But I wondered if he remembered that, or if he only recalled the lurid mud-slinging that the journalists had seemed to think was "investigative reporting."

He rattled on. "You simply *must* come to my lovely wife's birthday party this evening. We're at the Palais du Belle France in Cimiez. I'll be serving my *very own* escargots—something I've taken up since I moved here ... Oh, the things I've taught the locals up at my little snail farm in the mountains, you wouldn't believe it . . ." I could imagine how delighted the French must have been to be told by an Englishman how to raise snails. "You'll meet some *dear* friends of mine, Cait! Six for six-thirty. Don't be late! No, no, don't be late! Must be off—got a birthday cake to collect—very special— oh yes, very special!" Then he pushed himself out of his seat and was gone, as unexpectedly as he'd arrived.

As he was blathering on I'd been trying to think up any excuse to not go. A previous engagement? Bubonic plague? Instead, I'd folded like a cheap tent and accepted his invitation. I hit the shower at my hotel and caught a cab. That's how I came to be on the spot when Alistair Townsend died. Given how much I'd disliked him in life, and how he'd bullied me into being there, I'll call it ironic, because I don't believe in Fate.

"The ambulance is here!" wailed the freshly minted widow Tamsin, as though *she* wasn't the one who should tell them what had happened to her husband.

Before any of us could respond to her pathetic call, we were all taken aback by the sudden collapse of Madame Schiafino. Luckily she was standing near Beni Brunetti as she let out a little cry of surprise and grabbed at her left arm. She looked ashen as he helped her to a seat.

"Tell them to come here," called Beni authoritatively, "Madelaine needs help now!"

Of course, *this time* everyone was immediately concerned, and that concern grew as Gerard Fontainbleu suddenly sat down hard and lost *his* color, too.

"I, also, am not very well," the old man stated somewhat feebly.

I was wondering who'd be next to drop, and my immediate thought was "poison." I did a quick mental review of what we'd consumed that evening. We'd all drunk champagne poured from the same bottles, we'd taken slices of sausage or nibbled olives from the same plates, we'd helped ourselves from one huge bowl of salad and one huge platter of Alistair's escargots, and we'd ripped bread from the same loaves. If some sort of poison had already attacked three of our party, surely we would all be affected, sooner or later? I could feel panic grow in the pit of my stomach—at least, I hoped that was what it was.

Clearly, Beni was working through the same mental processes as me, and his expression showed concern. As one of the paramedics attended to Madelaine, Beni's commanding voice carried through the shimmering evening air.

"We must *all* be attended to, and the police must be alerted. I think we have all been poisoned." I hated to hear my own fears spoken aloud.

"Sure—poisoned," scoffed Chuck, then he turned pale. A fearful look crossed his face almost immediately. "You know, I don't feel too good myself," he admitted.

By the time the police arrived Madelaine was being given oxygen, Gerard was having his blood pressure taken, Chuck was squealing with terror and trying to measure his own pulse, and Beni was shouting loudly in Italian into his mobile phone. I was beginning to wonder if I was just getting caught up in some sort of mass hysteria, or if I was really experiencing palpitations.

To top it all, Tamsin was still waggling her smoking twigs about the place and wailing something about the "Curse of the Celtic Collar," which she seemed to be convinced had befallen our group. She was also ranting on that the "Celtic Collar" in question had been stolen. Not knowing anything about the missing item, nor believing in curses, I decided it was best to tune her out completely. I mean, her husband was dead and we'd probably all been poisoned—where *was* the woman's sense of priorities?

Luckily, one of the policemen spoke English: he immediately told Tamsin to extinguish her sticks and he quietened Chuck with some sharp words about "disturbing the peace." He ensured that the paramedics attended to us all before we were whisked away to the hospital for a battery of tests that left me feeling like I'd had a run-in with a particularly bad-tempered porcupine.

For hours I was told to *restez-vous* on an incredibly uncomfortable hospital gurney, endured being poked with syringes, and had innumerable little sticky patches attached to various parts of my anatomy, only to have them unceremoniously ripped off again without their seeming to have served any purpose.

I finally found myself being pushed by two giggling nurses into a corridor, where I was then completely abandoned, still hooked up to a drip that was feeding clear fluid into me and a monitor that had the most annoying habit of buzzing every few seconds. To be honest, I felt fine. Well, okay, I felt very annoyed and quite frustrated, but fine.

My annoyance must have subsided long enough for me to doze off for a while, because I awoke from a dream that involved my battling against giant wasps—some subliminal attempt to deal with the memories of lots of needles? I was now in a semi-sitting position in a large, echoing, grey-tiled room, with the policeman who had answered the call to the Townsends' apartment. He was hovering at my side, peering at me intently, with another officer who was his superior—judging by his manner and the fact that he was in "plainclothes."

The superior officer spoke in French, and the younger man translated into English, something for which I was grateful, because my French is somewhat limited. At any rate, I certainly didn't have the mental capacity, given my circumstances, to grasp what he was saying. I was informed that my various tests had been assessed and that, while I would have to spend the rest of the night in the hospital "under observation," I didn't show any signs of my life being in immediate danger.

So, the good news came first. Then came the inevitable bad news.

While not being in a position to specify, the "boss-officer" made it clear that we had all been exposed to the same toxin at the party, and that this toxin had, in all likelihood, killed our host. *I* could have told *them* that! He added gravely that, until more was known about the exact cause of Alistair's demise, I wasn't to leave Nice, nor would any other members of our group be allowed to do so, as we were all "persons of interest in a case of an unexplained death." I gave them my contact details and was "requested" to attend the police station the next morning at 11:00 AM for an interview. As they left me there on my gurney, I thought to myself, *What a great way to start a long weekend in the south of France!*

Mind you, if I'd known then just how much worse it was going to get, I might have seen being poisoned and becoming a murder suspect as high spots.

Friday Night

AFTER A LITTLE NAP, I was wide awake. You know, the sort of "wide awake" that means you're quite certain sleep is beyond your grasp. All I could do was try to ignore the buzzing machine next to me, *and* try not to worry about what poison I might have been served at dinner. Not easy.

My watch told me it was two o'clock in the morning. Nice is nine hours ahead of Vancouver, so it was only five o'clock in the afternoon there—a great time to get hold of people. My cell phone was in my purse, which was jammed beneath my body, but there were signs all over the walls making it clear that I shouldn't use it, even if I could have managed to get hold of it. Besides . . . who would I call? My mind leapt to Bud. He would be the one to talk to at a time like this.

For a couple of years Bud Anderson had been the head of Vancouver's Integrated Homicide Investigation Team, or Mr. I-HIT, as he liked to call himself. I'd been working with him over the past twelve months or so as a "sometimes consultant." Bud would call me if he thought I might be able to help his team, and I'd profile a victim to help gain an understanding of their life or life patterns. He'd recently taken on a Big New Job. He was setting up a unit to work out the way that gangs and organized crime worked in Vancouver, across Canada, and internationally. All very hush, hush.

I liked Bud and his patient, supportive wife Jan, but I hadn't seen much of them since he'd been promoted—or "given the Gangbusters job," as he put it. A dinner plan cancelled here, a coffee date postponed there. I missed the way he seemed to understand me, and how he supported my not always favorably viewed expertise. I also missed how much Jan spoiled me when I was with them—almost as much as they both spoiled their tubby black lab, Marty. I always got the "human treats," as she called them, lovely little nibbles made of chocolate and Rice Krispies.

As I squirmed to get more comfortable on the unyielding gurney, I wished I could hear Bud's calm, confident, commanding voice. He'd help me gain some perspective. But calling him would have to wait.

Generally speaking, I'm a "rule observer": the one and only time I ever parked in a disabled parking spot, I got towed—typical for me. Both my upbringing and my natural defense mechanisms have led me to try to not break the rules, if at all possible.

So I was on my own. What to do until I was unhooked and released? I resigned myself to reliving the events that had brought me to this situation.

Frankly, I shouldn't have been anywhere near Nice, let alone rolled up in a blanket having cheated death. My dear, but annoying, colleague Frank "I'm not afraid of mountain biking down Blackcomb Mountain at the age of sixty" McGregor, our Faculty's specialist in internet crime, had fallen off his stupid bike and broken his stupid collarbone and his even stupider right leg. So I had been "volunteered" by my Head of Department to fly to Nice to present daredevil Frank's paper at the symposium. Of course, at the time, I'd jumped at the chance of an all-expenses paid break in the south of France. I mean—who wouldn't?

"We'll cover your classes, Cait, and you can represent Frank and the Faculty. You'll fly out tonight, and arrive in Nice on Thursday. Frank's paper is due for presentation just before lunch on Friday. The University of Vancouver will be proud of you—I know you'll do a good job. You only have to formally present the paper and be prepared to answer some very general questions about Frank's methodology. You can read the briefing papers on the airplane. You'll have a marvellous time."

Those had been the words from my boss that had sent me home on a cloud of dreamy expectations to hurriedly pack and rush off to Vancouver International Airport to undertake the twenty-hour journey. Two changes of airplanes later, I finally emerged from Nice's airport bleary-eyed, heavily rumpled, and ready to savor all that the Cote d'Azur had to offer. After a good nap and a bit of a wash and brush up, that is.

If Frank hadn't gone mountain biking, and if I hadn't been chosen to replace him, I'd never have been sitting at that bar sipping a glass of wine in the warmth of the May sunshine when Alistair walked by. I wouldn't have been poisoned, or have been there when Alistair died. Clearly, it was all Frank's fault. At last—I had someone to blame!

Oh dear . . . poor Frank. He was probably feeling even more uncomfortable than I was at that moment: it can't be easy being almost totally immobile down one whole side of your body. For six to eight weeks, they'd said. They also say it does one good to think of someone who's worse off than oneself. Even though I'd been poisoned and was now a suspect in an unexplained death, Frank certainly fit the bill of someone worse off than me. As was Alistair. After all, whatever I might have thought of him—and none of those thoughts were good—he was dead. And that's about as bad as it gets.

I was back to Alistair again.

Alistair Townsend: I had hated him in life, and I suspected I was going to hate him even more in death. He'd screwed up a part of my life . . . well, okay, just a few years of it, while I'd worked for him. The advertising agency world has always been a pretty cut-throat business, but Alistair was much more of an "I'll find someone else to stab you in the back" type of operator. People had their careers ruined, they'd lost jobs and seen their marriages dissolve into chaos, and some had lost their homes and businesses . . . all because Alistair wanted to have everything work out to *his* advantage, and because he had knowledge about people that they didn't want him to share, so they did his dirty work for him. I'd been told at the time, by someone who had firsthand knowledge of such things, that more than one Alcoholics Anonymous group in London's Soho, the heart of ad-agency-land, had members courtesy of Alistair's machinations. And I, along with others I'd known back in those distant days, suspected that he was linked to at least two suicides—indirectly, of course.

Let's be honest, the world was unquestionably better off without Alistair Townsend. As I lay wriggling in my blanket I wondered if he'd "retired" from the ad agency world but had maintained his interest in "secret brokering."

That sort of habit is hard to break—and a skill set it must be difficult to put aside. Boy, thinking of it that way made Alistair sound like a character from one of Chuck Damcott's secret agent books. I wondered if that was why they'd become friends. Maybe Chuck was using Alistair as a model for a forthcoming tome. Maybe the world wasn't rid of the man after all—maybe he would be immortalized in print. I shuddered at the thought.

The policeman hadn't been very illuminating when he told me we'd all been affected by the same toxin. Had we all been victims of an intentional poisoner, or of an accidental one? Had we breathed in the toxin? Eaten it? Drunk it? Touched it? There'd been ample opportunity for all those alternatives. And he'd said nothing. Maybe they didn't know. Yet.

I began to seriously consider whether Alistair might have continued in his old ways, even while living his new life in France. After all, *someone* had poisoned him . . . me . . . all of us . . . Or maybe I was jumping the gun and we were all exposed to the same toxin by accident.

Some psychologists are very science oriented, while others stay mainly out of the lab and concentrate on the observations they can make, and the lessons they can learn, in the real world. I've never liked dissection or mathematics very much, so I guess I'm an example of the type of psychologist who believes that understanding human beings is as much of an art as it is a science. *Why* people do what they do is what fascinates and drives me. And *why* they might have become a victim has turned out to be my main area of focus.

While I'm no scientist, I know that tests take time: a lot longer than the thirty seconds they take on all those TV shows. Sometimes they take days. Given the number of times they'd stuck a needle into me and drawn blood, I was pretty sure that the hospital's pathologists would have their work cut out for quite some time before they knew exactly what had happened to me, or the rest of group.

Or maybe they *did* know already, and the policeman was holding back the information. If so, why would he do that? To keep us all off guard, I suspect.

My thoughts went back to Bud Anderson in Vancouver. I had a feeling that by the time I got out of the hospital Bud would be fast asleep and snuggled up to Jan and Marty (yes, they even have a set of steps to allow him to waddle up onto the bed). I'd have to wait, and then wait some more, until I could talk to anyone I knew or trusted. Bugger!

In the meantime, there was no reason why I couldn't still treat this as though it were a "proper" case. The way that I'd done for Bud in the past, and the way that I teach my students to do it.

The victim (let's call him that for now), Alistair Townsend: rich, relatively unhealthy, retired (from work at least), and living in the lap of luxury on the Cote d'Azur. If what I knew about him from his past was anything to go by, then he'd have accumulated a few enemies here, in his new life. Those people who worked at his snail farm, for a start: imagine showing up and telling the French how to farm snails! Then there was the swimming pool issue: I'd have to find out more about that. If Alistair had been the moving force behind digging up the gardens at the Palais to install a swimming pool, it might not just be the oldtimers Madelaine and Gerard who were against it; there could be dozens of other residents who didn't like the idea. Promising. And what on earth was his wife bleating on about when she said that a Celtic collar had been stolen? No one had mentioned such a thing at dinner, at least, not within my hearing. Or had they?

Maybe I should start by trying to work my way back through everything that had happened that evening, in detail. Maybe I'd missed some clues.

One of the great things about having what most people call a photographic memory is that I can sit quietly and recall certain things, or events, in detail. Now, being a psychologist I *know* that there's no such thing as a photographic memory, and that even the proper term, "eidetic memory," has not been "proven" to the satisfaction of many scientists. To be honest, I certainly cannot explain what I can do, nor, frankly, do I want to. I mean, can you imagine being studied and tested for years and years like a rat in a laboratory? Terrible. And that's what they do if you claim to have a special memory. Me? I *use* what I can do, but certainly don't advertise the fact that I can do it, nor do I mention it at all if I can avoid it.

I've always been able to recall things in an unusual way. As a child I thought that everyone could remember things the way I did. I used to get quite cross in school when a teacher would ask me to explain why I was contradicting something they said or did. I quickly found out that you get a detention for answers like "Because you said something/did something different two weeks ago." It can certainly be a curse (everyone's seen things in life they wish they could forget), but it *can* be useful. If used with care.

They say that hindsight is 20/20, but I've learned, to my cost, that my ability is far from perfect. If I haven't seen or heard something, of course I can't recall it; and those things I *have* heard and seen sometimes get a bit jumbled up. The human mind cannot help but make associations and links that might *seem* illogical, but which come from somewhere deep inside our psyche. I have to be careful with the "knowledge" that I have, because it might be something I have misremembered, or which I have imbued with my own values or judgements. That's why I'm fascinated by the reasons humans do what they do. The human mind is a wonderful thing—imprecise, complex, often inexplicable. I love the idea that a lifetime of studying it will never allow me to know everything. Though the thought that I might know nothing does alarm me!

One thing I have learned, however, is that focusing sooner rather than later on recalling things I've experienced helps me recall them more accurately. I decided to give it a go. I couldn't sit totally upright, due to my "attachments," nor could I lay down properly, nor wiggle my ample rear until it was comfy; I had little else to do but lay as I was. I screwed up my eyes to the point where everything goes fuzzy and started to hum softly (I don't know why that helps, but it does). If anyone had seen me lying there like that, they might have sought the attention of a doctor on my behalf, but I was still all alone, and even the distant clattering of efficient activity had fallen away. I could do my thing in private.

This time I would question everything. There might have been a look that was significant, a conversation that dripped with new meaning. This was my chance to ferret out possible clues to what had happened. I forced myself to revisit that evening, and experience it as though it were happening again . . . the sights, sounds, smells, tastes, and even my thoughts and feelings at the time . . . I would go back . . .

Friday Evening—Redux

THE CAB STOPS OUTSIDE THE tall, black wrought-iron gates. The driver is cross that he has to wait while I get out to push the little button to announce my arrival. Apartment 33. I push, and Alistair's crackly voice asks, "Who is it?"

"It's me, Cait Morgan," I shout. Even as I announce my presence, I acknowledge what I'm feeling: *I hate being here, but I want to be thought of as a good person.*

"Come to the front door and buzz again." Alistair is abrupt. The intercom squeals as his voice cuts out. *I want to run away. Alistair is a horrible person.*

The gates begin to open, soundlessly, and I jump back into the cab. We drive into the delightful, lush garden that sits in front of the fabulous Belle Epoque building. The pea-gravel crunches beneath the wheels. *I like that noise. I have always liked that noise.* The tall palms provide shade to the front facade, which is magnificent: plaster moldings, pilasters and curving iron balustrades adorn the front of the tall, shuttered windows that fill all six stories. The entire building is painted a rich cream. Yellow and cream awnings stretch out to offer shade to the apartments where dove grey shutters have been thrown open.

I pay the cab driver and climb the wide stone steps to the huge front door of frosted glass encased in more black wrought iron. I can feel the dead heat of the early evening sun on my back. I press number 33. Immediately the door buzzes and the lock releases. I walk into to the cool, cream and grey entrance hall. It smells of wax polish and moist soil. *That's a very curious thing to smell indoors.* The ceiling soars twenty feet above me. Palms in massive pots look glossy, well-tended and welcoming. *Now I understand smelling soil.* Ahead of me there's a winding stone staircase, but to the left there's a cage-like elevator. Just like the ones in the French movies. *I love these things—redolent of romance and stolen moments of passion.* I pull open the ironwork door and slide back the concertina inner gate. Pushing the button for the third floor, I feel the elevator jerk as it stirs to life. There's a slight smell of oil.

As I emerge onto the third level I see only one door. Dark, heavy wood. It opens slowly, and first Alistair's head, then large body, appears. I walk toward him, crossing cool marble, my heart sinking at his beaming smile. I sense a hug from those open arms. *Oh no, he's going to suck me in and suffocate me in his folds of flesh!* He's wearing a pink and white striped shirt and white linen pants. His clothes are tight on his flabby body. I'm caught with three revolting, wet kisses: left cheek, right cheek, left again. *Oh YUK! Shoot me now!*

"Three kisses in Nice! What! What!" he shouts into my still-close ear. He smells strongly of heavy, sickly cologne. *I cannot vomit on this man!* On his shoulders I can see specks of dandruff from his carefully styled, thinning, more-salt-than-pepper hair. "Come in, come in! You're bang on time."

I step into a small area with a coat rack, telephone table, and hat stand. Ahead of me I can see into a tiny kitchen with blue ceramic tiles and white everything else, beyond which glows the searing light of the sun on a stone patio. To my right is a bathroom, to my left the open expanse of a sitting room. Alistair's arm, still resting heavily on my shoulders, steers me toward the sitting room. *Impressive.* Dark wood floor; cream walls, ceiling and paintwork; grey shutters; creamy wicker furniture, cream upholstery and a large cream-painted dining table; subtle yet impersonal artwork is strategically placed both high and low on the massive walls; small tables are laden with Indian, Chinese, Indonesian, and Japanese trinkets. *Whoever planned this decor, it wasn't the people who live here— professional job.*

Two stories high, the room's windows must be fifteen feet tall; there are six of them, all with their shutters open and their gay striped awnings opened out. Four at the front of the building offer a magnificent view over the garden, to the Old Town and the sea beyond; the two on the right offer views of the curve of the Baie des Anges, out toward the airport a few miles away and the pretty buildings that nestle in the shadow of this wonderful old building. The smell of incense hangs in the air, mixed with cigar smoke, polish, and garlic. *It smells bizarrely pleasant.*

Tucked into the lefthand corner of the room, which extends farther into the building than the position of the front door, is a narrow, winding wooden stairway. Above it is a gallery, its balustrade hung with shawls and scarves of intricate patterns. Leaning over it is a young woman who seems to be swathed in a similar manner.

"You must be Cait! Hello, I'm Tamsin, the birthday girl," she squeals. *She's got one of those Minnie Mouse voices. Oh sweet Lord, no! It takes me about thirty seconds before I want to strangle your type.*

"Bull's-eye!" I say aloud. *I can be a complete idiot sometimes!*

"Champagne, Cait," says Alistair. It's clearly not a question, as he's handing me a glass.

"Thank you," says polite little me, as I flash a weak smile at him and look back, in horror, to see the Tamsin person literally bouncing her way down the stairs toward me. She's about five feet tall, must weigh all of one hundred pounds, is barefoot and brown-limbed, has a little beaded lariat tied around her long, sun-bleached blond hair, and is wearing a flowing chiffon something or other topped with a couple of long silk scarves and a shawl. *All very "child of the sixties" but a twenty-first-century version . . . Clean, healthy looking. Almost sterile. Fake. I wonder if the deception is carried through—maybe she's even a vegan.*

"Champagne for my little darling, what!" Alistair hands her a glass too.

"Oh, just a sip or two, darling," she replies, gushingly.

Maybe she doesn't drink, I think. It seems that Tamsin's idea of a "sip" is my idea of a great big glug, and her glass is finished in two mouthfuls. *Okay. Maybe she's a lush!*

Having drunk the champagne, she holds her glass for Alistair to take, which he does, smiling. An interesting insight into their relationship. She flings her little arms around me and gives me the three obligatory kisses. She barely touches my cheeks with her lips, but her hair fans my face. She smells of patchouli. *I remember wearing that back in my teens . . . At the time it seemed very cool.* Now the smell hits my gag reflex.

She's tiny. *I'm a big, lumbering giant in her fluttering embrace. I hate myself. I hate my weight. I immediately try to rationalize. I'm about five-foot-four, on a tall day, but I'm what my mum used to call "well covered." About thirty to sixty pounds overweight according to those devilish Body Mass Index things they've invented. Never been thin. Never will be. My boobs are too "fulsome." And my hips too naturally rounded. An ex-boyfriend of mine once said I looked as though I'd been made in the Rachel Welch mold, but they'd turned me out before I had set properly, so I'd spread. I'm pretty sure he'd meant it as a compliment. It was early on in our relationship, after all. No, I'll only ever be slim if I manage to give up everything I love. I love all the bad things too much. It doesn't stop me being on some diet or other, pretty much constantly, but . . . well, you know how it is, right? So tiny people make me feel . . . well, disproportionate is one way of putting it. I have no thin friends. Thin people make me nervous. Like they'll snap if I touch them. Much the same feeling I have around babies.* I feel all this as Tamsin stands back and giggles, like a child.

"Oh, she's nowhere near as big as you said she was," she stage-whispers to Alistair. To be fair, Alistair blushes.

I laugh as charmingly and operatically as I can and say, through gritted teeth, "Oh Alistair, you cheeky thing you!" *You rude old bugger! I hate you!*

It's the best I can manage. Don't let my eyes show the hurt I am feeling. I finish my champagne and hold out my glass to Alistair as though challenging him to fill it again. He looks almost apologetic as he pours more champagne. *But not quite.* He smiles weakly, and clears his throat awkwardly. *Got you!*

A buzzing sound rips through the air.

Saved by the bell . . . damn! Alistair bends his head apologetically and makes for the kitchen, champagne bottle in one hand, his own glass in the other.

"This is for you," I say to the tiny Tamsin. I hold out the parcel I've brought with me. *Another attempt at getting people to like me! Everyone knows you're supposed to take a gift to a birthday party, even if it's one you don't want to attend and you don't know the person whose birthday it is.*

I'm holding out a box of candied fruit because my Head of Department had written the address of a "Very Special Place" on a piece of paper and had begged me to bring a box of the confits for his wife. So I had found the shop in question in the Port area, had been amazed and entranced by the place itself, and horrified at the prices. But, having been educated by a wonderful assistant about the processes involved in making the candied fruits, petals, and peels, I could see why it would be so expensive. So fruits confits from the fabulous Confiserie Florian for Tamsin it was.

As Tamsin rips open the wrapping paper she squeals, "Oh, sweeeeeties! Lovely!" *You sound like a four-year-old. You and Alistair deserve each other—you each annoy me equally.*

"What's that? What? What?" asks Alistair as he re-emerges from the kitchen.

What an odd place to locate the intercom for the gate—I'd have it near the front door.

"Look, she brought me sweeties, darling," giggles Tamsin, holding the little basket for him to see.

"Ah, 'Florian.' Your favorites," he says flatly.

Tamsin is greedily eating a cherry. "Oh, yummy with the champers, Ally," she squeaks. "More bubbles, please." "Ally" obliges. *Why does he let this little slip of a thing address him with such a damning diminutive? Maybe he really loves her. Or maybe it's got more to do with what goes on in the bedroom . . . Immediately I try hard to wipe from my mind the thought of Alistair doing anything but sleeping in a bedroom. Ugh!*

"Beni's on his way," says Alistair. Again, flatly.

"Oh, lovely," squeals Tamsin. *She thinks of this other man as she thinks of another piece of candied fruit.*

"Mmmm." Alistair is almost growling. *Alistair doesn't like this Beni. Interesting. I bet he's more physically attractive than Alistair.* As Beni Brunetti enters the Townsends' apartment I allow myself to take in his physical appearance. He stands about five feet ten inches tall, so about the same height as Alistair himself, but this man is a magnificent specimen. Alistair's too-tight clothes look tacky when compared with the way that Beni's own impeccably cut linen pants and shirt hang beautifully on his well-balanced frame. He's broad-shouldered and quite slim-waisted, slightly muscular; his hair is longer than collar length—it's dark and thick and sweeps back from his intelligent looking forehead; his teeth glitter as he smiles broadly, with genuine warmth; he has slight dimples; his dark eyes twinkle. He smells of leather, musk, and lemon. *Fabulous combination—strength and freshness.* He greets Alistair heartily, kissing him, then booms a fatherly "Ah, my bambino," to Tamsin as he embraces her and kisses her too.

She beams and offers her cheeks in turn, pushing them against his lips. *Very forward!*

Tamsin finds Beni attractive, and Alistair feels threatened. How does Beni feel about Tamsin? I cannot see anything there that says "passion" or "desire." Rather, I believe he feels as he probably should—that, while she might be young enough to be his daughter (he strikes me as somewhere in his mid-fifties), she's another man's wife.

Interesting.

Alistair clears his throat, then introduces me. "Doctor Benigno Brunetti, Cait. He's quite the star locally." Emphasis on the *locally.* "He runs the Roman Museum just up the hill. Have you been there yet, Cait? Eh? Smashing place. Just stuffed with wonderful old things."

"It's a magical place," adds Tamsin dreamily. "Such wonderful bits and bobs. Such interesting stories." *I am wondering where in England Tamsin might have originated. I'm beginning to suspect somewhere north of London, with a few elocution lessons thrown in to take the edge off her accent.*

"Yes. Yes. Quite," replies Alistair absently. He turns to the Italian and says effusively, "And this is Cait, Cait Morgan—she used to work for me, but she's something to do with the police now, aren't you, Cait?"

Benigno Brunetti reaches for my hand, and I offer mine to shake his, but instead he turns my palm downward and kisses the back of my hand . . . where I can feel all the little hairs there standing to rippling attention. *Oh dear. Quite something.*

"Enchanted, Cait, Cait Morgan," he quips. "It's Beni, please." He looks up from my hand, and I see there are tiny amber flecks in his brown eyes, and green flecks too. I feel myself blush. And get warm.

"So you are a policewoman? Here in Nice?" he asks, now standing upright again.

I laugh. *Maybe a little too loudly. I know I am gushing. I cannot help myself. Oh dear.* "Heavens, no. I'm afraid Alistair has things a little mixed up. I'm a professor of criminology at the University of Vancouver. I presented a paper at an international symposium at the Nice Acropolis this morning. I'm only visiting for the weekend. And Alistair happened to bump into me and invited me here this evening. I leave on Tuesday. I did once work at his advertising agency in London, but that was a long time ago." *I am speaking quickly, and I am not being witty, engaging or even logical. I want to shut up, but it seems I can't.* "So are you an archaeologist?"

"Yes, I have been," replies Beni, "and I have also, like you, been a professor, but now I am mainly an administrator. They call me the director. It is a grand title for a person who sits in meetings. But I am fortunate to be sitting in meetings about things that fascinate me."

He is giving me polite attention. *Tamsin is on tenterhooks. She feels she should be the center of everyone's attention. It's her birthday: it's a fair expectation, but I suspect it's not confined to one day a year.*

Beni is carrying a heavy-looking parcel, wrapped in pink. His large right hand manages to hold it easily as all the kissing, hugging, and introductions take place, and now he offers it to Tamsin, who drops my little basket of fruits onto a nearby chair. *I suspect they'll stay there for some time. Clearly Beni's gift is far more important. Tamsin strikes me as having a fairly short attention span.*

"Ooooh, what is it?" she squeals. *Can this woman do nothing but be over-enthusiastically squeaky?*

"You should open it to find out," booms Beni. He's teasing her, just a little. *I wonder if he has children—he's treating her as though she's a child, and he seems to be used to that role. Maybe nieces and nephews? I can hope!*

Once again Tamsin sets about destroying the work of the gift-wrapper, dropping the paper and ribbons onto the floor (*Alistair bends to pick them up—very interesting)*, this time revealing a red velvet-covered oval box. She flips it open. It holds a beautiful silver-backed hand mirror.

"Oh, it's lovely," she coos as she looks at her reflection, all sense of irony lost on her.

"Beautiful workmanship," I observe, referring to the art-nouveau design of a peacock with a flowing tail that is chased into the silver back panel and down onto the mirror's handle.

"Oh yes," says Tamsin, still looking at herself.

Beni smiles at me, and winks. *He gets it.* I smile back, and raise an eyebrow.

"Have you seen the pattern on the back, my sweet?" asks Alistair, almost too cheerfully. *He gets it too, and he's embarrassed.*

Tamsin twirls the mirror in her tiny hand. Her eyes play across the back and onto the handle. "Look," she observes excitedly, "the feathers go all the way down. Isn't that clever?"

We all agree that it is. *Terribly* clever.

All of this I am certain about. Clear about. There isn't that much going on, so I can recall it clearly. *Now* things start to get more complicated.

Alistair hasn't closed the front door behind Beni, and through it rushes a slim, sandy, freckled man, probably somewhere in his late forties, wearing the North American uniform of khaki pants teamed with a striped, button-down collared shirt tucked into them and sneakers. He's sweating and red in the face.

The man looks panic stricken as he bleats in a reedy voice, "Oh Alistair, I'm so *sorry* to be late. I just *couldn't* get the elevator, so I had to run downstairs, and then I realized I'd forgotten Tamsin's gift, so I had to go all the way back up again, and now here I am."

He's a schoolboy apologizing to a headmaster for a misdemeanor.

Alistair looks at his expensive wristwatch for two long seconds, then says quite seriously, "Tut, tut, Chuck. Five minutes late. And you're the one who lives the closest—just two floors above us! Let's hope you're not catching the terrible Nicoise disease of arriving late for everything!"

The man looks even more horrified, but finally cracks a smile of relief when Alistair himself smiles and throws open his arms to him.

Unusual relationship here, I'd say.

"Come in, come in, Chuck—come and meet Cait Morgan. Cait—this is the world famous novelist C.T. Damcott—Chuck to his friends. You must have heard of him. They just did a film version of one of his spy books, didn't they, Chuck? Rolling in it now, aren't you old boy!"

Chuck holds his hand out to me, smiling with embarrassment, his already reddened cheeks blushing. *Not the kissing type. Good. Shaking his hand is like grabbing a bunch of wet cabbage. Yuk. His hand collapses in mine. Weak.*

Before I can say anything to him, a knock at the half-closed door brings the simultaneous arrival of two older people. At first I believe they are a couple. Alistair's introductions make it clear they are not.

"Ah," he says, kissing and welcoming first the woman, then the man, "welcome, welcome. I'll bring champagne while we all say hello." He moves to get glasses and the bottle, which is now all but empty. "You know Beni, of course," he says to the new arrivals, and I can tell they have all met before because of the polite passing of greetings in French, English, and Italian.

Alistair is handing around glasses with an inch of champagne in them. He continues, "Allow me to introduce you to *Professor* Cait Morgan, of the University of Vancouver." He nods toward me as he over-emphasizes the word "professor." "Cait, this is M. Gerard Fontainbleu, the man who is responsible for our wonderful gardens—he's been tending them since 1940, if you can believe it."

The weather-worn, wrinkled old man, whose eyes are barely visible within folds of sun-leathered skin, nods graciously toward me and raises his glass. "And this is the marvellous, the *unique* Mme. Madelaine Schiafino, our second-most well-established resident." He pronounces her name carefully—"Sha-feeno." *I think he has struggled with it in the past.* The woman is clearly ancient, and she makes Tamsin look tall. She must have been a handsome woman when she was young, rather than a beautiful one, and she holds herself with grace and elegance, despite a bowed back. She, too, raises her glass toward me. The two newest arrivals then sip in unison.

They are connected, these two, but not happily. I realize that I don't know why I think this, but I know that we humans constantly read people and situations based upon a myriad clues, many of which we perceive subliminally. I remind myself that it's not "instinct," it's a psychological process that can be investigated, assessed, and even learned and enhanced. I'm a pretty good "reader" and, as part of my training in criminal psychology, I have attended courses that helped me heighten my abilities. It's useful, but, like my so-called photographic memory, far from infallible. I use it—and allow myself to do so at this point.

And from here on I am struggling with a host of memories. Instead of being able to watch a movie unfold before me, I now enter the realm of a series of snippets from a greater work, like seeing tiny little parts of a narrative that not even the best film editor could work up into a cogent, fully told story. It's tough going.

I can recall chatting briefly with the elderly non-couple, both slightly deaf, both using their best English, she more successfully than him. Tamsin takes Beni to the kitchen—I cannot see them there, but I hear laughing and giggling. *Very cozy.* Alistair and Chuck draw aside and have their heads together. I compliment Madelaine on her expert coiffure—it is a work of art and she knows it. Gerard is looking a little lost. Beni joins Alistair and Chuck. Alistair lights a cigar, Beni a cheroot, and the men move to the balcony. We all follow. Alistair pours more champagne. The table on the balcony is set with little dishes: tiny brown Nicoise olives, salty and bitter; slices of dry sausage, not greasy but spicy; little square crackers sit beside pâté de foie gras. *Total over-indulgence—I love it!*

We all nibble and take in the view. Gerard points out landmarks to me: to our right the stubby towers and glinting domes of the Hotel Negresco on the Promenade des Anglais below us; the sun caresses the red-tiled roofs of the higgledy-piggledy Old Town to our left; and the Port area is beyond, nestling under the hill surmounted by the Chateau. I hear Alistair talking to Beni about me. They laugh. *I wonder what he has said. I suspect it is not good. For me.* With his English tested and having mainly succeeded, Gerard begins to talk to Beni in French.

I try to engage Tamsin. *I try again to work out where she is from. Then I ask myself why this matters to me, and I suspect snobbishness on my part. The same snobbishness I hate so much about the English themselves. I tell myself off.* I try again to make sense of what she is telling me. She is talking about how special the area is. How she is living her dream. *I cannot imagine Alistair Townsend being anything but a part of my nightmares, but I listen, patiently.* She wanders from one topic to another. *I lose the will to live.* Beni approaches and she tells us both how excited she is that it is her birthday, that she will be getting a wonderful gift, a magical gift, from Alistair, and that we will all be amazed.

Alistair calls us to the dinner table, we move inside, and he appoints us our places. Alistair is at the head of the table, Tamsin to his right, Madelaine to his left. Next to Madelaine is Beni, then Gerard, then me, then Chuck, who is next to Tamsin.

We are all passing bread from one to another, breaking off chunks and nibbling. There is no butter. We pour olive oil and balsamic vinegar onto our plates for dunking.

Chuck asks me about my work as a criminologist, but I deflect as much as possible. He needs little encouragement to talk about his work as a spy novelist. It seems it is his passion as well as his work. He tells me stories about the Palais during the Second World War, when it was Gestapo Headquarters for the area. He tells me that the Townsends' apartment, the one we are in, was the living quarters for the senior officer. He tries to explain the relationships between the SS and the Gestapo. *I can feel his enthusiasm for his subject, but do not share it.* He tells me about photographs he has seen of large swastikas flying from the Townsends' balcony, of how the local population grew to hate being watched over from the Palais by the secret police. He seems gleeful. *I try to imagine those times, but I cannot.*

Alistair brings a huge bowl of salad from the kitchen, and we all pass it around and eat. *The dressing is good.* We use the bread to mop it up. Alistair replaces the bowl with a huge platter mounded with steaming, garlicky snails, and a round of applause greets its arrival. Everyone comments on how wonderful Alistair's escargots always look. Apparently, he is famous for them. Alistair takes a huge portion and passes the platter to Madelaine, who needs help, it is so heavy. Beni stands to assist her. He serves her, then himself, passes the platter to Gerard, and it finally reaches me, Chuck, and Tamsin. Tamsin takes a tiny portion. Alistair takes more snails, then raises a glass of champagne and shouts, "*Bon appétit!*"

We all drink and eat. There are comments about how tasty, plump, and juicy the snails are. I agree. They are. *Alistair and his hill farmers are doing a great job!* More bread is passed around, more champagne. I speak to Gerard, who tells me about the gardens, and the way they have developed over the years into different sections—Italian, formal, Mediterranean, English Country, and so on, with all the different sections requiring different types of tending.

Alistair and Madelaine are disagreeing about something. Lots of "Non, non, it is bad for here . . ." from Madelaine, and "But it will be good—yes, yes . . ." from Alistair.

Gerard shouts, "It is sacrilege!" He slams his aged fist onto the table. *He is clearly very distressed.*

"Please stop fighting at my party," I hear Tamsin say. "The swimming pool is divisive!" I nearly choke with surprise, but all becomes calm again, and Alistair and Madelaine clink glasses by way of declaring a truce. Beni rolls his eyes at Gerard, who shakes his head in reply. Then Alistair coughs, drops his bread, clutches at his chest, and falls into his plate of snails.

Now . . . now I must concentrate. Who does what? I have to slow down the movie and study each face.

Tamsin: She throws down a morsel of bread and says "Ally! Stop it! Stop messing about!" *Her whole attitude says . . . annoyance.*

Madelaine: She brings her hand to her chest in surprise, almost matching Alistair's motions and says *"Mon Dieu!"* quickly, and quietly. *She is at full alert, leaning toward Alistair. She knows something is very wrong.*

Beni: He laughs and throws his hands up, booming "Alistair! No!" *His face shows amusement, but some annoyance.*

Gerard: He's looking intently at Alistair. *He's alarmed. Immediately.* His hands move to the arms of his chair, so he can rise. He says nothing.

Chuck: He's facing me, with a puzzled look on his face. "What's Alistair up to now—fooling around again, I guess?" He smiles broadly, then turns to look at his dead host.

There isn't one look of relief at the table. Not one hint of guilt. All the reactions are natural, or at least, explicable.

Then I leap up, quicker off the mark than Gerard, and I rush to Alistair. I lift him, with Beni's help. I feel no neck pulse. I shake my head. Tamsin starts to wail. Chuck comforts her, holding her in his arms . . . She pulls away and rushes to the staircase.

"He's gone . . . Ally's gone!" she wails as she runs upstairs. I wonder where she is going, but I am trying to lay Alistair back onto the table top, and deciding if we should move the plate of snails first. I think it best to move it to one side, wipe the garlic butter from his face, and replace his head onto the table—gently.

Tamsin arrives with her damned twigs, Beni suggests we leave the table, and we all agree. We troop through the kitchen to the balcony. Gerard comes out and announces the imminent arrival of the emergency services. Tamsin is last to join us, as she's waggling her sticks about. When we're all outside Beni goes back to make sure that she hasn't set anything alight with her antics. It appears she hasn't. *I suspect this is a miracle.* Then Madelaine collapses, the paramedics arrive, and all hell breaks loose.

There. That's it. I'm done. In more ways than one.

I must have slept then, because the next thing I was aware of was a dig in my ribs and a nurse telling me, "Go home."

Fantastic!

I was pleased to be getting out of the hospital at last—still alive.

Saturday Morning

I HAVE A SUSPICION THAT Nicoise hoteliers are used to seeing guests leave on a Friday evening and return on a Saturday morning, looking somewhat the worse for wear. The relatively disinterested yet knowing glance I got from the guy behind reception when I finally got back to my hotel implied as much. When I closed the door to my room and got a good look at myself in the full length mirror, I was surprised that the reception guy hadn't let out a cry of horror upon my arrival. I know that at five four, weighing one hundred and eighty pounds and being forty-eight years old with greying hair, I'm not anything to write home about at the best of times—but good grief, even *I* thought that I looked a state!

I usually keep my hair carefully swept straight back from my forehead into a ponytail and caught with a long scarf tied in a big floppy bow. But now it was a mass of ends and lumps and knots. Yuk. My clothes, my ubiquitous set of black bouncy, drapy layers, that suits most occasions, and which never, ever creases, looked as though I had slept in it—which, of course, I hadn't; they gave me a delightful little gown to wear—you know the type. My mascara had worked its way down to the middle of each cheek, and the eye shadow had somehow wound up in my hairline. Lipstick smudged my chin, but my lips were completely colorless. No wonder the guy downstairs had that knowing look. Little did he suspect that my state of disarray was not thanks to a session of unbridled debauchery, but courtesy of a night on a gurney. I'd have traded one for the other in a heartbeat.

I put aside thoughts of all the fun ways I could have ended up looking like such a mess, and set about cleaning myself up. An hour later I was feeling much fresher, and wondering what on earth to wear. When I'd packed my sadly shabby suitcase, I'd given thought to "nibbling salade Nicoise on the sea front" clothes, and even "enjoying a glass of rosé wine at a fine hotel" clothes. "Suitable for an interview as a possible murder suspect" clothes hadn't really featured in my planning. I was a bit stumped. I decided that navy linen pants and a navy and white striped, boat-necked, lightweight top would do. (Horizontal stripes, in case you're wondering—because whatever they say about them making you look wider, I still wear them: I firmly believe that people will look at me and think that it's the stripes that are making me look twenty pounds heavier than I am. Ha! Take that, fashion editors!)

On my way out of the hotel I stopped at reception to ask for directions to the police station. It hadn't occurred to me that this would give cause for concern. The guy who'd seen me arrive in such a sorry state earlier on was clearly trying to find out why I needed to know where the police station was. Was Madame well? Had Madame experienced anything unpleasant? Was everything acceptable for Madame at the hotel? His English was really quite good, if a little formal, which was very fortunate given that my brain still wasn't up to much real effort. I reassured him that everything was just fine, that I was in town to speak at the conference for criminologists, and that I wanted to go to meet with the police to help with some research I was doing. He looked relieved and satisfied. He was also kind enough to draw a map showing me the location of the address I'd given him.

I followed the little map easily, but I didn't arrive at the police station until five past eleven—it was farther away than I had thought, and much farther than the map had suggested. I'd asked the receptionist if he thought I could walk it in fifteen minutes and he'd said yes—but he was clearly a hopeless judge of distances. I'd been almost running for the last ten minutes and I was still late.

Having told the uniformed policeman behind the plate-glass divider who I was and who I had come to see, I still sat there for twenty minutes. Waiting. By the time the English-speaking policeman from the night before came to collect me, I'd had a chance to cool down, mop the sweat off my face, and tidy up my once-again dishevelled hair.

"Ah, Professor Morgan, please come with me," he said, as he opened a little side-door with a polite bow.

"Please, call me Cait," I replied.

He smiled and nodded, and drew close to me. "And I am Pierre," he whispered, "but here I am Lieutenant, or Officer, Bertrand," he added with a warm smile, "so you had better be Professor Morgan." He winked and opened a heavily embossed dark-wood door, holding it open for me to walk through. "Professor Morgan, Captain Moreau."

I walked into a magnificent room: a high vaulted ceiling with a deeply embossed cornice, tall double windows with shutters, walls with plaster panels and, a good twenty feet from me, a small man sitting at a large modern desk. His shirt sleeves were rolled up and his greying hair looked as though it had been freshly raked, leaving it delightfully messy.

"*Bonjour, Professeur Morgan. Entrez. Je suis le Capitaine Moreau. Asseyez-vous.*" His voice sounded gentle enough, as he motioned toward the seat he wanted me to use. Polite. He flashed his teeth, but his eyes were not smiling.

"*Merci,*" I ventured, as I walked across the expanse of the room. I hoped this man's English was better than my French. I suddenly felt nervous. Ordering food and getting directions, or even attempting to hold a polite conversation about the weather or the locale, are all within my grasp in French, but a police interview?

"*Parlez-vous français?*" he asked, reasonably enough, with some hope in his tone.

"*Je suis desolée,*" I managed, "*je parle français un petit peu seulement.*" I was pretty sure I'd said "I'm sorry, I only speak a little French" properly. His smile suggested that I hadn't *quite* got it right, but that he understood quite well what I'd meant to say.

He sighed. "*Ah, tous les mêmes, ces Anglais,*" he muttered under his breath. I wasn't letting that one pass!

"*Mais, Monsieur, je suis originaire du Pays de Galles et je vis maintenant au Canada. Je ne suis pas Anglaise.*" I smiled, knowing that I was being a little wicked in pointing out that rather than being English, I was originally Welsh and now lived in Canada. I wondered if he would know, or understand, anything about the feelings that Welsh people have when they are lumped in with the English.

He smiled and nodded. It seemed he understood something. "*Excusez-moi, Professeur, je comprends.*"

"*Bertrand, entrez. Traduisez,*" he called to Bertrand, who was still hovering at the open door. The young policeman, now designated the official translator, closed the door and hesitantly walked in. He stood at attention behind my chair. It felt a little intimidating.

Captain Moreau and I then spoke directly to each other, and we each waited for Bertrand to translate. It was an odd way to proceed, but that's how it went for the next twenty minutes. Through Bertrand the senior officer made it clear that he was making general enquiries into the events of the evening before; that I was being interviewed informally as a witness to those events; and that, while notes would be taken of what I was saying, I was not yet going to be required to make a formal statement, as there had been no decision taken as to whether an actual crime had taken place, or if our party had succumbed to a case of accidental poisoning. He further explained that if he felt that his investigations, and the results of tests being carried out by the police forensics department, suggested a crime had been committed, then I would be required to attend a more formal interview, at which time I would be required to make a legally binding statement, and he suggested I should then be aided by a French lawyer who spoke English.

Nothing like making a girl feel comfortable before you have an "informal chat" with her, eh?

I felt a bit flummoxed at all this explanatory preamble. Well, more than a *bit* flummoxed! You see, I'd been on the "right" side of the law for so long that I had forgotten how being questioned made me feel. For a moment or two I was right back at that police station in Cambridge, fifteen years ago, defending myself against the pretty heavy-handed assertion that I *must* have killed my boyfriend because I was the only other person present in our flat at the time of his death. I had been cooped up in that dreadful place for a terrible couple of days, with the entire weight of the police force trying to make me say or do something that would prove me guilty. The feelings of panic I'd had at that time were beginning to creep back.

I kept telling myself that I hadn't had anything to do with Alistair's death, and that the French police would quickly discover that to be the case. Though even as I ran these thoughts through my head, I only half believed them myself. I realized I was picking at the sides of my fingernails as the captain spoke, and I looked up to wonder if he could read the inner turmoil in my face and in my actions. I was probably looking as guilty as hell! And terrified too. I had to pull myself together. I gave myself a quick talking to, settled my shoulders and tried to keep steady eye contact with him as he asked me to recount the events of the evening before.

He asked fairly predictable questions: Why was I in Nice? Why was I at the party? How did I know Alistair? Did I know any of the other guests? Had we all eaten and drunk the same things? What had been my impressions when Alistair collapsed? Had I seen the stolen necklace?

It was at this point that I dared to ask a question, because I was getting quite curious about this stolen necklace.

"At the time that Tamsin Townsend mentioned the 'Curse of the Celtic Collar' there were people dropping like flies, so I dismissed it—but are you able to tell me what she was talking about?"

Moreau thought for a moment, then leaned forward across his desk and spoke rapidly, his fingers lacing and unlacing as he spoke.

"Monsieur Townsend was planning to give a valuable necklace to Madame Townsend for her birthday. We believe that the necklace disappeared from the apartment some time after lunch on the day in question. That is when Madame Townsend says she last saw it. Her husband then took it away so he could present it to her later that evening."

He might as well have said he couldn't tell me anything, because I wasn't much the wiser. Clearly, I was in the frame for theft, even if not murder.

"So there *has* been a crime committed," I observed, maybe a bit wickedly, "but you can't be sure if there's been a murder as well as a theft. Am I being questioned as a suspect for theft?"

The translation of my question clearly made my translator uncomfortable, and drew raised eyebrows from his boss, who pushed himself back in his seat, smiled wryly and said in a broad accent, "Ah, the professeur of criminology she is . . . mmm . . . sharp, I think."

I smiled back, but thought about the impression I wanted to make—I didn't want to seem to be a smart aleck.

"I sometimes work with the Vancouver Police Department," I explained. "I get called in to cases to help develop a deeper understanding of the victim. It's my specialty. And sometimes I can provide insight in questioning suspects—the more the investigators know, the better able they are to assess whether the suspect is lying or telling the truth. Now, personally, I know nothing about this necklace, but clearly you have more information about it than you are telling me. Should you be 'cautioning' me—or whatever it is you do in France when you are questioning a suspect about an actual crime?"

Captain Moreau nodded his head and drew in a long breath as Bertrand translated.

"Professor Morgan, I do not need to caution you at this time as we are still establishing if the necklace in question is missing or if it has simply been hidden by the dead man. We do not know if M. Townsend was poisoned intentionally or accidentally. It is all unknown. But, tell me, I am interested in the opinion of a criminologist—what do *you* think happened last night?"

I weighed my words carefully, and was as honest, and brief, as I could be.

"M. l'Capitaine, I think that someone poisoned something that we all ate or drank last night, and that, for some reason, the poison affected Alistair more than the rest of us. I don't know if he was the target of the poisoning, or if someone else at the gathering was supposed to die, or if we were all just supposed to become ill. As I have told you, I didn't know anyone else at the party other than Alistair, so it's difficult for me to be more informative. If I think about Alistair as the intended victim, I'd say that at least three people, Chuck Damcott, M. Fontainbleu, and Mme. Schiafino, disliked Alistair's involvement in a project to build a swimming pool in the gardens of the Palais. As for my own knowledge of Alistair—well, I might as well be open and tell you that he was known, during his working life, as a man who liked to have information about people that he could hold over them, in order to get them to do his bidding. I have no idea if that was a pattern of behavior he had continued into his retirement here in Nice."

The captain rubbed his hand through his hair as Bertrand translated. He looked thoughtful as he scratched the side of his nose and leaned closer to me across his desk. "Did you *like* M. Townsend, Professor?" he asked.

"No," I answered bluntly, "I disliked him intensely."

He nodded, appearing to have made up his mind about something. Then, quite abruptly, he stood up and held out his hand to shake mine.

"Thank you for your honesty, Professor Morgan," he said, looking down at the notes he'd been making. He looked me right in the eye as he added, "It is interesting to hear the point of view of someone who did not like the man whose dinner invitation they accepted, and who was the only guest unknown to anyone else at the table. You will not be leaving Nice until we have discovered the exact cause of M. Townsend's death, Professor."

I felt a chill run through me. Good grief—when he put it like that, I was clearly high on the list of suspects if Alistair had been murdered. A stranger at the table the night a man that I hated had died? I saw his point.

I was determined to not skulk out of Moreau's office. I held my head high as I swung my purse onto my shoulder and turned for the door, toward which Bertrand was rapidly marching.

As he held the door open for me to pass through, a thought suddenly occurred to me, and I turned back to see the captain making notes.

"M. l'Capitaine," I called across the wasteland of incongruous, fitted carpet between us, my voice echoing in the large room. His head popped up. "I have just remembered that Alistair *did* consume something that none of the rest of us shared with him."

"*Oui?*" he was clearly interested.

"While we were having drinks on the balcony he smoked a cigar." I felt pleased with myself.

"Was it his own cigar?" asked the captain.

What an odd thing to ask! I thought, but I then gave the idea some consideration, and supposed it was a reasonable enough question, though not something that had occurred to me. "I don't know," I replied truthfully.

"I saw a wooden box that could have been a humidor on one of the little tables inside the apartment, and I know that Alistair enjoyed his cigars, so I suppose, at the time, I assumed it was from his own supply. But I don't know that to be a fact. *I* certainly didn't give it to him, but I guess any one of the others at the party might have brought it for him. No one else was smoking cigars."

"Thank you," was the captain's curt reply, and he resumed his note taking. I was well and truly dismissed.

As we walked back to the main entrance, I thanked Pierre Bertrand for his efforts with the translation. He smiled and bowed politely, assuring me it was nothing at all. I also ventured to enquire about my fellow guests, and how they were faring after the medical emergencies of the previous evening. He looked uncertain and shuffled from foot to foot as he answered.

"I do not think I can do any harm by telling you that only Mme. Townsend is still at the hospital. She was sedated last night and is still being observed. But everyone else has been released, like you."

"Thanks for that," I replied gently. I could see he was concerned about how much information he was allowed to give me, and I didn't want to press him. You see, I was already beginning to think of this as a "real case," whatever the captain might have said, so talking to those who knew Alistair here in Nice, living his new life, was high on my list of things to do. That's what I do ... I learn about victims to help work out why they might have become a victim in the first place.

I didn't really need any inside information from Bertrand—I knew I could track down Beni Brunetti through the museum, and I knew that all the other guests lived at the Palais, so I *had* to be able to get hold of them somehow. And, giving myself the benefit of the doubt, I was truly concerned that the two older members of our group were, in fact, well enough to be at home, alone: they might have been released by the doctors, but were they feeling well enough to really look after themselves? Oh, okay then, I'll admit it—that was just my internal justification for wanting to talk to them about Alistair. Rationalization is something of a personal forte.

Rather than push for more from the young policeman, I decided to leave and rely upon my own investigative skills, some of which I have picked up by osmosis from Bud and his team. I looked at my watch and calculated the time in Vancouver. There were still a few hours before I could reasonably phone even an early riser like Bud, so I decided to fill my time the best way I could and find myself somewhere to eat. When in doubt, resort to food.

Saturday Lunchtime

I LEFT THE POLICE STATION as quickly as I could, and headed toward the sea. As I walked through the busy streets I was only vaguely aware of the sun in my eyes and the breeze on my face. I finally forced myself to become more alert to my surroundings as I was jostled by the crowds pressing together under the shaded walkway alongside the Galleries Lafayette. I decided to head to the Cours Saleya for lunch. I still felt robbed of my relaxation there the day before, so thought I'd try again, even though I knew that my enjoyment of *moules marinière* and rosé wine would now be tinged with—what? Sadness? Not really. Guilt? Certainly not. But . . . something. Call me selfish if you must, but I was beginning to realize that my position was far from enviable. I could end up stuck in Nice at the heart of a murder investigation for weeks!

Okay, so there are worse places to be, and I was pretty sure that they'd be able to organize someone to teach on my behalf at the university—but think of the cost! Good grief—it was all well and good the department covering my hotel for a few nights, but what if I had to stay longer? Who would pay then? I was pretty sure that my travel insurance wouldn't cover "out of pocket expenses incurred as a result of being suspected of murder."

That was a bridge to cross when I came to it. Rather than worry about things over which I had no control, I told myself to get my act together and get myself some lunch. I wandered past the bustling restaurants alongside the flower market and found myself an unoccupied table at one of the last eateries. Yesterday I'd sat at the one with the yellow awnings and chairs and today I thought I'd pick the one with the red awnings. The menus at both seemed to be pretty similar, and both offered what my palate yearned for—mussels. Having missed breakfast, and not having eaten much at all the night before, I was ravenously hungry. It's not a state with which I'm overly familiar, as I like to make sure there's always something around that I can snack on.

I settled down and accepted a menu from a young girl in a white T-shirt, black pants and a long white apron. Yes, I knew what I wanted, but I do so enjoy reading menus. I find I can eat my way through them in my mind, my mouth watering at the idea of all the lovely flavors and textures being offered. I was just enjoying the thought of *loup de mer* with *pommes frites* when there was a polite cough to my right.

"Professor Morgan, Cait, it is I, Beni Brunetti. May I speak with you?"

I looked around to see Beni standing there with his hand extended toward the chair opposite me, and a hopeful smile on his face. His teeth were magnificent. As were his eyes, and his hair and . . . well, you get the picture. Call me shallow if you want, but I couldn't see what harm it would do to allow an incredibly handsome, intelligent, and well-educated Italian to join me, so I smiled back and motioned for Beni to sit.

"How do you feel today? Well?" he asked, his rich tones resonant but quiet.

"I'm feeling fine, thank you, Beni. I seem to have rediscovered my appetite!" I laughed and patted my tummy. "Not that I ever really lose it," I added quickly. I always think it's better to get in cracks about my weight early—that way people get the idea that I'm comfortable with it. At least, that's what I hope.

"Ah, Cait—you must not worry about things like this. Body image is a cultural phenomenon, and it is also cyclical. Because we live in times of plenty, it is fashionable to be very thin. In times of great need it is fashionable to be plump. What matters is health and enjoyment. Eat, drink, be merry. The Romans had it right. They were, however, much healthier eaters than many think."

I was a bit taken aback by this opening. Considering that we had met under what had become such deadly circumstances, I had half expected Beni to only want to talk about the events of the previous evening. He seemed to be quite content to just sit and chat about food—my favorite topic.

"Will you eat?" he asked, picking up the menu himself.

"Oh yes," I answered quickly, "*moules* for me, I think."

"They are good here," he replied, nodding, "but I shall take the pasta with clams. The chef here is Italian and makes very good pasta. He knows the sauce I like."

As he sat there, completely comfortable in his body and his surroundings, I wondered what it must be like to be able to live like that. Don't get me wrong, I love my life, I can sometimes feel quite presentable when I'm all dressed up, and I can get along with most types of people in most types of situations. But he . . . well, he seemed to not just fit into his surroundings, but to epitomize them. The young waitress returned to our table with a notepad and a tray.

"*Moules marinière* for the lady, and I will take *linguini con vongole* . . . tell Toni it is for Beni. He knows the sauce I prefer. We will drink Cotes de Provence rosé. Right away for the drinks, please."

Beni spoke in a low, commanding voice. I was a bit annoyed that he'd ordered for me, but I calmed my natural desire to object by telling myself that he'd ordered for me what I'd have ordered for myself, so what was the point of even mentioning how rude I thought it was that he would just step in and take over? Sometimes I have quite long conversations with myself about such things, but it's not every time that I manage to hit the "edit" button before I open my mouth. Maybe it was the way that his eyes were smiling at me that stopped me from speaking out. Maybe it was just because I was so hungry that I didn't have the energy to object.

"It is a warm day for May," observed Beni as he turned his face to the sun and replaced his sunglasses. I reached into my big, messy handbag to look for my Guccis. I'd bought them about twenty years earlier, on a weekend trip to Brighton, in England, with Angus—that ex of mine whose death had caused me so much grief, and I don't mean grief because he was dead, but because the police had thought I had killed him. Of course, *he'd* called the Jackie-O specials a "waste of money." Spending money on anything but booze had always seemed like a waste of money to him. God—what had I been thinking, sticking it out with him for so long? I reckoned that by amortizing the original cost of those sunglasses over the years, they were now the cheapest pair I'd ever owned. It was strange, and a bit scary, to think of all that those glasses and I had been through together.

"Nice glasses," Beni remarked as I popped them on. "They work very well with the shape of your face."

You may keep on complimenting me that way for as long as you like, I thought. I smiled. I was beginning to warm to a man who knew what I wanted to eat and drink and who wasn't afraid to tell me that I looked nice. I wondered if these were abilities passed from all Italian fathers to all Italian sons, or whether it was more about Italian mothers teaching their sons just how to go about nabbing women with whom they could produce the next generation.

"We should talk about what happened last night."

Beni's remark surprised me. Of course, I'd suspected we'd inevitably end up doing just that, but he introduced the topic very abruptly. I was beginning to learn that this was his manner.

Before I could respond, the waitress returned with a curvaceous bottle of pink wine, two empty glasses, two more full of ice and an ashtray—all of which covered the small table completely.

"Thank you, no ice," said Beni, and she took away the ice-filled glasses. He poured the wine and pulled a packet of long, slim cheroots from his inside jacket pocket.

"You will smoke?" he asked.

At least you're not lighting two of them and handing me one, I thought, but I said aloud, "Not those, thanks—I'll stick to these." I dragged a somewhat squashed packet of super-slims from my purse. I *will* give up. One day. In the meantime I stick to the tiny slivers of cigarettes that are just about half the size of real ones. *And* I don't smoke them all the way to the end. *And* I hardly smoke in Vancouver at all—there really isn't anywhere to do it, except inside your own home, or in your car. In Nice—well, many places are designated "no smoking," but the outdoor terraces of the bars and restaurants are open to the elements where you're allowed to burst into flame if you want.

I lit up and just took it all in for a second or two. There are few things more glorious than sipping cool wine and inhaling smoke while listening to the jolly bustle of the Nicoise markets around you and smelling a hint of garlic in the air—the promise of a wonderful meal to come. For a moment, time seemed to stop . . . and I was blissfully happy. Then I opened my eyes, dragged myself back to the full reality of my situation, not just the fun bits. I thought I should reply to Beni's earlier statement.

"Last night was a first for me, Beni. I've worked on quite a lot of police cases, and many, many academic ones; I've been around bodies a fair bit, and I've even attended autopsies, but I've never seen anyone actually drop dead in front of me before. What about you?"

Was I trying to shock him? Was I just plain showing off? Either way, I didn't get the reaction I'd expected.

"I have seen three people die," Beni replied gravely. "My father, in a hospital bed, which was a terrible loss, and which upset me a great deal, even though it was expected . . . A trusted colleague who became trapped under a fallen marble column at a dig we were working on in southern Italy, which made me angry and frustrated, because I couldn't help him. And, now, Alistair."

He paused and seemed to be searching for words. I sat there chastising myself for making him think I was a completely heartless idiot.

"Alistair's death made me feel . . . relief," said Beni, almost with surprise at recognizing his own feelings. He drew deeply on his cheroot and nodded his head slowly as he blew smoke high into the air in a thin, blue stream. "Yes, relief," he muttered, huskily.

"That's interesting," I said. Aloud, as it turned out, which surprised me, because I'd meant to only think it.

"Yes, it is," he replied, slowly. "I thought his death would have made me feel . . . something else." He looked puzzled.

Of course, all the time that he was puffing and looking handsomely confused, I was wondering why he'd feel *relieved* about Alistair's death. It was intriguing, to say the least. A good-looking man with an air of mystery about him—how dangerous is that? I told myself to be objective, to try to find out more, rather than allow myself to be carried off into the realms of a romance novel.

I sipped at my wine, and simply watched Beni for a moment. Then I ventured, "Had you known Alistair for long?" I had to try to find out more, but gently.

"A couple of years, I think," replied Beni, still seemingly distracted.

"How did you meet?"

"It was a fundraiser for the museum. I cannot remember which one—we have many, you understand. There is a great deal of work to be done and not enough money from the government. I think it was a Primavera Evening. Yes. Two years ago, last spring. Alistair had been suggested as someone who might supply, or donate, food—the escargots from his farm. My assistant contacted him, he agreed, and, of course, he was invited to the evening. I met him and Tamsin at the event. After that, I was invited to their home many times, and Tamsin visited the museum often. Alistair came once or twice. They both liked it that I was able to get them VIP tickets for the jazz festival at the Cimiez Arena. I think that the music was not to Tamsin's taste: she attended because it is chic to do so, and she liked to be seen to be in all the fashionable places. Alistair seemed to be interested in the artists, but was happy to be seen at the concerts with Tamsin at his side."

That fitted with my assessment of both Tamsin and Alistair: a wannabe airhead with a rich, older husband, who was, himself, happy to show her off as the trophy wife she was. A cliché that exists because it's true in so many cases.

"Are both you and your wife friends of the Townsends?" I asked as innocently as I could. You can't blame me for wanting to know, can you?

Beni gently rolled the end of his cheroot against the inside of the ashtray, depositing a perfect column of ash, and smiled broadly, giving me a sideways glance that was almost conspiratorial.

"My wife is gone. She and I no longer live together. She lives in Milan. I live here. It is better this way. We will not divorce. It sits well with us both."

"Oh, I'm sorry," I replied feebly. I swear my stomach tightened at his response. I told myself it was because I was hungry, not because . . . oh, well, you know!

"Do not be sorry for me. It is life." He raised his glass to me and sipped.

His comments seemed very philosophical and wise. Not so very different from Bud, in many ways—but head and shoulders above him in the looks department, of course, Bud not ever having been "beaten with a handsome stick," as he himself put it.

I smiled as I thought about Bud, and wondered what he'd say about Beni. More to the point, I wondered what Jan's comments about him would be. "Oh Cait—I got married to Bud, I didn't go blind!" was something she'd said to me once when we'd been out having coffee and she'd spotted a good-looking guy in the crowd. *She'd* like Beni: she liked the tall, dark, and handsome types . . . which was odd, considering that Bud was quite short, very blond and more rugged than handsome.

My thoughts about Jan and Bud were interrupted by the arrival of our food, and the rearranging of the table that was required to allow our plates to be fitted onto the tiny space. Mussels and clams take up a lot of room because you need somewhere to discard the shells. The waitress managed, eventually, to place all the dishes, and she left us to the pungent aroma of garlic, wine sauces, and shellfish—and the embarrassingly loud rumbling of my tummy!

"*Bon appétit*," I said, deferring to my French surroundings. I picked up my glass and drank a mouthful, before peering into the huge bowl of *moules* in search of a shiny blue shell that looked about the right size to act as my "picker." Immediately my sunglasses steamed over, forcing me to take them off to wipe them with my napkin. I put them back on again. Then I dropped my napkin on the floor, so had to retrieve it before stuffing it into the neckline of my top, right underneath my chin. I know my own shortcomings when it comes to missing my mouth with food, and nothing *ever* has a chance to get as far as my lap, so covering my bosom with a protective layer is the best thing for me to do. Then I found a good-sized shell, popped the first fleshy mussel into my mouth and savored the deliciousness of white wine, pepper, celery, carrot, onion, garlic, butter and broth that coated the plump little mollusc in a totally blissful, utterly comforting taste sensation. Boy oh boy, I *love* good food! I know that I closed my eyes as I ate, and I opened them to see Beni smiling at me.

"You enjoy your food," he observed warmly.

I chewed greedily, swallowed reluctantly, and smiled back. "You're not wrong" was the only reply I was prepared to take the time to make, before picking up another beautifully marked shell in my left hand, plucking out its moist contents with the shell I now held in my right, and placing it onto my eager tongue. *Heaven!*

Luckily Beni surrendered himself to full involvement with his pasta and we both ate hungrily for a good few minutes. As I picked out mussels and tossed them into my mouth, Beni orchestrated the most amazing display of pasta eating I have ever seen—if you want to be truly mesmerized and entertained, watch a heart-wrenchingly good-looking Italian man eating linguine—the things he could do with a fork and his tongue! I kept thinking about the eating/seduction scene from the movie *Tom Jones*. Of course, Beni and I weren't seducing each other, nor were we tearing at chicken legs as though they were bodices and breeches, but I have to admit that my senses ran at "overload" for quite some time. Maybe the wine was going straight to my head. Maybe *that* was it. In any case, I loved every minute of it.

We managed to finish our bottle of wine before either of us had got as much as halfway through our respective meals. Beni motioned to the waitress for another. Should I have stopped him? Probably. Did I stop him? No. "In for a penny, in for a pound," my mother used to say. I'm pretty sure she hadn't had such circumstances in mind, but I felt justified in applying it to the situation.

Despite the overwhelming desire to capitulate to my sensory indulgence and simply enjoy the moment, I thought I'd better try to keep something of a conversation going, so I asked Beni about the mystery necklace. It intrigued me.

"Do you know anything about the 'Celtic Collar' that Tamsin said was missing? The police weren't very forthcoming, and she was wailing on about a curse, or something. It all sounds very mysterious."

Beni's reaction, once again, took me by surprise.

"*Quella collana!*" he shouted angrily, and he slammed his hand onto the table, causing a mini-tsunami in my mussel broth. I must have looked horrified, because he immediately apologized. Profusely, and with lots of hand waving.

"I am sorry, so sorry, Cait," he cooed. "I must not be angry, but it is this necklace. Alistair should not have it. He has no right to 'own' it. I am sure he has come by it illegally. I should have it. In the museum. It is an important piece. It is a piece for the world to see. It has a value beyond being a piece of jewelry! All that Alistair cared about was its monetary value!" His body language spoke of passion and rage.

"*I'm* sorry. I didn't mean to upset you," I said apologetically. "How do you mean 'it is important'?" Now I was really curious.

Beni took a final mouthful of wine as the waitress swapped our empty bottle for a full one, and brought fresh glasses. Very proper.

He smiled. He was regaining control and was more at ease. "Ah, I could speak about this piece for many hours, so I must try hard to not bore you. I can try to tell you the story briefly, if I may?" He raised his eyebrows and gestured with his hands by way of a query.

"Please, tell me. I'll enjoy every moment," I said. With him to tell the tale, a second bottle of wine at my elbow, and my delicious mussels to savor I wasn't lying—every moment was going to be an *absolute* joy.

As he began to speak in his rich, low tones, with his delightfully formal vocabulary and fascinating accent, Beni carefully selected a strand of linguine and started to twirl it around the tines of his fork. Instead of stopping to eat it, he just kept twirling absently while he told me about the necklace that Alistair had intended to give to Tamsin for her birthday.

"It is a piece with a long and bloody history," he began. "Maybe, after last night, it has another chapter. The necklace is written about in letters by a Roman centurion serving with the Second Augustinian Legion stationed in Isca Augusta, that is today called Caerleon, in the late part of the first century AD."

I had to interrupt. "Do you mean Caerleon in *Wales*?" It seemed bizarre to be sitting in the south of France, with an Italian, talking about my homeland, Wales.

Beni nodded. "Yes, the Celts were very troublesome to the Romans,

and they had major fortified encampments at both Caerleon and Chester."
Oh, the way he spoke those names—his rolling Italian "r's" seemed quite
at home with the Welsh words. "Of course, the Roman defeat of Boudica
allowed them to move the Second Augustinian Legion around the country,
but by the end of the first century they were based in Wales. They stayed
there for the next three hundred years then were moved north to build
Hadrian's Wall."

"Busy bunnies," I observed, with a mouth full of bread soaked in delicious broth.

Beni smiled and took a mouthful of pasta. He paused to chew, then took
a sip of wine, and continued.

"The centurion who was based in *Wales*—" when he smiled, his dimples
were almost edible, "wrote to his brother, a merchant living in Rome, that
he had taken a golden collar from the neck of a woman that he had killed
in a skirmish. There were dozens of nameless battles like this at the time:
the Celts would send out a raiding party to draw the Roman soldiers away
from the security of their camp, then they would set upon them. It was a
war that was fought in what we today call the 'guerrilla' manner. The native
population was, in many cases, treated well by the occupying forces, but
resentment ran deep. Pockets of resistance were many and widespread. The
letter from the centurion, itself, did not survive, but we have found refer-
ences to it in the archives belonging to his brother's family, which moved
here, to Cimiez. The archive is at the museum, which is why I know of it.
What is interesting about this necklace is the specific way it was acquired,
and what it might represent. You see, Cait—" Beni drew closer to me, and
his tone became conspiratorial, "the necklace *might* be the only item ever
found that gives the world physical evidence of the Druids."

He was obviously deeply knowledgeable and passionate about his subject. I was puzzled. As he said the word "Druids" I visualized a man with a
long beard, wearing a white robe, leaning against an oak tree and chanting
to the moon. A bit like Gandalf from *The Lord of the Rings*. Or Getafix from
the Asterix stories. I thought I knew a lot about Druids—but I decided I'd
take the chance to find out if what I *thought* I knew had any truth in it.

"Um, Beni," I hesitated: I knew I was on shaky ground, so I decided to give him a chance to fill me in. "Just because I was born and brought up in Wales doesn't mean that I know everything there is to know about Druids, although I've attended a few eisteddfods in my time. Don't we actually, I mean historically, know a lot about Druids? You know—oak trees, mistletoe, Stonehenge, full moon rituals—that sort of thing?"

Beni sipped his wine, refilled our glasses, and began to twirl his pasta once again. Then he stopped and pushed his food away. He lit a cheroot; he was obviously trying to assess how to proceed.

"You are an intelligent woman, Cait." I thought that was a good opening, but suspected it meant he was about to treat me like a child.

"I've belonged to Mensa for about twenty years, so I suppose that means you're right," I replied sharply.

"Ah, you are a *genius*," mused Beni smiling through clouds of cheroot smoke.

"Oh come now, Beni." I forced a smile to cover my embarrassment at trying to impress this man. "We're not having a conversation about my intelligence. You're telling me about the necklace that Tamsin was to be given. Are you saying that it was a *Druid* necklace? And, if so, what does that mean?"

Beni smiled. "You are correct, of course, Cait. I will continue, and I will trust you to keep up with me." His smiled widened as he grinned openly. Wickedly. It was lovely. I mopped my mouth, glugged some wine, then lit up a cigarette. I sat quietly, mesmerized by the way his mouth moved as he spoke and the way he expressively threw his hands about in the air as he enlarged on the points he was making.

"The Romans, like Julius Caesar, and the Greeks who wrote about the Druids and their rituals, had their own political agenda: they demonized them, so we are not sure about the *real* life of the Druids at all. We do know, however, that on what is now called the Island of Anglesey, yes, in *Wales*—" he nodded graciously and smiled again, "there was a stronghold for the Druids, and the Second Augustinian Legion was sent there to break them, early in the first century AD. It was very a difficult time for the people on that island, and the Druids never forgot the brutality of this particular legion. Thus, it is said, the Druids made it their particular mission to defeat the Second Augustinian Legion by a process of attrition: they plotted and planned many of the raids on the legion that took place over the next hundred years or so. Indeed, many of the battles with this particular legion were seen as 'holy battles' by those opposing the Roman occupation, their efforts being blessed by the Druids, and the Romans being cursed. For example, we believe that the Druids supported Boudica in her famous confrontations with the Romans, which the Second Augustinian Legion eventually won."

Ah—Boudica! Good old Boudica! I'd read a lot about Boudica, or Boadecia as she'd been called when I was at school, because I loved the idea of a strong woman fighting and sometimes defeating an overwhelming enemy. I grew up in a poor household (you never know if you're poor or rich when you're little, do you—however you live, it's just 'normal') where library books had been about the only thing I could have as many of as I liked, because they were free. I took full advantage. And so it went for the rest of my life, which, given my apparently unusual memory and my voracious appetite for knowledge, has led to my possessing a wide, if eclectic, range of knowledge gleaned from books. Unfortunately, quite a lot of my so-called knowledge has since proved to be completely wrong, because of new discoveries or reinterpretations of existing evidence. It *can* be confusing, especially when you're talking to an expert with up-to-date knowledge on the topic.

Rather than launch into an enthusiastic conversation about my childhood heroine, I thought I'd just let Beni get on with *his* story and not side-track him. I might discover that Boudica wasn't that wonderful after all; we all want our memories of our heroes to remain unsullied, don't we?

"The letter referred to in the archive tells the story of such a 'holy battle,' and it seems it was a very bloody one. Many Romans were killed as they slept in what the locals believed was a sacred grove. Somehow the wine the soldiers drank had been drugged. The Druids were believed to be masters of mixing potions. They were the members of society who possessed knowledge about plants and herbs, and how they could be used to help or harm humans and animals, and drugging enemies was a popular method used to undermine forces. So this rings true.

"The soldiers could not fight back, their limbs were too heavy. Only those who had not drunk the wine the night before could fight back—or take flight to save themselves. This is what the letter-writer did, much to his shame. He wrote to his brother that it was this shame at having left his fellow soldiers that made him take vengeance on the first person he saw after he had fled the site of the massacre. He encountered a young woman who was bathing in a stream by moonlight, and singing. He was angered that she should be doing something so idyllic while his comrades lay dead and dying, so he attacked her, without warning or provocation. He wrote that he regretted his actions as soon as he drew his sword from her flesh. She lay dying in his arms, and, as he tried to staunch her blood, she begged him, in his own language, to cut off her head when she died and throw it into the stream—this way she would find peace and happiness in the afterlife."

"It doesn't sound very peaceful or pleasant to have your head hacked off and tossed away," I interrupted. Because it didn't. Of course, once you're dead, you're dead. That's it—as far as I'm concerned. Your corpse is still a biological wonder, no question about it, but it isn't something you're going to need again. (Mind you, I've still got the ashes of my mother and father sitting in two urns on my mantelpiece at home, so I guess I shouldn't labor the point too much.)

"Ah, but this is why it is an interesting story," replied Beni sharply. His eyes were visible above the lenses of his sunglasses, and they were aglow with passion. While I might have wished it was for me, I knew it was for this story. I sighed and let him get on with it.

"From the various writings we have, and from our studies of the continuing Celtic belief systems that grew from this Druidic base, we believe that running water, moonlight, and the reciting or singing of mystical odes, or poems, were all very important to the Druids. We also know that women often had a role within the mystical life. The head was seen as the most important part of the body—many stories about how the spirit lives in the head, as opposed to any other part of the body, abound in Irish, Scottish, and even Welsh mythologies—but I assume you know this of your own history." Charming though his smile was, I knew he was patronizing me.

I snapped back, "Well, I've read *The Mabinogion*, of course, and a few other pieces of medieval Welsh literature—but those are mythologies, not histories. There's a big difference, isn't there?" Whenever I'm feeling defensive I slip back into Welsh mode. In other words, I start asking rhetorical questions that don't assume the need for an answer. (In Wales almost every part of a conversation is wound up with "is it?" or "isn't it?" or "shall we?" or "didn't I?" or the ever popular "eh?" The "eh?" thing at least allowed me to fit right in when I moved to Canada.)

"Ah-ha!" replied Beni loudly, which made me start. "Yes, you understand our problem. What part of a mythology is based on a historical fact, and what part is pure fantasy? The word 'myth' did not always mean something bad or made up and untrue, it has also been used at different times in history to mean 'news' or 'history' or even 'a search for the inner truth.' What was viewed by a Victorian scholar as a 'myth' might be a historical fact, or vice versa. You see that, yes?"

Fascinating though all this was, a full tummy, a light head, and the warmth of an early May afternoon were taking their toll, especially given the night I'd just had. I had to get Beni back on track or he'd never get to the important bits—the bits about Alistair, and how he came to have such a necklace.

"Would you like some coffee?" I asked. I thought it might help keep me focused.

"*A, si, buono,*" replied Beni, lapsing into his native tongue. He reached into the air, waggled his hand, and the waitress appeared, as if by magic. "Espresso for me, and for the lady, a cappuccino—"

"I'll take a double espresso, thanks," I interjected. I knew what I wanted and it wasn't a cup of foam—I needed caffeine and I needed it strong and black!

As Beni waved to someone across the marketplace, I took my chance to steer the conversation back in the direction I wanted it to take.

"Beni—listen, if the Roman soldier took the necklace off a woman's body in Wales almost two thousand years ago, then how on earth did Alistair get his hands on it? I mean, I understand what you're saying, but, if it's so important, and old, and rare, why *isn't* it in a museum?"

"Oh Cait, it *should* be, this is what I am telling you. The soldier told his brother he did as the woman asked—he cut off her head and threw it into the stream—and he then wrote something that the brother's record is very precise about: *he said that the head spoke to him as it was carried away in the water.*"

He seemed to be waiting for some response. I obliged by raising my right eyebrow. I can raise either eyebrow, at a pinch, but I tend to let the right one do most of the work.

Beni appeared to realize that this was all he was going to get, so he continued. "The dead woman's head said that a curse would be upon the solider and his entire family until his bloodline had died out completely, that the necklace was magical and would kill everyone who owned it or wore it, unless they were of true Celtic blood."

"Ah," I nodded, "the dreaded Curse of the Celtic Collar." I was pretty sure I'd loaded my voice with as much irony as possible. Beni nodded back. Earnestly. Oh dear. "So, what happened?" I continued, "I am guessing he took the necklace in spite of the curse, then met some horrible end?" Call me cynical, but that had to be where this story was going.

"Sadly, yes," replied Beni seriously. "But not just him, many of his comrades died also, very soon afterward."

"Another battle?"

"No, they died of what the record speaks of as a dysentery type of disease. We now believe it to have been an outbreak of a waterborne disease, maybe cholera."

"Ugh. Nasty. But surely a coincidence? There must have been lots of outbreaks like that in those days." I was *not* going to get sucked in. There are no such things as curses—just idiots who believe in them, and then usually make them come true by their own actions . . . or *inactions*.

"This is true. Though the Romans were very particular about their water, they did not understand about such diseases. They knew how to manage it, how to use it, and how to ensure its general cleanliness. In fact, water management is one of the reasons they were so successful in growing, and keeping, their Empire. But, yes, cholera was common." He pushed on. "As was the custom, all the possessions of the dead soldiers were sent back to their families. Of course, this took some time, but eventually the necklace arrived back in Rome, where the brother decided to keep it hidden, and not allow his wife to wear it, because he was worried by the story of the curse. Then as I said, the family moved here to Cimiez to live and the necklace surfaced in the family archive again as the cause of a feud between the two nephews of the centurion, who discovered the necklace upon their father's death and fought over who should have it."

I opened my mouth to speak, but as if he had read my mind, Beni added, "The eldest *should* have had it, by the rules of inheritance, but, because the boys were twins, the father had written a will saying that his possessions should be divided between them equally. They could not decide on the value of the necklace, neither of them having seen it before and not knowing anything about its history—they were young men, they had no time for reading family archives—so they fought. One died, one lived. The one who lived gave the necklace to his new wife as a wedding present. Within a year she had died giving birth to a son, who, in turn, stole the necklace from his father to give as a gift to a slave-girl he was in love with. Days later, the slave-girl disappeared, along with two other slaves. Blood was found, a great deal of it, but no bodies. The young man was tried for murder, found guilty and put to death. His father killed himself. The original Roman centurion had no wife or issue, and, with the deaths of his brother and nephew, the entire bloodline had died out. That is all that is spoken of in the archive. Except for one thing that I have not mentioned—there was a description of the necklace. It is said to be a gold collar, that sits flat around the neck, ornamented with oak leaves, mistletoe berries and ancient writing, as well as some Latin inscriptions scratched rather crudely inside it that apparently said 'True Blood or Spilled Blood,' 'Before Luentinum,' and 'Arawn Sees.'"

I waited, but he didn't explain. He just looked pleased with himself. So I asked, just as the coffees arrived, "And what does all that mean to *you*?"

He actually looked over each of his shoulders in turn, waited for the server to leave, then leaned in very close to me (he smelled good) and whispered, "I think I know . . ."

Oh good! I thought, but just as he was about to share what he thought he knew, we were accosted by a tattooed young man in shorts and a T-shirt, with a Mohican haircut, lots of piercings, and a rather frightening demeanour, who screeched to a halt on his bicycle beside us, jumped off and started talking to Beni, very fast and very loudly, in French.

I managed to understand that there had been some sort of break-in at the museum, and that people had been trying to get hold of Beni on his cell phone. Beni pulled his phone from his pocket and swore at it, explaining he must not have turned it back on that morning. It was clear that lunch was over: Beni turned on his phone, dug around for his credit card, motioned to the waitress to bring the check, and told the young man he would be at the museum as soon as possible. All this as though I didn't exist. Which hurt.

As the young man rode off, and Beni all but threw his credit card at the waitress explaining that he needed his bill *pronto*, he pulled on his jacket, which he'd removed to be better able to relax in the sunshine, and took his seat next to me. He wasn't relaxed anymore!

"Cait, I must go. It is terrible. They have discovered a theft at the museum. We have lost a valuable vase, some small figures, and maybe more. I must go. It happened last night, they think, but it was not discovered until before lunch. I *must* go. I am sorry. We will meet again," and he reached for my hand, as if to kiss it. Despite this gallantry, I could tell that he was hiding something.

"I'll come with you; I might be able to help," I said boldly, standing and making sure I'd gathered up all my bits and pieces.

He looked taken aback. He seemed to be struggling with trying to appear to be polite and his need to take charge of the situation. "But I cannot attend to you there. I must give my attention to the situation and the police. Ah, again the police!" He rolled his eyes heavenward and raised his hands as if pleading with the sky. "It will be a difficult situation."

I suspected he was right, but I wasn't going to be put off. *Something* told me that I should go, so I stuck to my guns—as sweetly as I could, of course. Initially.

"Oh Beni, I don't *know* anyone else in Nice, and I can't just wander the art galleries and museums, not with a possible murder charge hanging over me..." Was I batting my eyelashes? I suspected I was, though I've never really been sure what that's supposed to achieve—make someone feel sorry for you because you've got a nasty eye infection?

"But it will be *difficult*..." he sounded feeble.

"Oh come on, Beni." I thought I'd just go ahead and challenge him. "There's something you're not telling me. What else has been taken?" I was pretty sure I could guess.

He looked defeated.

"I believe they have taken the family archive that tells the story of the necklace. It was stored in that area of the museum. But I cannot imagine why—"

"Oh, come off it, Beni!" The camel's back was well and truly cracked. "Do I really have to spell it out for you? Alistair, who owned the necklace, died at the dinner table last night; the necklace itself disappeared the same day. Now the archive, the only record of its existence, is stolen from a museum that must house things much more valuable than a humble merchant's family history." How dumb did he think I was? "These are *not* coincidences."

He nodded his head. "You make good points," he said, sadly.

Damn right I did. Unfortunately, I'd made them rather loudly, and heads were beginning to turn.

He held out his arm toward me. "You are involved, you should come. We will take a taxi. Come, walk with me to the Promenade des Anglais, it is the nearest place to find one." He grabbed my hand. Under any other circumstances I'd have been in seventh heaven. He had lovely soft, strong hands and nicely manicured fingernails, with no rough skin, just a firm grip, but all I could do was hope that my palm wasn't sweaty and rush to keep up with his long strides over the cobblestones. I was glad I'd worn pants and flats. It wasn't long before a taxi was whisking us up the hill toward the Roman Museum in Cimiez.

Early Saturday Afternoon

BENI WAS OBVIOUSLY DISTRACTED AS we sat in the taxi. Such a state of mind is useful to the person who wants to winkle information out of someone who might not otherwise divulge it. I didn't want to lose what might be my last chance for a while to speak to him alone.

"Beni—how did you get on with Alistair? Did you like him?"

He thought for a moment, looking out at the scenery passing us by, and then he turned to me and, again, took my hand. This time it seemed that this was a contrived action. I was on full alert as he started to speak; I was pretty sure that as soon as those beautiful lips began to move, they'd start to lie.

"I liked Alistair. He had a real love for life. He lived well. Everyone found him good company. He was a very generous host—as you saw last night: he spared no expense for his guests."

While it was true that Alistair *had* served us Dom Perignon and the very best sausage and olives, and there was no shortage of fine crystal and bone china at the table, his manner hadn't been generous, nor had it ever been, to my knowledge.

"He'd changed a lot since the days when I worked for him," I responded bluntly. "Back then he was a ruthless, unpleasant man, who'd use everyone and everything to his own advantage, never thinking about, or certainly not caring about, the consequences for others."

Beni cleared his throat with embarrassment and looked for an escape. There was none. We were still winding our laborious way up the lower levels of the hill, and in heavy mid-afternoon traffic at that. I wondered if he was used to mixing with people who were incapable of being honest, like Alastair.

"I do not wish to speak badly of a man who has just died. I knew him well. He will be missed," was Beni's politically correct reply. His body language, however, spoke of such inner turmoil that I felt it was my duty to address it.

"Beni—I understand that maybe you spent many hours, or even days, in Alistair's company, and that he might well have shone the beam of his bonhomie upon you for most of that time—he was good like that. Always was. But you strike me as the sort of man who can sum up the character of another. You have intelligence and insight—" I think it's always best to flatter someone into telling you the truth, rather than bully them, "so you must have known that there was another, darker side to Alistair. I'm not saying that he had anything on you, personally, but to be honest, his stock in trade had always been to get people to tell him their secrets, then use that knowledge against them. Surely you saw *that* Alistair, too?" I'd opened the door as wide as I could. I hoped that Doctor Benigno Brunetti would walk through.

"Cait—I know that the death of Alistair is important. He was a man. He was alive. Now he is dead. But I must also consider his connection to the necklace. Cursed or not, it might have led to Alistair's tragic end. And I might be responsible, in part. I did not take it. I did not kill Alistair. How I felt about him is not important, though I can tell you that he was hated by most of the people sitting at his table last night. We cannot bring him back to life, but we can maybe find the missing necklace. This must be our focus. I think that this way we will find who killed Alistair."

"You think it *was* murder?"

"You said yourself that it does not take a genius to link these events. I have to agree with you. Alistair was killed so the thief could steal the necklace. Maybe the same person has now stolen the record of the necklace. This means that this person is not only a thief and a murderer, but they also have a very valuable item that they can sell, with some provenance."

"Would it be easy to sell?" I asked. I honestly had no idea.

"Yes, it would be easy to sell. There is a huge increase in modern-day Druidic-type societies. Even a knowledgeable collector of Roman antiquities would pay handsomely for it. There are no known pictures or photographs of the piece. There is only the description in the archive. And now that is gone."

My mind was whirring. "Could a clever operator make several pieces that were all similar and sell them to different people at the same time?" I'd heard of schemes like this before, but would it work in this case?

Beni considered for a moment, then replied thoughtfully, "No, I do not think this would work. If a person wanted to buy the necklace, they would also want to buy the archive—the provenance. It might be possible to reproduce a gold collar, if you spent enough money doing it, but it would be much more difficult to produce a fake Roman family archive that would stand up to expert scrutiny. I think that anyone buying this piece would certainly seek authentication of the archive."

"Who might they call upon to do that?"

"The greatest expert on such documents is me. But, obviously, they would have to find someone else."

"What about students of yours? People you know in the business? If you gave it some thought, I bet you could put together a list of everyone in the world who might be able to do that. A potential buyer would have to ask one of them. You could tell the police. That might help." It seems I can never stop my natural tendency toward problem solving.

Even as I was saying the words, I realized that Beni himself was as much of a suspect as anyone else at that table last night. If Alistair had been murdered, and by this time I was pretty convinced he must have been, *and* I was leaning toward poison as a method—though which one I had no idea—then Beni could have waited for the poison to work, and then taken the opportunity to steal the necklace while we were all distracted.

On reflection, I was pretty sure he'd been the one who'd led Madelaine Schiafino out onto the balcony after Alistair's death, and he'd certainly been with her when she collapsed, so he'd been in my sight the whole time since he'd arrived at the apartment. Well, except for the time when he'd popped to the loo, and when he'd gone outside onto the balcony to take that phone-call. Okay, there were two chances there for him to have—well, *that* was the question, of course. For him to have *what*?

Another question occurred to me. "Did you visit the Townsends' apartment yesterday, before dinner, at all?"

Beni seemed to be in a world of his own. Possibly he was thinking through a list of Roman scholars, or maybe he was just trying to make sure that he was looking suitably distressed.

"Ummm . . . Pardon?" he asked, sharply.

"Did you go to the Townsends' before dinner last night?" I tried to not sound irritated.

"No. Ah, yes. No. Not really."

I was confused.

"I'm confused," I said, sensibly. "What does that mean?"

"I did go to the apartment. I delivered the bread we ate. Well, no, that is not true. I did not deliver the bread." I looked at Beni as though he was mad.

He flapped his hands around, seemed to organize his thoughts, and continued. "There is an excellent *boulangerie* close to the museum, so I offered to Tamsin to get the bread for the party. You cannot be sure that there will be enough fresh bread for everyone at six o'clock on a Friday. It is a very busy time for people to buy bread. It was risky to say I would buy bread on the way. But this is Tamsin's favorite bakery, so I promised Tamsin I would collect the bread at four o'clock and bring it to the apartment. I buzzed at the gate, but there was no reply. I buzzed for Gerard, who lives in a small apartment at the rear of the Palais, and he let me into the building. He took the bread from me in the entrance hall and said he would bring it to Tamsin. I phoned Tamsin as I drove away and left a message telling her that Gerard had the bread. So I meant to be there, but I was not. Though I was at the building. You see how it was?"

I saw. Suddenly I saw that two people had the chance to somehow poison the bread. Though I was at a bit of a loss as to how someone might do that. I supposed many poisons could be made up in such a way as to be brushed onto a stick of bread. It would have to be a totally tasteless poison to go unnoticed when eaten with such a bland item. That would help me narrow it down. I remembered feeling the bread as I broke it in my hands. It had been dry and floury. Whatever it was would have to not interfere with that finish and texture. A bit of a tall order. Or it might not have been "floury bread"—the "flour" itself might have contained the poison. Hmm. Interesting.

"Here is the bakery now," said Beni, rousing me from my thoughts. I looked up at where he was pointing and saw a tiny shop front, with dozens of cars triple-parked outside it. Yep, it *had* to be a good bakery! No sooner had I noted its name and location than we were turning into the car park adjacent to the huge, open-air site that comprises the greatest part of the Cimiez Museum of Roman Antiquities, and Beni started to shout parking instructions at the cab driver. There were several police cars littered about the place, and the cab driver seemed to become suddenly interested in our destination, and our links to the place. He feigned shock and dismay that the police should need to be at the museum at all, but Beni was out of the car too quickly to be able to answer any of the man's questions, and I decided to hotfoot it after him. I didn't want him getting away from me.

Sticking close to Beni, I was ushered into the museum buildings under cover of his credentials. As entered I watched Beni's movements minutely. If he'd set up this break-in himself, he was a very good actor; nothing about his posture suggested that he was afraid of being found out. Nothing indicated he was afraid, full stop. Instead, his body language suggested "indignance." I thought that was very interesting, and that it gave a great insight into his personality.

The scene was one of chaos. Policemen in a variety of uniforms hung about, seemingly doing nothing; various people in civilian clothes were scurrying around, their reaction to Beni's arrival suggesting they were members of his staff. Beni himself went into full Italian Opera mode— throwing his hands in the air, booming his rich, deep voice around the echoing display areas, and I—well, I decided that, now I was in, I'd try to find out exactly what had happened.

I wandered up to a young man wearing a short, suede jacket, jeans, and cowboy boots. I introduced myself in a way that I hoped would encourage him to accept me.

"Hi! Beni and I just got here. What's happened?"

He couldn't wait to tell me. He spoke hurriedly and quietly, and the gist of it was that the break-in had been discovered just before lunch, but that it likely took place the night before. It was clear that the place had been abuzz with discussions about what had happened, and how it might have happened. The agreed theory among museum staff was that the theft must have taken place at night, otherwise the point of entry would have been clearly visible from the car park, which was used all day from about eight in the morning onward. The break-in hadn't been discovered until late morning because it affected only the office area of the museum, rather than any of the display areas and, because it was Saturday, no one had been using the offices, until one of the researchers had arrived to take advantage of some "quiet time" to work on some artifacts. The other fact I gleaned from the young man was that the thief had, somehow, managed to pick the one window in the whole museum that wasn't hooked up to the alarm system. When I asked why it wasn't connected, he answered matter-of-factly that the window had just been replaced the day before, but that the window fitter had been delayed because he had arrived without one of the parts he needed for the installation. *Oh good*, I thought, *so that happens all over the world then!* The window hadn't been fitted in time for the alarm company workman to hook up the new window.

"The alarm company guy just left the window un-alarmed?" I found it hard to believe.

"Yes. He had finished his hours. For work. It was the weekend. Besides, it was a very small window that only gave access to a little corridor that leads to the offices. All the doors to the display areas are alarmed, so the thief could only take what we might have left at our desks," replied the young man casually. It all seemed quite natural to him. I mean, I know that the French have a really short work-week, but this whole thing was screaming "law suit" to me. Maybe the French just aren't as litigious as we North Americans, though.

"I will sue you!" Beni screamed in French at the end of the room. He stood about half an inch from the nose of a short, fat man in a badly cut suit, who I suspected might represent the alarm company. "This is all *your* fault.

You are to blame. Why did you not instruct your workman to fit the alarm? Why not send someone else to do it if he could not?" I was quite impressed with how my French translation abilities were coming along.

"It was the window fitter at fault," replied the rotund little man. He, too, was angry, but his anger smacked of desperation. Oh dear. Poor thing. And poor Beni. He looked very flushed, and in fact I was surprised his feet weren't beginning to leave the floor, given the way he was flapping his arms about.

"You will wait. I will deal with you later. Now I must find out what has been taken." Beni motored toward a door at the far end of the display hall. I thanked the young man who'd been so informative and rushed after Beni. I wanted to know if the archive had been stolen—that was my only interest. I knew I had to stick close to be sure I could see what had happened.

As we left the large open area filled with display cabinets and artifacts, we walked through a small door into a long, dark corridor. Ahead of us was a tiny window, set about five feet high in the end wall of the building. It couldn't have been more than eighteen inches square. The broken glass that had fallen to the floor in the corridor surrounded a rock about the size of a fist, and the frame of the window had been opened inward and now swung on one broken hinge. The police had taped off the end of the corridor, so we peered into the offices that had their doors open. Each room we could see into was in some sort of disarray. In one a computer screen lay on its side; in another papers had been scattered around the room; and in yet another, an earthenware pot lay broken on the floor; the greatest amount of damage was in the largest office at the end of the hall.

Beni wailed as he looked into the room. "Oh, my office!"

"Can you tell us what is missing, Doctor Brunetti?" asked the policeman who'd been leading our sad little guided tour of destruction.

"May I enter?" asked Beni, sounding unhappy.

"Yes, but do not touch anything, and please be careful where you tread," replied the policeman. I had to content myself with craning my neck around the door jamb to see what Beni could see, but it was only a moment or two before he emerged, looking crestfallen.

"A small alabaster vase that I kept in that niche is missing," he said, pointing to a little space above his desk, "two stone tablets with inscriptions that came from the wall of the baths outside have disappeared, and some papers that I was working on at my desk yesterday have gone." He looked at me as he mentioned this last item, and I knew he meant that the archive was missing.

"Are the missing items very valuable?" asked the policeman.

"Not in themselves," answered Beni. "It is surprising that such ancient and rare objects as the vase and the tablets often bring only small amounts of money. The papers were the archives of a family that used to live in the area. They are rare in that they were domestic writings and were on papyrus, rather than on wooden or wax tablets. But, when I say 'papers' I do not mean it in the sense we would use the term today: what is missing is a wooden box filled with rolls of papyrus."

"The box would have been heavy, and bulky to remove?" asked the policeman.

Beni shook his head.

"And how big?"

"About so big," Beni answered, holding his hands about a foot or so apart. He looked distraught and asked the officer, "What else is missing?"

The policeman referred to his notes and replied, "Apart from your box, tablets, and vase, a statue of Aphrodite has gone from this office," he turned and pointed behind him, "and a pair of . . . ummm . . ." He struggled a bit as he said, ". . . millefiori pyxis?"

Beni nodded. "The ink-wells. I know them. Small and, again, not very valuable. Is that it?"

"Yes," replied the policeman. "It seems that the thieves did not gain access to any of the other areas. The alarm was not tripped, and there appear to be no attempts to reach anywhere other than this part of the complex. They took small items that could be easily removed. It looks like a crime of opportunity. Your colleagues have all told me that the offices with the disturbances were not locked. Did you lock your own office when you left here yesterday?"

"I thought that I did," answered Beni slowly, "but I had a lot on my mind, so maybe I did not."

"It does not look as though the door was broken," added the policemen significantly.

"Then maybe I did not," replied Beni quietly.

"Sir—outside, they have found something," came a shout from a young policeman at the other end of the corridor.

"What is it?" asked the more senior officer.

"Some sort of wooden box, sir. It looks as though it has been discarded in the parking area."

Immediately I saw a brighter look appear on Beni's face and he mouthed "The archives," at me. I, too, wondered if that might be what they'd found.

"We will come," replied the policeman, and we all retraced our steps back toward the display hall, then out through the fire exit to the parking area. Beni was clearly excited, and trotted ahead of the policeman, to where a little knot of uniformed officers were gathered around a large recycling bin.

"In here, sir," said one of the men to his superior, nodding toward the bin, then opening its lid with latex-gloved hands.

We all arrived at much the same time and peered into the receptacle. Sure enough, inside was a large wooden box, bound with metal strips, with the lid levered off and discarded at its side. The box was empty.

"The scrolls . . . has anyone found the scrolls?" asked Beni sharply.

"We haven't examined the other contents of the bin yet, sir," the young officer replied.

Beni's voice was commanding. "When you do, please be very careful. If the scrolls are in there they are delicate and could break apart easily."

The young officer looked at his superior who nodded back, obviously signifying that the search should begin.

"We will let you know what we find, Doctor Brunetti," said the superior officer. "But now, could I ask you to come back inside with me so I can get some more details from you about the items that are missing?"

"Yes, yes of course," replied Beni, "but maybe we could sit in the sun and smoke while we do that?"

The policeman smiled and nodded. Having moved to a low wall that surrounded the parking area, both sat and smoked as Beni spoke and the policemen took notes. When Beni had turned to leave, I'd gestured to him to show that I was going to make a phone call. I was of half a mind to call Captain Moreau to tell him about the theft of the archive, but, since it might be sitting in a big plastic bin just yards away from me, I thought that I should wait until we were sure. I decided to call Bud instead. It would be about seven in the morning in Vancouver, still early for a Saturday morning phone call. I knew for a fact that he and Jan were always up at six with Marty because dogs don't know it's a weekend. Besides, he called me at all hours when there was a case he needed my help with. I wandered off to another part of the little wall and turned my face to the afternoon sun. I pulled my phone and my cigarettes out of my purse, which I dumped on the floor at my feet, lit up, and punched in Bud's number. To hell with the roaming charges—I needed to talk to someone about all this, and Bud Anderson was just the man.

Late Saturday Afternoon

I IMAGINED THE PHONE RINGING in the Anderson household. Bud and Jan's two-bedroom apartment on Quayside Drive in New Westminster wasn't small, but it struggled to accommodate two busy adults and a very rambunctious Labrador. It always felt as though it was ready to burst at the seams. Funny, that. Bud was known as a stickler for neatness, accurate record keeping, and meticulous attention to detail in his work as a police officer. Jan, on the other hand, seemed to have lots of hobbies that required large quantities of "stuff." She belonged to groups that did scrapbooking, weaving, quilting, candle-making, soap-making, knitting and photography, and probably a lot more. It made for a snug home.

They had loved their place since the moment they'd first seen it, right on the riverfront, with great walks for the three of them on the doorstep, as well as a fantastic view of the "Mighty Fraser River," as Monty Python once famously put it. And at night, you could see the lights of the city beyond. It provided Bud with a relatively short commute to Downtown Vancouver—where his new office was based. I knew that he'd accepted his new job as "Head Gangbuster" on the basis that it was likely to offer slightly more regular hours than his last position. When you head up a murder investigation team, you know that murder won't wait; it has to be dealt with whatever the hour. Longer term investigations into gang affiliations and drug routes can, apparently, be managed more within what the rest of the working world thinks of as "normal office hours."

The phone rang for the fifth time before Jan's breathless voice answered.

"Yes—who is it?" she panted.

"Hi Jan, it's me, Cait. Sorry to bother you so early on a Saturday, but I guess Marty has you up and about already, eh?"

"Oh, you're not kidding! He's all over me right now to take him out. It should be Bud's turn, but he's off on some urgent call. My morning off has turned into an extra walk with Marty this week. Never mind. I'm meeting some friends down at Crescent Beach for coffee today, so I'll take Marty with me and he can have a long run on the sand. Then he can sleep while we girls catch up on all the gossip. I hope Bud took the car and left the truck for me. Marty prefers the truck—more space for him in the back seats than in the car."

Jan always referred to herself as a "girl." Her friends too. To be fair, she's only six years older than me, so she's not "old," but I'd run into her and her "girlfriends" in Kitsilano once, and had been delighted to find that Jan was the baby of the group, at fifty-four, and the oldest "girl" was approaching seventy! Mind you, they were a fit bunch; they only sat and chatted for a "coffee and a gossip" after walking about three miles.

"So Bud's gone already?" I was disappointed. I could have called earlier, after all.

"Yes, long gone, but he's driving out to Chilliwack, so he'll be on the road for a while yet. You could call him on his cell. It's him you're after, I guess?"

I only knew Jan because she was Bud's wife, but I liked her a great deal. I'm a natural loner, so I shy away from any sorts of gatherings that I don't *absolutely* have to attend. To be honest, the idea of spending time with a bunch of women, the way Jan does, fills me with horror. So, even though Jan and I always got along really well, we hadn't really clicked. No reflection on her. Just me. We both knew it. The only time I ever called was to talk to Bud. I hadn't anything to talk to Jan *about* except Bud, his work, my work . . . oh, and Marty. He and I seemed to have struck up a friendship on first meeting, and it was tough to resist his unquestioning enthusiasm and affection. Especially since he didn't require me to engage in conversation!

"Yes, you're right—it's Bud I was looking for. I'll try his cell. Thanks, Jan—talk soon . . ."

"Well, aren't you coming next week?" she asked.

I wracked my brain. Next week? What was happening next week? I paused as I thought. She noticed and jumped in.

"Next Saturday—a week today—it's Bud's get together at the old office. Remember? They're doing it now because they couldn't do it when he left because of that big case on the Downtown Eastside, then MacMillan was off on leave for a month, then Bud was off on that big 'fact-finding' thing . . . So it's next Saturday. Terminal City Club. Six-thirty for seven. You will be there, right? You said you would, and it'll be great to catch up . . . It's been an age since I saw you, Cait. You haven't forgotten, right?"

"No, Jan, I haven't forgotten, and I'll do my best to be there. It's just that, well, I'm a bit stuck at the moment . . ." I *had* forgotten. What to say? What not to say? "I'll do my best. But I can't leave Nice right now."

"What? Did you say 'Nice'?" Jan sounded puzzled. Not surprising.

"Well, that's what I want to talk to Bud about. You see, the university sent me to Nice to present a sick colleague's research paper at a criminology symposium, and I ran into an old boss of mine and ended up being at a birthday party he was giving, where he died. I think we were *all* poisoned, and now I'm a suspect in a murder case. Oh, and an ancient Druid necklace has been stolen . . . and there's this really gorgeous Italian professor who's the director of the Roman museum here who took me out to lunch, but then the museum was burgled . . ." It all sounded a bit far-fetched when I put it that way.

"Oh, Cait my dear, this could only happen to you, eh? That house party in Kelowna last year where you were snowed in with the dead body of that romance novelist? Now this! Only *you* could go to the south of France and get caught up in a murder. I can quite see that you'd want to talk to Bud—so you do that, and I'll take Marty out for a quick pee . . . he'll give me no peace until he's relieved himself and had his food, then we can get ourselves ready and set off for a good long beachy walk! Tell Bud I'll call him when I'm on my way back from Crescent Beach. Maybe by then he'll have some idea of how long he'll be out in the wilds of Chilli-wack-wack-wack."

"Chilli-wack-wack-wack?" I was puzzled.

"Yeah—they call it that because of all the 'whacking' that goes on out there—a lot of killings this past year, Bud says. More than usual. Seems it's working its way out into the Valley from Abbotsford and Mission. I don't know, Cait, the world is changing so fast. Now that Bud's working on this gang stuff . . . well . . . it *feels* different . . . I don't know how to explain it . . . It used to be he'd come home and talk about some terrible murders—but they weren't like the stuff he's working on now."

"How d'you mean?"

"Well, it's real sad when someone is murdered, of course, but so often he would be dealing with a killing resulting from a fight that got out of hand, or a crime of passion, or something that happened in the heat of the moment. This gang stuff . . . It's all so businesslike . . . so planned. I know you guys haven't been working on it together, because I guess they don't need a victimologist when they know exactly who the victim was and why they were killed—they usually know exactly who's done it too. That's the other thing, Cait. I know the hours are better, and there's more opportunity for us to plan time for ourselves and be more of a couple, but he's getting so frustrated. Already! He's only been at it two minutes, but already he can't cope with how tough it is to pin anything on these guys. He just keeps pushing and pushing. In fact, I think that's where he's gone now: they've been watching some group out in the Valley that's up to its ears in marijuana grow-ops and guns, so it sounds like they might be about to swoop. But there, I'm the last to know. Typical that they'd decide to do it first thing on a Saturday morning!"

Lovely though it was to talk to Jan, I really wanted to get hold of Bud.

"Yeah, bummer, Jan. He'll probably be home soon so you guys can have a nice walk later on with Marty, then G&Ts to watch the sun go down—"

"Sun? Sun? Oh, of course, you're not here! The weather here is pretty grim. It might be early May but you'd think it was November. Still, Marty and I can move at quite a pace, so we'll wrap up warm and march on. Go on now, call Bud. And take care of yourself. I know you're bright Cait, but you sure do know how to get yourself into some trouble! Oh—and watch out for that Italian. Yes, I heard what you said, and I'm guessing he's gorgeous . . . So watch that heart of yours, madam—take it right off your sleeve and pop it into an inside pocket, where it's safe. Make sure you're back for Bud's party. It wouldn't be the same without you. Bye . . . Marty's got his leash in his mouth—I am about to be taken for a walk!" And she was gone.

I looked around and could see that Beni was still closely engaged with the policeman. Jan and I had only spoken for a few moments, so I still had ample time to call Bud, which I did immediately.

"Hello Cait—how are you? And what are you doing up at this hour?" was his jovial reply. He was clearly using the speakerphone in his car.

"I'm not there. I'm in Nice. South of France. It's gone three in the afternoon here. How are you?" I thought I'd get the pleasantries done with before I blurted out my sorry tale.

"I'm good, thanks Cait. Did you speak to Jan?"

"Yep. She told me where you were. On your way to Chilliwack, I hear."

"Yeah. I'm about half an hour away. So we can chat. Haven't seen you in a while, Cait. I miss working with you, you know."

"Yeah. Right."

"No. Seriously, I do. You can be fun to have around. Pleasant change from the usual lot. You see things so differently. Sadly, we know only too well what we're going to face in this gig. I'm afraid that all those 'consultancy fees' are a thing of the past, my Deario." I liked it when he called me his "Deario": it made me sound like a small child, and him like my grandfather . . . though, like Jan, he was in fact only six years my senior. "If you're in France and you're calling *me*, I'm guessing you're in some sort of trouble that Uncle Bud might be able to help with—would that be right?"

I took a deep breath, then began to relate the events of the last couple of days. Briefly. But with all the necessary details. It took a little while, but it went quicker because Bud didn't interrupt. "So there you have it. The archive might have gone, the necklace might have gone, Alistair has *definitely* gone, and I am most definitely *not* going anywhere!"

"You know, I don't think we should let you out on your own," were Bud's first words.

"Thanks, Bud. I appreciate the vote of confidence," I replied sullenly.

"Okay, so there are a few things I might be able to help with," he added. "I can certainly call the lead detective, Moreau, as one cop to another, and fill him in about you. They shouldn't be allowed to think of you as a real suspect, because it'll take their efforts away from finding the real perp. So that'll help them, and it'll help you ..."

"Oh no, Bud—please don't do that ..."

"Yes—I *will* do that, Cait, and, given that my French is a whole lot better than yours, I'll be able to do it directly on the phone with the guy himself—so when we're done, you call me back immediately and leave a message with his number, 'cause I can't write it down while I'm driving—right?"

I capitulated. He was right. "Yes, I will. Of course, you're right, Bud. Thanks."

"You're welcome. Next, I can give you my opinion about what you've told me."

"Great. Thanks, Bud. So what do you think?"

"It'll come as no surprise to you that I think that you *were* all poisoned at the party, and that *that* means whoever did it either gave Alistair an extra dose of the poison, or was sure that the same amount for all would affect Alistair more—so you need to find out if he was on any medications, what else he ate or drank that day, where and when, and if the stuff in his system was stronger than what was in your system. Hopefully, when I've spoken to him, the captain guy will take you into his confidence."

"Well ... he didn't seem to be a particularly *warm* character, Bud," I added hesitantly.

"Look, Cait—and don't take this personally—I know how defensive you can get—"

"I do *not* get defensive, Bud!" As I heard myself whine, I knew I was proving his point for him. Bugger!

"Hmmmm ... well, *whatever* you might bleat at me, my Deario, you must realize that the cop was looking at you as a possible murderer. He doesn't know you from a hole in the ground, and you're the only character on the scene who arrived, out of the blue, on the day the Townsend guy shows up dead. You have to admit, the optics are bad. See it from his point of view. Who else is in the frame? An old couple—"

"No, Madelaine and Gerard are not a *couple* ... most definitely *not* a couple," I interjected. I didn't want Bud getting the wrong impression.

"Okay, then—in this case the immediate suspects are an old man and an old woman, neither of them overly mobile and, presumably, they're well known in the area and they've had many chances before to kill Alistair. The dead man's wife—who you've painted as a dotty airhead, who may or may not have the wits about her to be an honest to goodness gold-digger. There's a world famous American author, who fawned on the dead man. Oh, and just one more pillar of the community—the director of the local museum! Not very promising as a list of suspects when running against a criminology professor who hated the victim and is visiting town on the very weekend when he drops dead, eh?"

"Oh Bud . . . don't put it like that."

"No Cait, *I'm* not putting it like that—but I am guessing that that's just how that captain saw it. Like I say—I'll talk to him about you, then we can get on with thinking about the others. You know what you should do?"

"I don't know—do my 'thing' on Alistair?"

"If by that you mean work up a victim profile on your old boss, then, yes, that's what I mean. I know you knew him once, Cait, but things might have changed."

"I doubt it . . ." I mumbled.

"Cait—don't do it! Don't let your judgmentalism cloud your objectivity. You have to find out about Townsend as he was, there, in Nice, now. Unless you think it's something from his earlier life come back to haunt him?"

"You know, Bud, it could be anything . . . but I think there has to be a connection to the necklace stuff, so it's rooted in the present, and his own-ership of the necklace." This conversation was helping me feel more certain that my thinking was right about this whole mess.

"I agree, so treat the necklace as though it were a victim too. Do a 'victim profile' for the necklace as well as one for the Townsend guy."

I thought about it for a moment. "That's a really good idea, Bud! Thanks!"

"I do have them, on occasion, you know," was Bud's wry reply. "You've helped us so often on cases to understand the life of the victim. You know it's often helped us narrow the field of suspects, or even work out where to start looking for a possible perpetrator . . . so, yes, do that for the dead guy, by all means . . . but also do it for the necklace. If he was killed only in order to facilitate the theft of the necklace, then you might get more of an idea of who might be to blame by understanding the history of the necklace—*its* life if you like—rather than just the life of the man. He *might* just have been collateral damage. Or else, and I'm just throwing this one out there, his death might not have been connected with the theft of the necklace at all. It *might* just have been a huge coincidence."

"Since when do *you* believe in coincidences?"

"Yeah—you've got a point. Anyway—I'm nearly where I need to be and I've got to get right into this one when I arrive, so I gotta go now, Cait. Don't forget—call right back with that number and I'll get on it as soon as I can. I'll call you. Remind me about the time difference?"

"I'm nine hours ahead of you," I replied.

"Right, I'll make that call as soon as I can," said Bud, in his "office voice." I pictured him getting close to his destination.

"Oh, Bud . . ."

"Yeah?" I could tell he was distracted.

"Jan said to tell you she'll call you when she gets back from some girls' get-together at Crescent Beach today."

"Oh yeah—she was still pretty much asleep when I left. Glad you reminded me. I'd forgotten that was today. I'm sure she'll have a great time . . . They always do, those girls. No Men Required. The NMRs, they call themselves. Bless 'em! I *would* say why don't you ever join them, Cait, but I know you a bit better than that, eh?"

"True," I had to concede. "Good luck with whatever it is, and be safe. Is it a Kevlar vest day?"

"Yep—Kevlar, guns, dogs . . . the lot. I get to sit on the sidelines and watch it unfold these days, Cait, so don't worry about me. Jan keeps telling me how much better she feels knowing I'm so much more likely to come home alive now that I'm basically in an office job, rather than out on the front line. Though this feels pretty front-line, today. Big grow-op. Big players being drawn in. Long-term planning coming to fruition—we hope! We'll see. Somehow they always seem to wriggle out of it. But we've gotta keep bringing them in if they're ever gonna get convicted of anything that'll take them out of circulation for a good amount of time. Wish us luck, Deario . . . gotta go now. Talk soon. Bye!"

"Good luck, Bud. Thanks—and bye," I said, but the line had gone dead. I quickly called the number again and left Captain Moreau's contact info. Then I was on my own again—no longer speeding along the Trans-Canada Highway across the Sumas Prairie with Bud and his clever ideas and comforting voice to help me see the wood for the trees, but sitting in the still-warm sunlight on a wall built thousands of years earlier by Roman hands.

Those wall-builders had been strangers in a foreign land back then. Probably thinking of the homes they'd left behind as they'd laid each brick and slapped on the cement. I knew how they felt. Despite the fact that this was supposed to be one of the most glamorous places in the world, I'd have given anything to be curled up on the sofa in my little house on Burnaby Mountain, with the wind and the rain slamming against the window and good old Mark Madryga telling me on Global TV that it wasn't going to let up any time soon. Bliss!

As it was, I was being hailed by a gloriously handsome, impeccably dressed, and possibly murderous Italian. He motioned to me to join him, against a backdrop of the ancient white stones of ruined Roman baths awash in the pale buttery glow of the late afternoon sunshine. It should have been idyllic. It wasn't. Bugger!

Beni walked away from the group of policemen who'd obviously gone to their superior to tell him about what they'd found in the recycling bin. Clearly it wasn't good news, because there was still only the broken wooden box sitting on a tarpaulin to one side of the bin, and a huge pile of paper, cardboard and other recyclable materials on another tarpaulin opposite.

"There are no scrolls. There are no artifacts," stated Beni bluntly, sounding and looking miserable. "They have taken them." He made it sound very final.

I felt as though I should comfort him in some way. If this had been Bud, I'd have given him a big hug. I suspected that wasn't quite appropriate, so I settled for giving Beni a pat on the arm. It was really quite maternal of me. *Very odd.*

He acknowledged my pat with a sad nod, then looked at me with pleading eyes.

"Will you come with me to collect Tamsin? She has called me from the hospital. They say she can go home. They are finished at the apartment. She wants me to be with her." *I bet she does,* I thought, somewhat bitchily. Instead, I said, "Do you *really* want me to come?"

Beni looked a little worried. "I think it would be good if you are with me. It will not be so . . . intense."

I allowed myself a tiny, internal smile as he selected the right word. I got the impression that Tamsin frightened him a little. I'd seen how she'd looked at him when her husband was standing right next to her. Goodness knows what she'd be like as a young, beautiful, and, let's not forget rich, widow. As I thought all this I caught myself, and tried, as Bud had reminded me, to be more objective and less judgemental. Maybe Tamsin would be in bits. She might have *really* loved Alistair. It was possible that her flirtatiousness had been totally innocent—that's often the case with flirts. They do it because it's "good, clean fun," only indulging when they know that nothing will come of it. Or she might be a cold-blooded killer who'd only married Alistair for his money, and was sick of waiting for him to die. Anything was possible. After all, I knew almost nothing about the woman.

If I went to the hospital with Beni to collect Tamsin, I could pump him for information about her, and Alistair, and we'd have a chance to discuss the necklace. Or I could get a cab back to my hotel and sit there counting my toes. It wasn't a difficult choice.

"Of course I'll come, Beni, but would it be okay if I used the washroom before we leave? All that wine . . . all that coffee . . . It's got to go somewhere, you know!"

Beni looked slightly embarrassed, which I thought was hilarious. He walked with me toward the fire exit door, which was still wide open, and directed me to the public washrooms that weren't being examined by the police. I thanked him and ducked into a very tastefully decorated and well-appointed room. I used the facility for its major purpose, washed up, and then took full advantage of the large area set aside from the wash-basins for the hasty reapplication of my lipstick and a quick touch-up of my hair.

I re-emerged feeling a great deal fresher and drawing the comment "Bella" from Beni. That guy knew how to make a woman feel special!

We headed outside. I expected Beni to call for a cab, but instead, we walked toward a long, sleek, midnight blue convertible BMW.

"Is this yours?" I was puzzled.

"Si, it is mine," he said casually.

"Why is it here?" We'd come by cab, after all.

"I left it here after work yesterday. I do not like to drink and drive. It is not good. And I know that I drink with Alistair. Sometimes too much. When I left hospital this morning I wanted to go straight to my home, which is much lower down the hill than here and, because I had to meet with the police at the police station this morning, I have not had time to collect it yet. It is lucky, because now it is here and we are here."

"You were just drinking with me at lunchtime," I remarked.

"But this was just wine," replied Beni calmly.

Obviously, wine didn't count.

We both got into the car and I asked, "You saw the police this morning?"

Beni nodded as he started up the motor. At least, I think he did—it was so quiet and smooth it was difficult to tell.

"Captain Moreau?"

Again he nodded. "He was very pleasant. His Italian is very good, but I think my French is better." He wasn't even being arrogant, so I'm glad he didn't see me roll my eyes or smirk.

"Did he tell you anything, or did he just grill you?"

"Grill me? I do not know this."

I wondered if he was deflecting, or if my use of language had been too colloquial. I gave him the benefit of the doubt.

"Did he ask you lots and lots of questions?"

"Ah, yes. Many questions. About me, about Alistair, about last evening, about everybody at the table. Of course, I could not tell him much about you, because we did not talk together very much. I am glad we have talked more now. Though it does not seem to have been very much about you. Except to establish that you are a genius, of course!"

"Oh, touché, Beni! I'm not really very interesting, though. But I bet Tamsin is . . ." Had I managed to steer him toward one of my desired topics of interest?

Beni smiled broadly as he negotiated a very tight turn (for a car the length of his, anyway) as we left the museum. "Ah Tamsin . . . the Widow Tamsin . . . is she interesting? No, I think not. But I think that *Tamsin* thinks that Tamsin is interesting. She is young. She has not lived. She is fresh faced with no lines or wrinkles, but she has nothing to say. She is like a child. A greedy child. She used Alistair to do everything for her, or to buy everything for her. Even if she has all of his money she will not be happy unless she has people around her she can control. She makes eyes at me because she cannot control me. She wants what she cannot have, then she is bored with it as soon as she has it."

"Boy, oh boy, Beni—why don't you just come out with it and say what you think?" I quipped.

"But I *have* said what I think," he replied, sounding a little hurt. Clearly, he didn't get the irony. I decided to rescue him.

"I know you did, Beni—I'm sorry, I was just playing with you. I shouldn't do that." I still couldn't help but smile, though, as I added, "So you're not very keen on Tamsin, eh?"

"She can be difficult," he replied a bit sulkily.

"Do you think she might have killed Alistair?" I thought I might as well get right to it, and I'd expected a quick response from Beni but he actually mulled it over for a moment.

"I think she might want to. But I do not think she would know how to."

It was funny, because that was pretty much what I'd been thinking. "What about her smoking sticks, and chanting all those weird words when he died? Is she into mysticism or something? Do you think she'd know how to mix a potion to poison him?" I'd been intrigued by that at the time, but now all I could think of was "the pellet with the poison's in the vessel with the pestle," à la Danny Kaye. Shameful of me, really, given the circumstances.

"Ah, yes, her beliefs." Beni sounded exasperated, and I didn't think it was because of the early evening traffic that was beginning to slow our journey to a snail's pace as we wound down the hill toward the Old Town. "Tamsin is a person who likes to call many things magical. I believe that is why Alistair wanted to give her the necklace."

"Did Tamsin know about the necklace? Had Alistair shown it to her?"

"Oh yes. But she had not been allowed to wear it."

"How did Alistair find out about the necklace? How did he even find it, or know about its history as a Druidic relic?"

Beni began to shift in his luxurious leather seat. It couldn't have been because he was physically uncomfortable, because that would be impossible in his beast of a car.

"I might have mentioned the necklace when Alistair and I were talking about the work I had been doing on the archives," replied Beni, sheepishly.

"You *might have*? Or you *did*?" I wasn't letting go of this one.

"*Si*. I *did*. It is true. Sometimes Alistair and I spoke about my research. I thought it was a good way to encourage him to make donations to the museum. We happened to be talking about Roman family life—he was amused by the idea of the Romans eating so much that they had to leave the table to vomit. He had been told this as a boy. I had to correct him and tell him that a 'vomitorium' is simply a means of allowing a lot of people to leave a place quickly, and is nothing at all to do with vomiting, in the modern sense. It was a very silly discussion—but, for some reason, the family archive was mentioned, and I then told him about the necklace. I do not know why." *That was Alistair's famous "Silver Tongue" at work for you*, I thought. "He said how wonderful it would be to own such an item, and I think then he started to try to find out more about it. But Alistair seemed to be very interested in all sorts of stories about the Palais and the general area. I think he was trying to establish that there was no reason why the gardens couldn't be dug up to install a swimming pool—he wanted to prove that there was nothing of historical importance there, except, of course, maybe the old wine cellars. He had already been told by the authorities that it would be acceptable to dig into a part of those as they were not of any real importance."

I wasn't as interested in wine cellars as I was in the idea of Alistair hunting down the necklace.

"Beni, you say that Alistair believed he had found this Druidic necklace, but didn't he tell you *how* he had found it?"

"No, he would not tell me. He promised he would tell the whole story at the birthday party, when he gave it to Tamsin."

So, that was a dead end.

"Maybe he told Chuck?" added Beni casually. I perked up.

"Why? Were they close?" It seemed an improbable partnership.

"Ah, *this* I know!" Beni seemed excited that he could finally contribute something he felt was concrete. "Chuck wanted very much to own an apartment at the Palais. He is very interested in the Nazis and the Gestapo. The Palais was headquarters for the Gestapo here in Nice during the Vichy years . . ."

I let him carry on—I didn't have the heart to tell him that Chuck had given me a very detailed insight into the Gestapo life at the Palais at dinner the night before. "It is difficult to buy an apartment at the Palais: the Syndic—or the residents' management group—controls who can buy. They hold interviews; they have to accept the buyer. It can be problematic for those who are selling—but selling does not happen often. It is a very desirable building. Alistair knew Madame Schiafino, through some friends in Cannes, and she spoke for him when he purchased his apartment. She was a famous lawyer for many years and can be very persuasive. He had the best apartment, you know: it is the only one with so large a balcony. I have spent many evenings there with Alistair and Tamsin admiring the view. It is very good, as you saw. So Alistair had his apartment, and immediately became involved with the Syndic himself. So he spoke on behalf of Chuck when he wanted to buy *his* apartment."

"How did Alistair know Chuck?"

Beni replied, "I am sorry, but this I do not know for sure. But Chuck is famous, and Alistair liked to know famous people. They could have met at any one of the events to which rich and famous people are invited. Since Chuck moved to the Palais, he and Alistair have worked on the Syndic together. Chuck and Alistair disagree about the swimming pool. It is strange: usually Chuck agrees with everything that Alistair says, but on this they do not agree. Me? I think that a pool will increase the value of the apartments even more: people like to have a pool these days. Though I do not think that everyone who lives at the Palais really cares about the value of their apartment, some like to see their investment grow. Others hate the idea of a pool. They believe it will change the character of the building because it will change the use of the gardens, which are very peaceful. Chuck, Gerard, and Madelaine are against the pool. Alistair and Tamsin were for it. I believe that the Syndic had agreed to a vote by the residents. But you must get this information from Chuck. If you think it is relevant."

I wasn't sure about the relevance of the pool. Of course, if someone hated the idea of it enough, they might kill Alistair, its main champion, to try to halt the project. It seemed a bit far-fetched, though. Besides, who was to say it wouldn't go ahead without him? Beni might not think that many people were interested in the potential resale value of their apartments, but, in my experience, greed can be a great motivating force. There might be a resident counting on that extra value for some reason. I'd once worked on a case with Bud in the Downtown Eastside of Vancouver where one man killed another over five dollars. Sometimes the amount of money isn't important—it's what it means to the person who needs it that matters. I chose not to answer Beni, but decided I'd grill Chuck about the pool issue as soon as I had a chance.

In terms of suspects, all I had to go on was the fact that Beni had made no bones about wanting the necklace, and not liking Alistair. I hadn't really got very far with what Bud had encouraged me to think of as "my investigation." At this rate I'd never be leaving Nice, and I didn't like the idea of that at all!

Beni concentrated on swearing in Italian at every driver on the road. I watched the wonderful Belle Epoque architecture crawl by as we descended toward the Old Town, and I tried to come up with a plan of action.

We were going to collect Tamsin. Somehow I had to try to find out how she really felt about her dead husband, and work out if she might have killed him, though I couldn't think of any reason why she'd want to steal a necklace she was about to be given as a gift in any case. After that, I'd try to get to see Chuck Damcott: maybe he could enlighten me about the pool, and any enemies that Alistair might have made on that front . . . though, again, how the swimming pool might be connected to the theft of the necklace left me puzzled. I could try to pin down Madelaine, to find out all I could about Alistair, and the mutual friends they had in Cannes: maybe there'd be some clues there about whether Alistair might have been up to his old tricks. What about Gerard? Might he know something about Alistair that would help me?

It was all so very confusing. Nothing seemed *connected*. Well, the thefts of the archive and the necklace were certainly connected, but were they connected to Alistair's death? Was the swimming pool involved? Or Alistair's propensity for blackmail?

Early Saturday Evening

WHAT I REALLY NEEDED TO do first was sit and get this all on paper. It really helps me to *see* something, to work out relationships between things when they are there in front of me in black and white. That wasn't going to be possible for some time, though, because we'd just arrived at the hospital. Tamsin stood in the middle of the drive, gesturing frantically at Beni to pull right up to her. An oncoming ambulance didn't look as though it was about to stop, and she leapt up onto the pavement just in time to avoid being run down. She hovered there as we pulled forward. Without waiting for Beni to get out of the car, she opened the back door and jumped in.

"Beni, take me home, now, before they change their minds and drag me back to that horrible little room again," she whined as she flopped across the rear seat.

At least you had a room, not a corridor, like me, I thought. "How are you, Tamsin? You must be exhausted," I said. I strained around in my seat to make sure that she hadn't gone sliding onto the floor as Beni slammed his foot on the gas and we took off into traffic. Do all Italians drive like that? If they do, remind me I never want to drive in Italy . . . I wouldn't last five minutes.

Tamsin's response was to wail and cry. She sobbed for a few minutes into paper tissues she tore out of a surprisingly large box she produced from her handbag. Eventually, she blew her nose and managed to say, "He's gone, my Ally is gone . . . What will I do?" And she was off again. She was posing a rhetorical question; no one could be heard above the din of her distress.

Beni's driving, as we made our way back up toward Cimiez, was a lot worse than it had been on the way down. The traffic seemed to have dispersed, so he was able to put his foot down and swerve from lane to lane, which resulted in Tamsin's tiny body slithering across the wide expanse of leather in the back of the car. She stopped crying and began to look rather alarmed instead. She even tried to strap herself in with a seatbelt, steadying herself against one of the doors. By the time she'd found the buckle for the strap, Beni was asking if she had her remote control to open the gates to the Palais.

"I don't know. I don't think so. I was in an ambulance," came Tamsin's weak reply. "I'll look," she added, and she started scrabbling about in her handbag again. Until that point I'd always thought that mine was bad—but hers was huge, and a total mess. She dumped all its contents onto the back seat and started sorting through them. I cast my eyes across the collection and announced, almost immediately, that there was no remote control.

"It might be here, somewhere . . . You never know," replied Tamsin.

"Tamsin, you have five lipsticks, all the same color; six wads of used paper tissues; a dozen pens and pencils, most bearing restaurant or hotel logos; two notebooks—both small, one ragged, one new-looking; a very large, overstuffed Chanel purse; a Louis Vuitton credit card wallet that has seen better days, and obviously a great deal of use; two sets of keys, one a duplicate of the other except that it has an extra key; a bottle of water, given to you by the hospital when they discharged you—" I had one the same, "and what looks like a handkerchief tied at one end to form a little bag with some lumpy contents. *No* remote control."

Tamsin and Beni both looked at me open-mouthed. I could have kicked myself. It's all a little bit *Rain Man*-ish, but it's one of the things I can do—I can *see* things, really fast. It's another thing I don't really understand about myself, and something I try to keep quiet. Sometimes it gets the better of me and I just do it, but the reaction is always predictable. Beni and Tamsin both chorused the same thing. "How did you do *that*?"

"Oh, it's nothing," I said, trying to brush it off, "it's just a thing I can do. Nothing special . . ." I hoped they'd let it go at that.

As she began to gather all the bits and pieces together, stuffing them back into her bag, Tamsin muttered, "Ally said you were weird," under her breath, just loud enough for me to hear. Then, louder, she said, somewhat imperiously, "Buzz for Gerard, Beni—he'll let us in. He always lets me in when I forget my remote."

Beni jumped from the car, pressed some buttons on the keypad, spoke into the little microphone, and the gates began to open. We crunched along to the front door, where Beni parked. I got out, but Tamsin waited until Beni opened her door, when she swooned just enough so that Beni had to support her.

As Beni helped Tamsin toward the front door, and I collected the purse she'd just let fall to the ground, Gerard came though the front door and down the steps to greet us. I thought he looked a lot paler than he had at dinner the night before, but, I told myself, he was a relatively old man who had probably had as good a night's sleep as I had. He just needed some rest.

His voice croaked as he said, "Ah Tamsin, 'ow are you? You look weak! Ah, it is terrible. Terrible. We all miss him so much already!"

"Yes, I am weak, oh Gerard, they took so much of my blood, and they didn't let me sleep at all. I have cried and cried all night. I'm so tired. I can't cope! How will I cope?" squeaked Tamsin, in that annoyingly high-pitched whine of hers.

"Come inside," said Gerard, reaching to take the arm that Beni wasn't supporting. "It will be better when you are in your own apartment."

"I need to shower. I need to take a bath. I stink of the hospital," she wailed back.

"Ah yes, you will feel better when you are clean and warm," replied the old man. "I will make tea," he added, as we all made our way up the steps toward the front door.

"Oh God, no, I need something stronger than that," replied Tamsin. "I'll drink some champagne in the bath—that'll help," she added. It seemed a strange thing for a newly widowed person to want to do, but merely the thought of it seemed to infuse her with more energy to climb the steps unaided, as she pushed both Beni and Gerard away and launched herself though the doorway.

That's a pretty quick recovery, I thought to myself. "Careful now," I said aloud, "you don't want to tire yourself!" Everyone was ahead of me so I was sure they couldn't see the look on my face.

When we were all inside the apartment, we clustered in the little entryway. None of us seemed to want to go farther. I have to admit it was eerie, and, frankly, more than a bit of a mess. Gone was the casual elegance that had greeted me at the same door the evening before—now the place looked as though a small nuclear device had detonated at its center.

I've seen a lot of crime scenes in my time, and this wasn't much different. The police, the paramedics, and the forensics people don't actually clean up after themselves—that's not their job. They get there, do what they have to do, make as much of a mess as they need to, then they leave. It can be a bit of a shock.

"Oh my God!" wailed Tamsin, holding her little face in horror. To be fair, the mess entitled her to some dramatics. "What have they done to my home? It's terrible! *I* can't clean this up! Who's going to do it? They can't leave it like this! Daphne doesn't come until Monday. I'll have to get her in for an extra day."

I surmised Daphne must be the cleaner. *Of course* Tamsin had a cleaner. I mean, why *wouldn't* a woman who didn't work, married to a man who was retired, need a cleaner? I assumed they must both be far too busy relaxing all day to actually do any housework. Perhaps Alistair and Tamsin both had very time-consuming hobbies I knew nothing about or spent all day working with the city's homeless. I could feel my judgemental streak getting wider by the second. I decided to step up and take control. Whatever! I spoke with as much enthusiastic vigour as I could muster.

"Oh, come on, it's not as bad as it looks. Here's what I suggest: Tamsin, why don't you go and have that bath you've been promising yourself, but first tell us where all your cleaning stuff is, will you?"

Tamsin looked blank for a moment, then squeaked, "It's all somewhere in the kitchen—under the sink, I think. The brushes and things may be in the cupboard under the stairs."

I sighed inwardly. God, I *hate* pathetic women!

"Okay—I'm sure we'll find everything we need. We'll clean up down here, so that it's good to go by the time you're done. Okay Beni? Gerard?" The two men nodded. "Go on now, enjoy your bath," and I waved at her, just to make sure she knew that she should leave. She took her cue and disappeared upstairs. Shortly thereafter, we heard water running and, I'm pretty sure, a champagne cork popping.

The two men and I managed to find large refuse bags, dusters, cans of spray polish, rags for wiping and drying, and several rolls of paper towels, all of which we put to good use for the next fifteen minutes, clearing up the detritus from the paramedics, the police and the fingerprint guys. (Here's something I learned that day: Always wipe off fingerprint powder with a damp cloth *before* attempting to use spray polish—what a mess I made.) We all got on with our own areas. Gerard worked around the dining table, Beni saw to the sitting room, and I tidied the balcony. I was the lucky one; I watched the light change from day to night on the horizon, and I got to enjoy the cooling air—just as we had all done the evening before.

Gerard had shown us how to use the chute in the kitchen that sent the refuse bags plummeting to the basement for collection there by the janitor. After we'd all washed our hands, Beni announced that he should move the car to a visitor parking spot. Gerard and I decided to try to find what we needed to make a cup of tea and something to eat. Beni headed out, and I proceeded to open and close doors in the kitchen, discovering that the Townsends seemed too live exclusively on tinned pâté de foie gras, crackers, assorted nuts, and cheese straws. The contents of the fridge didn't help much either: lots of champagne, six bottles of beer, smoked salmon, a couple of plastic containers of cooked lobster, a variety of cheeses, some eggs, milk, spread, toasting bread, and cream.

There *were* fresh beans with which to make coffee, but the coffee maker looked like it had been designed by NASA. You'd probably need a degree in engineering to be able to make it work at all. Gerard looked flummoxed by it all. Once again, I came up with a plan.

"Well, we'll work with what we've got. They've taken all the flatware and glasses we were using last night, so we'll just use whatever is left and I'll lay out an assortment of things so we can all snack. Okay?"

Gerard nodded. "I will prepare the table—the settings are all in the other room, under the stairs," he said gravely, and off he went.

I started to pull out tins and packets (making sure they were all sealed . . . after all, we'd probably been poisoned by something we'd eaten there the night before!) and then began to ferry serving platters to the table on the balcony. On balance, I thought it would be better than eating at the table where Alistair had died. Five minutes later the balcony looked quite festive. I'm not the world's most highly domesticated creature, so I allowed myself to survey the table with pride, even though under the circumstances it seemed inappropriate somehow.

Gerard and I both sat down outside, and I lit a cigarette.

"It is terrible, this," said Gerard quietly. "Terrible."

"Yes, it is," I replied. Taking my chance, I added, "You were fond of Alistair?"

"He will be missed" was Gerard's safe reply, with a great emphasis on the "h" of "he." Beni had said much the same thing: funny how neither of them had said that *they* would miss him, but rather that the man would be missed, in the abstract sense. I decided to try again.

"Had you known Alistair for long?" I, too, spoke quietly. It seemed a shame to disturb the peace of the evening.

"Since 'e moved 'ere, five years past," replied Gerard factually. Not only did he have trouble with the English "h," he struggled with tenses, too. But, bless him, he was trying very hard to speak his best English. "*He* is a good man. *He* loves life," he added.

Again, it struck me as odd that Gerard would say much the same about Alistair as Beni had, earlier in the day.

"Were you friends?"

Gerard thought for a moment then said, "No, not friends. He is very kind to me. We know each other a little. He likes it when I tell him stories about the old days. But we are not friends. I have always work in the gardens, and now I live in an apartment at the back—at the discretion of the Syndic. M. Townsend, Alistair, is a wealthy man. He invites me to his home, but we do not mix outside of his home and some of the Syndic meetings."

"I bet he enjoyed your tales about 'the old days' here—Alistair was always a bit of a history buff," I lied.

"Ah yes, he is," replied Gerard smiling. "We sit inside in the shade, or maybe out here, and he asks me to tell him all the stories I know. It is good to think about old times. Sometimes I remember things I have forgotten. He is . . . gracious."

I opened a bottle of champagne and offered Gerard a glass. Well, if Tamsin couldn't drag herself away from her bubble bath, why shouldn't I act as the hostess? Besides, I fancied a glass myself, and I had *only* brought out the Veuve Cliquot, rather than the Dom Perignon, after all. Gerard smiled an affirmative, and I poured. As on the previous evening, my knowledge of etiquette for bizarre circumstances was letting me down. I wondered if it would it be alright for us to begin to eat, or whether we should wait for the widow to join us. As I felt my tummy rumble I decided I would just dive in. I loaded up a cracker with pâté de foie gras and had at it. Oh my God—I *love* that stuff... However politically incorrect it might be to enjoy the product of force-feeding fowl, I cannot believe there is a taste in the world more wonderful, more satisfying, or more haunting, than foie gras. Once tasted, always desired. *Bliss!* I relished the flavors bursting in my mouth, as Gerard copied my actions, and we both gave ourselves over to a moment of indulgence... tinged with only a little guilt.

I knew I had to apply myself, so I pulled myself back from the brink of disappearing into paroxysms of delight. I asked, as innocently as I could, "Was there anything about the Palais that particularly interested Alistair?"

"Oh yes," replied Gerard, swallowing quickly, "he is interested in the man who was the architect—he wants to know all about the building from the time when it was built until he arrives." Gerard spoke slowly, his French accent guttural but understandable, his words chosen with care and pronounced carefully. "My father comes here as a gardener before the First War. I live here all my life, always in the same apartment. My father and mother live here. Now I live here. My father knows men who work on building the Palais when they are boys. They tell him stories, and he tells me. Ten men die building this," he waved his arms around him, "it is very sad. But more blood than that is spilled here, as I tell M. Townsend."

"Really?" I encouraged him. "In what way do you mean?"

"Ah, in many ways. The men who die building it, and, to be sure, there are more deaths here since—some are natural, as you expect; there are two duels in the gardens in the early years; in the 1960s a man kills his wife, then his mistress, then himself—all of them are residents here and, of course, there are the terrible things that happen in the war. But even before it was built there is a scandal. They are digging the foundations, and there are bodies. Not graves, but bodies. My father tells me all about this. M. Townsend says this story is most interesting. It is a tragedy."

"Oh, I love an old story like that," I lied, again. "Do tell me about it."

Gerard pushed back in his seat and looked up at the dark sky, then directly at me, and slowly began. "The architect is appointed by the owner of the land. He is well established and, as you can see from the building, he favors the classic look for the Belle Epoque buildings in this area, which is very fashionable. He arrives from Paris in 1878 with his bride, who is very beautiful and thirty years less in age than him, and they set up home lower down the hill in the Carabacel area. They have a baby—a boy, but it is not an easy birth. The woman she can have no more children. She breaks down, as you say, and is not seen much from that time. Soon afterward they find the bodies. A workman who sees them tells my father they are four bodies. They are bones only. They are in a hole that is not deep. It is at the edge of the site for the building. One body is a woman—this they know because she wears jewelry. One is a man, who has a sword, and two look like children. The men who find the bones are afraid, so the architect he comes and takes them all away himself. Later, my father is told, the workers they see the wife of the architect at a party, and she is wearing the jewelry from the bones of the woman. They think that this is bad. They think it is against God. So they all give up their jobs and go to work on another building."

"It must have been a difficult choice for them to do that—to leave steady employment," I commented.

"No, it is not. There are many jobs in Nice at this time. This is 1880, the start of the Belle Epoque, when the railway is here from the north, the city grows very fast, and it is full of the English, the Russians and the Italians. Everywhere there is building. In any case, it is good that they leave because very soon there are many problems here. It begins with the young wife. She is having an affair with one of the assistants to her husband—a young man from Germany, of about her own age. There is a story that the architect challenges the man to a duel. In any case, the man disappears, and the wife as well. The child is still with the architect. Then men fall sick, there is talk of cholera—which kills many, many people in Nice fifty years before. There is terror. Many workmen leave the building. The owner of the land replaces the architect and gets another man to manage the making of the building, the architect has nothing left but his son, who dies when he is very young, then the architect himself is sick, and he kills himself at the building site one night." Gerard's eyes were sparkling and he was slightly flushed. It seemed that he thrived on tragedy.

"They all died? Very Shakespearean! Very sad." What else could I say? "Did anyone see the jewelry again?"

"Ha! This is what Alistair says to me! All this sadness and you ask about this thing. Maybe you are like him?" I could see what he meant. I had to put him right on that one.

"Oh, no, Gerard—I'm sorry, I don't mean to appear to be heartless, but I was talking to Beni about the necklace that is missing, the one that Alistair was going to give Tamsin for her birthday. And I wondered if that necklace might be the jewelry of which you speak."

"Huh! I do not know this," was Gerard's somewhat sulky reply. "It is just a piece of metal, in any case. It is not beautiful. It is ugly. It is not as important as a human life. Why would anyone kill for a piece of metal? *Life* is what matters. Life is not to be replaced."

Well, he wasn't going to get any argument from me on that one, but, again, I'd seen people kill for "pieces of metal" before—and they hadn't been priceless, ancient, and possibly mystic pieces of metal, either!

"Did Alistair really seem more interested in the jewelry than the lives lost?"

"Always. He is always asking more and more about the jewelry. But I know no more. This is what I know. It is what my father tells me. I do not know more than he tells me. It is impossible." Gerard was starting to get a bit hot under the collar on the topic, so I was actually quite relieved when the buzzer sounded in the kitchen. I let Beni back into the front door of the building, and a few moments later he came out on to the balcony, looking pink in the face and huffing and puffing that he'd had to park at the bottom of the gardens because it was very busy at the Palais that evening. He wasn't kidding—he'd been gone for *ages*.

It was almost as if Tamsin had been waiting until her entire audience was assembled ready for her entrance *(in fact, I'm sure she was)*, and she wafted out onto the balcony almost immediately after Beni's arrival, wearing something loose, flowing, and black. She looked appropriately tragic. I only shook my head in disgust internally.

"Hello. Ah—I'm *famished*," she announced dramatically, waving a black chiffon scarf imperiously at the table, and she sat. Not *one* word of thanks for all the cleaning we'd done, not even a nod in my direction for having laid out what was, in my eyes, a feast. Ungrateful so and so! I seethed, and sipped my champagne. At that moment I was sorry I hadn't opened a bottle of Dom after all. I was 300 per cent certain I wouldn't be pouring her anything, anytime soon. Of course, Beni did the honors, pouring her champagne, trying to "tempt" her with the morsels in front of her and telling her how marvellous she looked, given the circumstances.

I was about a nanosecond away from needing a sick bag—I hadn't over-indulged, I just find all that sort of hypocritical crap totally nauseating. I pulled myself together, kept repeating, internally, what Bud had said about *not* being judgemental, and decided to smile at the Widow Townsend.

"Come now, Tamsin, you must eat *something*. I've done my best with what's here, but, at some point, you're going to have to get some real food in so that you can look after yourself properly. Would you like me to get some groceries for you tomorrow?"

Tamsin looked puzzled, then she smiled, dabbed at her dry eyes, and said, "Oh Cait, I don't really cook, or anything like that. Ally said I made good reservations so I didn't need to be able to cook, and he was right. I do make good reservations. Don't worry about me, I can manage to eat very well, thank you."

"What if you don't feel like going out?" It had to be asked.

"Oh, *everyone* will deliver to us. It's not like England, or America, you know—all the *good* places deliver here . . . It's not just pizza or curry, absolutely *everyone* will deliver *everything*."

Well, that was me well and truly put in my place. After all, how could I have *not* known *that*? Bitch! And that was my *considered* judgement of the woman.

Beni came to my rescue. Or, at least, he tried to. "Cait would not know this. She does not live here like us. She lives in a part of the world where this is not usual." It was something of a back-handed compliment.

"Doctor Brunetti is correct, Tamsin," added Gerard, "you must eat something. You must be strong for these days ahead. They will be difficult. There is much to arrange." He nodded his head sagely. I wondered how many funerals he'd had to arrange in a life of more than eighty years.

"Oh no," said Tamsin quite lightly, nibbling on a cracker and sipping champagne, "Ally made all his own arrangements. It's a service in Holy Trinity Anglican, cremation and an urn to be kept here with me. He wanted to make sure it was all as he wanted, so he chose the hymns and wrote his eulogy for the Rector to read. All I have to do is to decide the date, and that's it."

I was pleased to see that I wasn't the only one at the table to be stunned by this. Both Beni and Gerard were, literally, open-mouthed. I made sure I shut mine quickly. I don't think they noticed. Tamsin's body language spoke of no discomfort, no stress or even sadness. She was quite calm about the whole thing.

"You are very calm about the whole thing," I said. It made sense to say what I was thinking, for once.

"Well, of course I am, silly, because it's just his *body*. Ally's gone. There's no point worrying about arrangements for the leftovers, is there? All *I'm* concerned about is Ally's spirit, and I know *that's* gone to a good place. He was a good man. He loved life. He'll be missed. To Ally!" She raised her glass by way of a toast.

As I raised mine I thought how remarkable it was that Tamsin, Beni, and Gerard had all used *exactly* the same phrases to describe Alistair. *Quite remarkable.* I'd have to give that some thought. I decided that, at that moment, it was more important that I took my chance to talk to the person who had, presumably, known Alistair the best—his widow. I suspected that she and I wouldn't have many more chances for a heart to heart; our personalities did not promise a flourishing friendship, if you know what I mean!

"When will it be, Tamsin? Do you have to wait until the hospital knows how Alistair died?" I asked, trying to sound sympathetic.

"Oh, I know that already," she replied casually. Again, the rest of us looked very surprised, and this time she saw it and reacted. "They told me at the hospital. Well, they would, of course, because I was his wife. He died from something digital."

Well, given my size I know you could never *really* knock me down with a feather . . . but this was about as close as you'd ever be likely to come.

There was a trio of "How?" from the three of us, each in our own native tongue. Clearly, none of us understood what on earth she'd meant.

"They said it was *digital*," replied Tamsin, blithely. "It can kill some people, you know, but if we're all alright now, we'll be fine," and she ate another cracker.

Frankly, I was completely exasperated with her. *Stupid woman!*

"Tamsin, what do you mean, it was 'digital'? He was zapped with something? What? *Please* explain yourself!" I knew I sounded cross, but, come on, I mean what *was* the woman prattling on about?

"Was it a poison or not?" asked Beni, in rather more measured tones than my own.

Tamsin put down the sliver of cracker she'd been holding and wiped her fingers on a napkin. She looked as though she was concentrating intently, the way a small child might look when you've asked them to spell something like "antidisestablishmentarianism." When she spoke it was slowly, though still in that godawful Minnie Mouse voice of hers.

"The doctor came to me and said that the blood tests and the heart thingy tests showed we had all been affected by something digital. It had killed Ally because of his heart tablets. I asked would I be alright and he said we'd all be alright because otherwise we'd be dead already. There." She looked very pleased with herself, and resumed her nibbling.

A lightbulb clicked on in my head.

"Do you mean 'digitalis,' Tamsin?" I asked as calmly as I could.

"Oh—yes, that's it. Silly me. Digital-*is*. Don't worry—we'll all be just fine."

"Digitalis, it is very dangerous," said Gerard in something of a panic. "And this has happened to us all?"

"Don't worry, Gerard," I said calmly. "Yes, digitalis can be dangerous, but you need a pretty big dose for it to kill you and the doctor was right—if our bodies have coped with the initial dose, we'll be quite alright now. It gets metabolized relatively quickly." I could see confusion on the old man's face, so added, "Our bodies take care of it quite quickly, so we are all as safe now as if it had not entered our systems. We must all have good hearts."

"Yes, maybe," chimed in Beni, "but Alistair had a bad heart. He took medication."

"Did everyone at the dinner know that?" I must have sounded a bit sharp, but I didn't care.

"Alistair made no secret of it," answered Beni.

"I think everyone knows he has a weak heart," added Gerard. "M. Townsend likes to play at it . . . to make us sorry for him, then laugh at himself."

"Ah yes, that's very true," nodded Beni, "he would beat at his chest and say 'Got to keep the old ticker going—what, what' very often."

I could imagine Alistair doing that. To the point of annoyance, I'd have thought.

"He was afraid, that's why he made fun of it." It was a comment I thought quite out of character for Tamsin, and it was spoken in a voice that was lower than her usual register, and seemingly more thoughtful.

"Why was he 'afraid,' Tamsin?" I asked.

Tamsin shot a glance at me that suggested she was the one who was afraid—but afraid of what? She answered me in her normal, dimwit tone, "Oh, you know, just afraid. Afraid he'd have a heart attack, I suppose . . ." She trailed off into shoulder shrugging, head bobbing, and a vacuous smile. "He didn't like pills. Sometimes he didn't take them, then he'd feel bad and take extra ones."

I was pretty sure that, whatever he'd been prescribed, Alistair's decision to fiddle with the doses wasn't a good one. Maybe he'd contributed to his own demise by taking a high dose of something before dinner that then interacted with the digitalis, or maybe he *hadn't* taken the pills that he *should* have taken, and that was why he died.

"Did the doctor say if he had a very high amount of digitalis in his system, Tamsin? Compared with the rest of us?"

"Yes," she replied earnestly, with that look of concentration on her face again, "he said about five times more than any of us."

"That sounds like a lot," remarked Beni.

"Obviously, it was enough," I said. I hadn't meant to be flippant. It just came out.

"Yes, obviously," replied Tamsin quietly, nodding. The heartlessness of my comment seemed to have passed her by. "It was in the food, of course, the snails, but they don't know how, yet."

At last! So we'd all been dosed on digitalis, in the snails. It was definitely murder, and by someone who knew enough about Alistair, his medication, and the effects of digitalis to be able to subject us all to its effects while only killing Alistair. I felt a great relief at knowing this, though it didn't, on the face of it, seem to get me any closer to identifying the killer. While I pondered this, and while we were all, it seemed, deep in thought, the doorbell rang.

"I shall go," said Beni, standing, apparently glad to leave the table. He returned moments later with Chuck Damcott at his side. Chuck was carrying a massive bunch of flowers, which he presented to Tamsin with a tragic look on his face and shaking his head.

"My dear, dear Tamsin . . . I am so sorry . . . We will miss him so much, but none of us as much as you. Here you are, my delicate one—these are to show you that there is still beauty in this world, even though Alistair has left us." Yuk!

Tamsin took the flowers from the American. The bouquet looked even bigger in her tiny hands, and she was able to bury her entire face in the flowers, re-emerging with a beatific smile and a tear in her eye. I lit a cigarette in disgust.

Smiling, Tamsin looked up at Chuck and said, "Oh, they are so beautiful. You are right. Ally would want us to enjoy life. Won't you join us for champagne?"

It was as though she were simply inviting the man for cocktails!

"I will get a glass," said Beni, turning back toward the kitchen.

"Thanks," called Chuck toward his receding back. He pulled a chair to within inches of Tamsin's and sat down beside her.

Interesting.

"Tamsin's been telling us that we were all dosed with digitalis in the snails last night, Chuck," I offered by way of an icebreaker. I wondered how he'd react.

Chuck looked shocked. "Digitalis? Oh, my. I guess that's why Alistair . . . um, died . . ." He seemed embarrassed to say the word. "I guess it overdosed him because of his medication. It's just awful. Awful. We'll all be the poorer without him." I wondered if he meant because of Alistair's wealth of bonhomie, or because of something else.

"Here is a glass," said Beni as he offered a beer glass to Chuck. "I cannot find any more champagne glasses," he added.

"I know where there are many," replied Gerard, and he began to push himself up from his chair.

I shot to my feet. "Please, let me," I offered.

Gerard smiled and shrugged. "It is easy for me to get them, but not easy to tell you where they are. *Merci*," and he moved slowly toward the door of the kitchen.

I sat back down and returned my attention to Chuck. "Do you know what medication Alistair was taking?"

"Oh yeah, he was always waving that little silver box around. He was taking a digitalis-based medicine; he told me so. Helped with his heart arrhythmia, he said. Though I know he liked to mess around with his dosages. Thought he knew better than the medics. Alistair was kinda like that." Chuck's accent seemed to come from somewhere on the East Coast, rather than the West, and I was reminded that "where are you from" hadn't been one of the questions I'd asked him the night before. Where we were at the time had seemed so much more important to him, in any case.

Beni nodded, as did I. Tamsin seemed to not be listening. Or maybe she was. It was hard to tell, since little seemed to register on that vacant face of hers.

"You say it was the snails?" Chuck seemed surprised. "I guess it had to be in something. But *how*? Anyone know?"

I looked across at Beni, who shook his head and shrugged, "I do not know how this was done. Is it possible that someone took Alistair's pills and put them into the snail dish?"

To be fair, it was a good idea, but I wondered how practical it would be. "To be able to do that, someone would have to have gained access to his pills. Did Alistair have his pills on him when he died, Tamsin? And are there more in the apartment?"

She thought for a moment, then replied, "Yes, and yes... or no. The police told me at the hospital that they'd taken his little silver box to check it out, and his big bottle is in the master bathroom ... at least, that's where he kept it. The police told me they took away the big bottle too." I suspect that Beni might have seen me roll my eyes at this one. When I caught his expression out of the corner of my eye he was trying to not smirk.

"They're obviously thinking along the same lines we are. I guess they'll check what Alistair had at the time of his death against what he was pre-scribed, and when, and compare the two. Of course, given his erratic dosing, they might not get a clear answer," observed Chuck.

Chuck was beginning to interest me greatly. At dinner he'd been cogent and passionate, but somewhat dry, and I hadn't thought of him as someone who might be able to think quickly and clearly. I suspected that this was the sort of "judgmentalism" that Bud was always warning me about. I was beginning to realize that Chuck was bright. *Possibly very bright.*

Not to be outdone I added, "You're right, Chuck. Whether it was the pills or not, somehow the digitalis got into that dish of snails. Anyone got any ideas?" I thought it best to try to find out what other people were think-ing before I said anything myself—after all, I was the only person there I knew for certain hadn't done it!

Beni sucked on a cheroot and looked thoughtful. Chuck scratched his head, and Tamsin poured herself more champagne. Gerard was heading back toward us with a champagne glass in one hand and a wireless telephone handset in the other. I hadn't heard a phone ring, so I was puzzled.

"I have telephoned Madelaine to tell her the news about Alistair, but there is no reply. I have not my spectacles. Will someone please call her again? I might not have the right number."

"*Si, buono,*" said Beni, holding out his hand for the phone. "I do not know her number . . ."

Gerard rattled off what seemed like a thousand syllables in French, and Beni poked at the keypad, then listened.

"She has no machine?" he asked Gerard in French.

Gerard shook his head. "Too modern," he replied.

"Is it usual for her to be away from her home at—" Beni looked at his watch, "seven on a Saturday?"

Chuck shrugged. "I don't know, Beni. I only ever see Madelaine when she's here at Alistair's."

Gerard was shaking his head. "It is not usual. She stays at home at this hour. Maybe she is sick from last night? She arrives home before me, I know. They say at the hospital that she is sent away before me. She is a very healthy woman."

I looked over at Beni as he disconnected the call, and I said what I suspected he was thinking. "I think we should check on her to make sure she's okay, Gerard. How about Chuck stays here with Tamsin, and Beni and I run along to her apartment, with you to show us the way?"

Everyone except Tamsin, who seemed to be in her own little world, nodded in agreement, so Beni and I stubbed out our smokes and headed off with Gerard. We took the elevator to the ground floor, then walked the entire width of the building and circumnavigated the mirror-image elevator in the other wing, to find ourselves facing a tiny door that led into a narrow corridor, which then turned, and began to run back in the direction from which we had come.

"This is where we rent apartments, not own them," said Gerard, quite proudly. "Madelaine, she is in number eleven, and I am along farther in number seventeen." About three doors along we stopped and Gerard knocked, quite loudly. "She is deaf," he announced, "though she does not think so." This made me smile—I was thinking that much the same was true about Gerard!

There was no reply, so Beni knocked—with rather more force than Gerard had managed. Beni also put his booming voice to good use by calling "Madelaine! Are you at home?" in French, of course.

There was still no reply. There was no handle on the door, just a lock let into it.

"Is there a key anywhere?" asked Beni of Gerard, who thought for a moment.

His eyes lit up and he replied, "Maybe with Daphne! She is along here, in fourteen. She cleans for Madelaine and some other ladies. She will have a key."

We knocked at her door. After Beni explained why we wanted the key, the short, round, mousy woman, who was obviously Daphne, gladly handed it to him. She insisted that she came with us to check on Madelaine.

I acknowledged to myself that I was getting a bit worried. My main concern was that maybe something had happened to Madelaine as a result of the digitalis. I knew quite a bit about it from my toxicology classes, but I certainly wasn't an expert. I mean, there might have been a whole raft of nasty side-effects I knew nothing about that could cause real problems for a woman in her nineties. I had that nervous tummy thing again, and I kept telling myself it couldn't be because I was allergic to foie gras . . . or champagne (oh heavens no—that would be a real tragedy!). I was really quite apprehensive as Beni handed me the spare key so I could open the door to Madelaine Schiafino's apartment.

The Middle of Saturday Evening

THE FIRST THING I SAW when I pushed open the door was all four of us reflected in a full-length mirror. It was a bit of a disorienting vision. To the right was a blank wall and the rest of the apartment ran off to the left. I swear I could feel the hairs rise on my neck. I knew there was something very wrong. I pushed in. I wanted to see whatever there was to see *fast*, and for myself.

It was one of those sights that I'm always going to wish I could forget, but never will. Not because it was gory—just the opposite. Everything looked so normal.

The room was small, the walls a discolored beige. The furniture must have once been grand, and was certainly of a scale that suggested that in years gone by, it had graced much larger spaces. The walls were covered with sepia photographs, landscapes in oils, portraits on canvas. The whole place smelled of garlic and mothballs—not a pleasant mixture. I stepped farther inside to see what had become of Madelaine herself.

She was sitting in a large, wing-backed armchair that had been arranged to get the best view through the window. At least, it would have done if the shutters had been open, or if poor Madelaine had still been able to see. Her head lolled forward onto her chest. Her hands were folded in her lap. She looked as though she might be asleep. I knew she wasn't. She was dead, and I felt a sadness wash over me. Yes, I've seen a lot of bodies in my time, but I hadn't been sharing small talk and appetizers the night before with any of the corpses I'd seen on the body farm. *This* hit home. So much more than Alistair's death had done.

Of course, the question in my mind was about what had caused her death. Was this natural, or had she been murdered?

We all *knew* she was dead, without anyone saying it. Behind me Daphne let out a high-pitched scream and Gerard started praying in French. Beni let loose some choice Italian before he pulled Daphne away and started to punch at numbers on his cell phone. I wondered if he had the police on speed-dial yet.

Dragging my eyes away from Madelaine's body, I looked around the room. Nothing was disturbed. It really looked as though she'd simply sat down and died.

I swung around to see Gerard crying, and my heart went out to him.

"I'm sorry, Gerard, I know she was an old friend of yours."

"No, more than a friend," he said, then added, "much more."

I wondered exactly what he meant by that as I watched the man wipe at his eyes with a large, grubby pocket-handkerchief. He looked around, as though in a daze. He seemed to be smiling as he cried. He seemed . . . relieved. It was odd. I gave him a moment.

Beni's head reappeared around the corner of the room. "The police are on their way. They say to leave and do not touch anything. I am taking this lady back to her family. It is best," he said, and was gone.

I looked again at Gerard. His expression puzzled me: it looked as though he'd won something—his eyes shone with victory.

"Are you feeling alright?" I asked.

"Yes. It is finished. She is gone."

He didn't seem to be referring to an old lover.

I looked around the room again and walked a few steps toward the kitchen. On a little side wall there was a large rectangular mark on the wall-paper—it was darker than the rest of the wall. Something that had hung there for years was gone.

"Gerard—there's something missing from this wall. What used to hang here? Can you remember?"

Gerard walked up beside me and looked at the wall.

"I have not been here for many months, but every time I am here there is a photograph of Madelaine here."

"It was a large picture?" I asked. The mark on the wall measured about two feet by three.

Gerard nodded. "Yes, large. Head to toe." He used his expressive hands to illustrate. "A photograph. A portrait. She is in a fine gown, with feathers." He waggled his hand above his head. "She is a good-looking young woman. This picture is taken in the war. But after the war, then she is not so beautiful anymore."

I didn't understand. I'd thought of her as a handsome, if aged, woman the night before. "Why was she less beautiful after the war?" I asked.

Gerard looked back at the body in the chair and wiped his eyes again, then almost whispered, "When the women in the town they get hold of her after the Germans leave, they shave her head, and beat her and kick her until she is broken in many places. She leaves and goes away. She cannot be in Nice anymore. She is known. She is hated. She becomes 'Madame' Madelaine Schiafino. But no husband. But her name is Mademoiselle Madelaine Roux. Always. She is a prostitute for the Gestapo. She informs on other women. She lives here at the Palais in the war, now she comes back to die. It is right. The picture . . . that one—" he flung his arm toward the empty space, "she is showing how proud she is, how clever. Women come here to the Palais and are never seen again. She tells the Gestapo where to find women for this. My sister . . . my sister is one of these women, she disappears . . . My father, he has hidden her away from the town when the Germans come, but one day we see her come back here in a truck, then she disappears, and from then my father is never the same . . . Always he cries for my lost sister . . ." He subsided into sobs. I had a feeling they were for his sister, not Madelaine, who I was beginning to see in a whole new light.

Considering that things couldn't get much worse for the poor chap, I decided to strike while the iron was hot. "How did the hated Madelaine Roux manage to become the lawyer Madelaine Schiafino? It can't have been easy . . . or cheap! And didn't anyone around here recognize her as the same woman? You did, after all."

"She takes the money, the gifts, that the Germans give her and goes to Paris to study law. She comes back to Cannes after many years, and she has everything different about her: her name, her hair, her shape . . . she is much thinner than in the war—in the war everyone was thin, but she was not. No one thinks of her as Roux. It is when she comes here, back to the Palais that I meet her, but even I do not recognize her, until I see this picture. She tells me it is someone from her family, before the war. But I *know*. I have seen her standing on the balcony that is now the Townsends' with the Gestapo and the SS officers. I never tell anyone, until M. Townsend asks me about her. He knows her from Cannes, I think, but I do not know how. I tell him about the picture and the way she is dressed, ready for a ball, showing off the fine gifts the Gestapo give her . . . So much gold, so very fine in her . . . sin."

"Did you ever confront her about this, Gerard?" I was curious. The man was old, but his hatred was clearly still strong. Had he acted upon it? I found it hard to believe.

Gerard shook his head. "I do not need to. She knows me, and I know her. The only time it is ever mentioned is when I am here, and I see the picture and ask I her about it, and she says, 'Sometimes we must do things we know are wrong to save ourselves.' I ask her if this is what she accepts when she is a lawyer and she says no, so I say that God knows sinners and will find them out, when it is their time. She says she knows this is true, and that she is happy to meet her Maker. She is not afraid. I think it is for God to punish her. Not me. These women, who are beating her after the war, what they do is wrong too, and I must not do wrong. We answer to God, that is all."

"Any idea who might have removed the picture?" I asked, doubting he'd know.

He shook his head. "All I know is my enemy is gone." It was a statement with a sense of finality.

"Nothing else is gone?" I asked quickly. "What about in the other rooms?"

"I only see this room when I visit," was Gerard's guarded reply.

"Okay," I said, and with that I tiptoed across the carpet to peer into the tiny kitchen. There *might* have been something so obviously out of place that even I would spot it. Gerard followed, timidly, and peered in too. He shook his head and shrugged. Before we could make it to the bathroom, I heard footsteps clattering along the little corridor. I motioned to Gerard to follow me back toward the front door, which he did with a surprisingly agile step.

There I came face to face with Captain Moreau.

"Ah, Professor Morgan, we meet again. This is not good." I was sure he was referring to the circumstances, rather than meeting me—at least, I hoped that was what he meant.

"It's terrible, Captain, but I am glad you are here. We waited—we didn't want anyone to see the body by accident. Doctor Brunetti is farther along the . . . um . . ." I stopped there. I had no idea what the French for "corridor" was, and I knew was making a mess of all my tenses. Thank goodness Gerard stepped in to explain, and the puzzled look on the captain's face cleared. He thanked us both with a little nod, then asked Gerard where we could be reached. I understood quite clearly that Gerard told him that we would all head back to the Townsends' apartment, if that was acceptable. It seemed that it was, and that Moreau would meet with us there, so we were dismissed, just in time for the forensics guys to arrive.

Beni walked up to us as we exited the tragic scene, and Gerard explained to him what was going on. We made our way back toward the Townsends' wing of the building, being passed by new arrivals every moment. As we walked, none of us spoke.

I was deep in thought about the scene we'd just left. I knew something was odd about it, and I was trying to work out what it was. I wanted some space, just a few minutes alone so I could think about it clearly, but that wasn't likely to happen any time soon.

Soon we were back upstairs at Tamsin's front door. Chuck opened it.

"How is she? Okay?" he asked, cheerily enough.

"Dead," said Beni.

"What?" Chuck squealed, blocking our way inside. He looked horrified.

"Let us in, and I will tell you," replied Beni, pushing past Chuck, who seemed to be supporting himself with the door. "I need cognac," Beni added tersely, and he walked in, striding toward the drinks cabinet, where he swept up a bottle and headed for the balcony. "I will sit, and drink, and smoke, and I will think about this terrible day," he said, very dramatically. I thought that was the best idea I'd heard in a while, so decided to follow suit. Of course, we had to deal with Tamsin first, who, upon hearing that

Madelaine was dead, started wailing and weeping, and had to be the first served with the cognac. Typical!

We gave the bare details to Chuck and Tamsin together. Tamsin's responses were, needless to say, all about how this news affected her, whereas Chuck's reaction was less about himself and more about Madelaine, which was refreshing.

"Does she have any relatives we should get in touch with? I mean, is there someone we should call?" Chuck sounded distressed but keen to do something.

I deferred to Gerard, who shook his head and replied, "She is alone. No friends. There is no family. She is the last." It sounded terribly final and bleak. I felt pretty low. The cognac wasn't working. I poured another, just in case the first one hadn't been big enough. It had certainly been quite a day, and, given Moreau's promise to talk to us when he had left the late Madelaine Schiafino's apartment, I was certain that it wasn't over yet.

Oh yes, and I was hungry.

Late Saturday Evening

I DON'T MEAN TO SOUND heartless, but I really *cannot* think straight when my stomach is panicking that my throat might have been cut. I spent a moment grappling with how to raise the subject of eating. I was a "guest" at someone else's home, I couldn't leave because I was due to meet with the police, and I knew for a fact that there was nothing of any substance to eat on the premises. I decided I'd just say what I thought and hope it wouldn't sound too rude and that I wasn't the only one rumbling out there on the balcony. Luckily, there was a bit of a lull in the conversation, so I took my chance. I used my "apologetic but firm" voice—the one I usually reserve for explaining to a student that I cannot give them a higher grade just because they'd like one.

"Excuse me." I thought I'd try to get everyone's attention before I began. "I don't know about anyone else, but, if I'm going to have to wait here until Captain Moreau arrives, and none of us have any idea how long that might be, then I really am going to have to eat something approaching a proper meal."

Everyone's eyes were on me. I wondered if anyone was thinking that I could probably afford to live off my own fat reserves for a week or two. No one spoke. I carried on.

"Tamsin—you and Beni mentioned earlier that restaurants can deliver any type of food. Is there, maybe, some place locally that could deliver something we could all share?" I didn't go as far as to suggest pizza, but frankly, the thought of a large, thin-crust pepperoni with extra cheese appealed enormously!

Still no one spoke. The expressions around the table suggested that everyone was thinking it was Tamsin's place to take action, but she didn't speak. I piped up again, "You see, I wouldn't know who to call, Tamsin. Do you have a list somewhere? Or Beni, could you suggest a place?"

At last Beni spoke. I'd given him the chance to do something positive. "Of course I know a place—the place where we had lunch today. As you know, Cait, the food there is very good and I know the chef. I can call him. He will send whatever we want. So, Cait—what will make those beautiful blue eyes sparkle again?"

I felt myself flush—that second cognac must have reached my cheeks at just that moment. Damn!

"Pasta? Chicken? Steak? He can make them all. Though I do not think that fish is good if it is delivered—it will be cold too quickly. And you, Chuck? Gerard? And poor Tamsin—you must eat. I will order for you all if you like."

Ah, good old Beni—back in control.

I'd been cross when he'd ordered my lunch, but now I didn't give two hoots what he had in mind for me—I'd have eaten a pair of old boot soles glued together with jam if he'd put them in front of me at that moment. Given that I was in one of the world's centers of culinary excellence, I didn't feel too guilty hoping for something a little tastier.

There was a general nodding around the table, and Beni marched toward the kitchen, announcing loudly that he would make all the arrangements. I could hear his voice booming into the telephone as he barked rapidly in Italian to someone for whom the last twenty-four hours had *not* been a rollercoaster of murder, poisoning, police, robbery, death, and more police. No wonder I was hungry!

"That was a good idea, Cait," commented Chuck quietly. "We could all do with something. And even if Tamsin says she's not hungry, she has to keep her strength up."

For what? She doesn't actually do anything. I looked at the waif-like blond to my right who was nodding off in her chair, her head bobbing down then popping back up. What I actually said, sounding concerned, was "Yes, of course."

Chuck nodded toward Tamsin and whispered, "Sedatives?"

I shrugged. "I guess," I replied, although I didn't think that sitting in a hot bath and drinking champagne had helped very much. I smiled at Chuck. I tried to look sympathetic. It's the sort of response I knew would be expected.

Chuck then nodded in Gerard's direction. He, too, was doing the head-bobbing thing, but in his case it was understandable. He was over eighty; he'd spent the night in hospital—probably getting as little sleep as I had; and he'd just had a pretty big shock . . . and a couple of pretty large cognacs, too.

I smiled at Chuck, "I know how he feels—I bet we could all do with a nap at some point. How did you get on at the hospital? Did they keep you in all night?"

Chuck seemed distracted, and answered absently, "Yes, they let me out around six this morning. I came home, showered, and tried to sleep, but I couldn't. I kept thinking about Alistair." He fell silent for a moment, then added, "Cait, what do you think happened to Alistair? Do you think that Madelaine's death can possibly be connected to his in any way?"

I felt my multi-purpose right eyebrow lift as I said, "I think someone wanted to kill Alistair and poisoned us all to achieve that, and, yes, I think that Madelaine's death is connected to Alistair's in some way." I trailed off, realizing that I was, after all, talking to a suspect. I didn't want to give too much away, even if Chuck did look more like the all-American everyman who disappears into the background than a violent killer.

"Did Beni tell you about the robbery at the museum?" I asked. I didn't think he had. Chuck looked surprised.

"Today?" he asked, sharply.

"Well, the thinking is that it took place last night, but, yes, it was discovered earlier today." I could hear tiredness in my own voice. I lit a cigarette—that would keep me focused.

"What did they take? I've been there a few times—though it's not really my era—and they've got some great stuff there. I'm sure a lot of it is very valuable." Chuck wasn't wrong.

"They took a couple of statues, and some little ink-wells I think Beni said they were, and some papers that Beni was working on. They only got into the offices, not the actual display areas."

Chuck nodded sagely. "They were lucky, then."

I decided to not tell him about the archives and the necklace. My natural inability to trust a stranger led me straight to the thought that I really wanted to talk to Bud about Madelaine's death. But I knew that before I did that, or spoke to Moreau, or even ate, I had to find a place where I could be alone and get the events of the last hour or so into a proper perspective.

Beni's reappearance from the kitchen, proclaiming that food would arrive in half an hour, snapped both Gerard and Tamsin out of their torpor. I got to my feet and ground out my half-smoked cigarette. Then I grabbed my handbag.

"Just got to use the you-know-what," I said, and I headed off toward the downstairs bathroom. As I walked through the kitchen I glanced about and spotted a little notepad, which I picked up. I locked the bathroom door behind me, turned on the extractor fan to create some noise, took the only seat available, and tried to concentrate on what I'd seen at Madelaine's apartment. I screwed up my eyes, started to hum . . . and I was there once more . . .

I can see my hand putting the key into the lock—the lock is perfect, no marks or scuffs: it hasn't been forced or picked. The door opens silently. I smell mothballs and garlic . . . and something else . . . what is it . . . *Gerard's cologne.* He's standing next to me. Very close. I can hear him breathing. We see our reflections, and Beni gasps. I move forward and to the left where I can see the room. It is clean, well dusted and polished and, though everything in it is old, it is well tended. No—not everything is old. The television is new and large, and, now that I see it again, it is quite out of place here. Very flat. Very expensive. Tucked into the corner is a laptop computer, hooked up to various cables. *All very high-tech for a woman in her nineties.* The chair in which Madelaine is sitting is new, though its style is old, as is the pattern on the upholstery fabric. Is there anything else out of place? *No.* It all seems to be a variety of furnishings that were once costly and are now well worn and much polished. I look again at the space where the missing photograph once hung. It is only visible when you walk to, or from, the kitchen. Madelaine doesn't sit and see her young self while looking into the garden, or watching the television; the picture is behind her then. She only sees it when she's bringing something from the kitchen to the living room, or standing at the window or TV and looking toward the front door.

Madelaine's body is upright in the new/old chair. The angle of the chair is slightly reclined. I look at her feet and ankles. They are dark and mottled with lividity, which means she's been dead at least thirty minutes, but probably not more than twelve hours, and she likely died in this position. Her hands have fallen into her lap. Were they placed there? I don't think so, I think that's where they fell naturally. Now I can see what is wrong. If she had simply died as she sat there, she would have fallen forward, or at least sideways. *Someone has propped Madelaine in her upright position after her death.* She didn't just die—someone killed her, then rearranged the body. She is wearing the wedding band and gold watch she had on at dinner the night before, but her clothes are different. She has changed her clothes since leaving the hospital that morning. There are no signs that would suggest a corrosive poison or something that would have made her convulse. It seems she died quite peacefully.

Now I think about the kitchen—I can see two bowls that have been used and washed but not put away, a cup and saucer, a mug, and a coffee pot, too. There's a huge, stainless steel refrigerator squashed into the tiny space. *That's new: there are still traces of the plastic coating around the trim.* Is there anything else here that's odd? No . . . but the smell of garlic is not strongest in the kitchen—it's strongest in the living room. Why would that be? *I'll think about that.*

Is there anything else to see? Or smell? Or touch . . . No, I am careful to not touch anything. Do I feel anything? Yes . . . I feel the air move; there's a through-draft. I take myself back into the kitchen, and I see that the top portion of the window is open, though the shutters are almost closed. Like the window in the museum, it is tiny and high up. Why do I think of the museum? It must be the window.

I'm tired. I'm done. I'm hungry.

I got up from my "seat" and leaned on the edge of the basin, looking at my reflected self in the harsh lights and thought, *Oh, Cait—you look exhausted.* My God—little had I thought, when I'd got on that plane a few days ago, that *this* would be my experience of the fabulous Cote d'Azur!

Rather than wallowing in self-pity, I looked at my watch and decided to give Bud a ring. I pulled out my phone and dialed his cell, but I only got voice mail. Of course, he was out in Chilli-wack-wack-wack doing his Gang Busters thing and probably all the paperwork accompanying an operation like that. I left a message.

"Hi Bud, it's Cait. I hope your Chilliwack thing went okay. It's about eight at night here now, on Saturday of course, and I have to announce another dead body. The elderly woman, Madelaine Schiafino—though apparently that's an assumed name to lend an air of respectability to a woman who gave herself to the Gestapo, then ran off with German booty at the end of the Second World War. We've got to hang around to speak to Captain Moreau . . . I wonder if you've spoken to him about me yet? I guess I'll find out soon enough. Anyway—it was digitalis that we all got dosed with, Alistair more than the rest of us, which is why he's dead and we aren't. I don't know about Madelaine: hers might have been a natural death, but I doubt it, because I think her body was rearranged after death. If you fancy giving me a ring I'd say that I'm likely to be up and about until at least your three o'clock today . . . but, honestly, call any time. It would be great to hear a friendly voice about now. I'd really like to talk about all this with someone I trust. Okay. I'll bugger off now. Hope to hear from you soon . . . Byeeee."

I pushed the off button. I know I'd only been talking to an empty line but, somehow, I felt as though Bud had been with me, and had gone. I felt very alone.

I used the loo, washed up, put on some more lipstick, and hoped that by running my fingers along the dark circles under my eyes, they'd magically disappear. They didn't. At least I'd made the effort and, when I smiled at myself, I looked relatively perky. I was ready for dinner and the people out there. But first I asked myself if I'd made any sense of the Madelaine thing. I realized immediately that nothing much made any sense at all. So I held my head high as I marched back through the kitchen. I hoped the food would arrive quite soon because I was reaching a place I had never thought existed—I *wasn't* looking forward to nibbling any more pâté de foie gras!

Saturday Night

AS I REJOINED OUR "PARTY" on the balcony, Tamsin was whining that she was cold. Chuck tried to pacify her and offered to bring her a shawl. Beni suggested everyone should move inside. Gerard sat quietly, and I could see his eyes glistening with tears. I wondered what I'd missed. I moved toward Gerard and asked, "Are you alright?"

"I am very tired," he replied heavily. "I wish the policeman comes soon. I feel I must sleep."

I patted him on the arm and suggested that I might make some coffee, though I was a bit apprehensive about doing so because I remembered how very complicated the coffee maker had looked.

"Coffee will come with the food," was Beni's response to my general enquiry.

"Did you order decaf?" asked Tamsin sharply. Personally, I've never seen the point of decaffeinated coffee—it's just hot, brown liquid that tastes like . . . well, not coffee, in any case.

"For you, I did," replied Beni, smiling graciously. Obviously, he knew her preferences. I could only imagine they were numerous and demandingly precise.

"Good," replied Tamsin. "Caffeine is very bad for you, and if I drink it now, I'll never sleep. My mind's racing as it is."

That must be a novelty for it, I thought. "That's only natural, Tamsin, given the circumstances," I said. "You must be desperate to know what happened to Alistair, like we all are," I added.

Beni, Chuck, and Gerard all nodded, but Tamsin's response floored me. "I know what happened to Ally. He died because of the digital-*is*."

I couldn't leave it there, now could I? The woman was a complete idiot!

"Tamsin, if the snails were somehow dosed with the digitalis, aren't you the least bit curious about how the digitalis got there? Or who might have done it? And what about Madelaine? Don't you think that her death is somehow connected to Alistair's?" I knew I was raising my voice, but I'd reached the point where I felt that was all I could do to get through her thick skull.

"Well, I sort of thought Ally died because he ate so many more snails than us. He always eats fast, and he was on his second bowl when I'd only just started eating. *And* he'd been eating them in the afternoon. He said he had to try out his butter stuff, so he made himself some while I was getting ready. He said he didn't feel very well, so he took his pills. I told all this to the policeman!" She seemed annoyed that we might also like to know.

"As for how the poison stuff got there, well, I don't know. Ally got the snails delivered here from the farm on Monday and they sat in their box things over there all week," she waved her arm airily to the far corner of the balcony. "I don't know all the ins and outs, but he always seemed to be hosing them down and feeding them, then he kept going on about how well they were 'drying out,' though I don't know what that means. He got them ready on Friday morning. It took ages! All that boiling, and pulling them out of their shells—yuk! I know he'd finished before he went to the Cours Saleya for his drinky-poo because he took the shells with him in a big bag to give to a friend of his who has a restaurant there."

"What about the snails after they were prepared? They weren't in plain sight when we all came through the kitchen to the balcony on Friday evening, were they?" I was quick on the uptake because I thought I might be able to discover something useful.

Tamsin furrowed her pretty little brow and then replied, "Well, I know that Ally cooks them with all the butter and wine, and bits and pieces, in a really big pot. It's blue. Le Creuset."

"Okay, it was on the cook-top," I interjected. Everyone gave me an odd look. I let it pass. "Any one of us could have put something into that pot, if we'd known what was in it. I know that every single person left the group at one time or another, so everyone had the chance to slip in the poison."

"What do you mean 'any one of us'?" wailed Tamsin. "None of *us* wanted Alistair dead!" She seemed genuinely taken aback at the thought. I found it hard to imagine it hadn't already occurred to her. It had certainly occurred to everyone else! She carried on, "*I'm* his *wife*! *I* loved him . . . and everyone else there was his friend. Well, except *you*!" She stabbed a perfectly manicured fingernail in my direction as she spoke. Of course, everybody turned to look.

Beni furtively lit a cheroot, thereby avoiding all eye contact, and Chuck elaborately cleared his throat. Gerard nodded his head sagely. I felt I had to respond.

"Which means that I'm the only one who didn't know him well enough to want to kill him. Whereas each of you—" I didn't point, but I made sure I looked at them all in turn, "had a good reason to want him out of the way. There's his money, the swimming pool, the missing necklace, and let's not forget Alistair's unusual ability to get people to tell him their darkest secrets." *Ha! Take that!*

They all exclaimed that I was talking rubbish . . . each in their own way, which was good, because that's what I'd wanted them to do: I wanted to try to get them to defend themselves. I kept going, regardless of their cries of protestation.

"Beni—you said you were 'relieved' about Alistair being dead," Tamsin looked shocked at my comment, and I could see Beni blush, even in the dim light that washed across the balcony from inside the apartment. "What did you mean by that?" I didn't expect a straight answer, but I knew that whatever his response was, it would be interesting.

I got no answer from Beni at all. Instead, Tamsin piped up and said, "You never forgave him for telling your wife about that red-headed girl he saw you with in the Place de la Magenta, did you, Beni? Apparently she was *very* young," she added, almost as an aside to the rest of us. "That's what sent wifey running back to her mummy in Milan. It's why you're on your own now. He told me all about it. Or was there more? Ally was clever about knowing things. People liked to tell Ally stuff. Like Cait said." She sounded quite pleased with herself. I could picture her pulling the wings off butterflies.

Beni huffed and puffed a bit, then replied sharply, "There *is* no girl. There *was* no girl. Alistair did not speak to my wife. She is in Milan because of her work. She designs clothes, as you know. That is where she needs to be for her business. Besides," I sensed he was about to retaliate, "with Alistair gone, you get all this—" he waved his arm in the air toward the apartment, "and all his money too. You like money. You are very good at spending it. Good at making Alistair spend it on you. He must have spent a *lot* of money to get that necklace for you. You do not even know what it is. It should be in a museum!"

Ah, good, we were back to the necklace again.

"I *do* know what my necklace is . . . it's pretty, and gold, and magical, *and* it's a part of history. I should have it, but my necklace has gone, and Ally has gone. How can you be so cruel, Beni? I thought you liked me! I like you!" Tamsin was whimpering like a child, and employing much the same sort of logic as one. "Maybe," she added with spite in her voice, "if you wanted that necklace for your precious museum so much, *you* stole it and killed Ally too! He told me about what you said about the necklace—that you'd do *anything* to have it. He *told* me!" I was surprised she didn't poke out her tongue as a parting shot.

"Me!?" cried Beni, "I did *not* steal the necklace! I *did not* kill Alistair and I *did not* kill Madelaine!" That just about covered it . . . well, he'd left out the theft at the museum, I supposed, but he *was* in a temper.

I jumped in. "So who did, eh? What about you, Chuck? You were against the swimming pool. And I get the distinct impression that you'd like to own *this* apartment—the one with its famous balcony and the truly grisly history. Well, maybe now Tamsin will be persuaded to sell."

"So I killed Alistair for a *balcony*? *This* balcony?" Chuck's already high register was even higher. "I'd be more likely to kill for the *Kragen des Todes* than a goddam *balcony*!"

Gerard gasped and roughly grabbed Chuck by his arm. "The *Kragen des Todes*? What do you know of this? Why do you speak of this? It is a terrible thing!" Gerard was horrified at what Chuck had said, but I had no idea what either of them was talking about.

"What's the *Kragen des Todes*?" I asked. Beni responded with a shrug, and Tamsin shook her head, indicating she didn't know. I said to Chuck, "Come on, spill!"

I could tell he wished he could take back what he'd said. His eyes darted about, as though he was being hunted and looking desperately for an escape route.

"Ummmm . . . It's complicated," he replied, weakly.

"It is *not* complicated," boomed Gerard in a surprisingly loud voice, "it is death. Death is always simple." It was a bold statement, and he certainly had my undivided attention.

He drank down the last dregs of his cognac, slammed his glass on the table top, and said, "The *Kragen des Todes* is what the Germans called the *Collier de la Mort*. It is the same thing. The Collar of Death. It is what Madelaine is wearing in the portrait that was taken," he added, more to me than anyone else. "It is a terrible thing that the Gestapo do when they are here. Them and the SS. They bring young women, some are just girls, like my sister, to this place. They make them dress like a queen. They make them wear fine clothes, jewels, and the *Kragen des Todes*, then they treat them as slaves, then the women, the girls, they are seen no more. Not by their family. Not by anyone. They disappear. They are dead. This happens many times. Stories come down to us, from the servants who work in the Palais. As soon as a woman wears the necklace, she is dead. And you," he looked directly at Chuck, "you think this is interesting. Ha! Interesting? It is *real* people. It is my family. It is not history, it is real. You make the Gestapo seem glamorous! You want to live here because you are captivated by them. You are a terrible man!"

Chuck leapt to his feet. "I'm not 'captivated' by the Gestapo! My grandfather helped Robert H. Jackson lead the prosecution at the Nuremberg Trials, for God's sake! Nazism was a terrible blot on the history of mankind. I truly believe that, but we cannot ignore history. We must learn from it! That's why I write the books I write, so people can learn."

"Why mention this Collar of Death at all?" asked Beni, now totally engaged and apparently confused.

Again, Chuck looked at his feet and didn't answer, which was fine by me; I was pretty sure I'd worked it out. The necklace part, anyway. Chuck, Beni, and maybe even Gerard, had equally strong motives for wanting to own it: either because of its role in history, ancient or more recent, or because of a personal connection.

"I don't know why people always talk about the horrible things that happened here," said Tamsin plaintively. "This is my home. You'll give me nightmares."

Once again Tamsin had managed to take a conversation about man's inhumanity to man, and make it all about her. Wow!

The doorbell rang, and Beni leapt to his feet. "It is the food," he shouted, looking at his watch. "I will arrange all this," and he took off toward the kitchen. Meanwhile, Gerard looked sulkily at his empty cognac glass, shooting Chuck the odd disparaging glare, and Tamsin began to whine again that she was cold.

"A good meal will warm you up," said Chuck.

"Yes," I added, keen to make at least something of my surroundings, "it's a lovely evening, and it would be a shame to be indoors." I suspected that my life on Burnaby Mountain meant I was just a bit hardier than our delicate little flower, Tamsin, who had obviously become acclimatized to the warmth of the south of France. Just to be sure, I added, "And I, for one, would rather eat at this table than the one where we ate at last night."

"Absolutely!" agreed Chuck, a little too loudly.

"Chuck, will you help me carry this?" called Beni from the kitchen. Chuck dutifully helped Beni carry foil containers, plates, glasses, and cutlery from the kitchen, as well as a couple of bottles of champagne and some red wine. We all pulled our chairs to the table, and soon we were tucking into a wonderful choice of pissaladier (a local onion and anchovy tart), salade Nicoise, Provençal stuffed vegetables, veal Milanese, pasta, and gnocci with three different sauces—creamy, meaty or spicy, and bread and cheeses, of course. For me, it wasn't so much a question of choosing as of having a bit of everything. In my own defense, it was all so good it would have been a sin to miss anything.

Tamsin nibbled at the stuffed vegetables; Gerard said he didn't feel up to much more than a little gnocci, then ate a great big pile of it; and Beni and Chuck "grazed," though less voraciously than I did. Chuck hit the meat in a big way, Beni more the pasta. We were all pretty quiet for a while which might have been a good way to ratchet down the tension, but it meant I didn't have as much of a chance to gather new information.

We were all ready for the cheeses and coffee when the doorbell rang again. It was gone ten o'clock, so I couldn't imagine who it could be but Moreau. I was quite glad, because I wanted the day to end, but I knew it wouldn't until he was done with me . . . with us all.

"I'll go," said Chuck. Beni and I didn't object because we were smoking, Gerard seemed to be glad to let his food settle, and Tamsin . . . well, it would be unlike Tamsin to volunteer to undertake any sort of action at all, as far as I could tell.

Captain Moreau walked out onto the balcony, just ahead of Chuck. I wondered what his thoughts were at the sight that greeted him; it must have looked as though a wonderful dinner party was just wrapping up. Beni politely rose to greet the policeman, and he pulled an empty chair up to the table.

In French Beni invited the man to join us for some cheese, or bread, or maybe a glass of wine. Moreau sat in the seat he was offered and accepted a glass of red. He pulled out his cigarettes, raised them toward Tamsin with a query on his face, to which Tamsin didn't react at all, but to which Beni responded telling him to go ahead and smoke. He did.

"*Bon soirez*," began Moreau.

Beni immediately looked at me and Chuck and said, "Captain Moreau says 'Good evening.'"

A feeling of dread crept over me as I realized that we might be in for a very long night.

"I speak only very little French, as Monsieur l'Capitaine knows from our meeting this morning," commented Chuck.

Moreau had a busy morning, I thought to myself. Aloud I said, "Mine's okay, but I don't get every word when people speak quickly. Maybe Chuck and I could just ask you if we don't quite catch something?" Beni nodded. "Do you speak French, Tamsin?" I continued. I could guess her response.

"*Mais bien sur, je parle français couramment*," was Tamsin's incredible reply.

"You speak French *fluently*?" I asked her. Maybe I had misunderstood.

"Of course, you have to if you want to go shopping," she replied innocently.

Well now, *that* threw me! I've heard of idiot-savants, of course, but who'd have thought that *this* twit would be able to master a second language? Not me, for one! It certainly put the pressure on Chuck and me to keep up with Moreau. I concentrated hard, and, to be fair, I think Moreau was making a real effort to speak quite slowly and very clearly.

"You all know of the death of Mme. Schiafino," he began, and we all nodded gravely. "She died some time between three this afternoon—that is when she was last seen alive, by a neighbor—and about half an hour before the body was found. I know that she was a guest at the party last night where M. Townsend died. We now know *how* M. Townsend died; at least, we know what caused his death. I am still investigating how the digitalis was introduced to the escargots. Two unexpected deaths in the same building within twenty-four hours is not likely to be a coincidence—" I could imagine Bud saying much the same thing, "so I am interested in understanding how Mme. Schiafino and M. Townsend were connected. This might help us to understand why they both died. I have had the opportunity to speak with you all about M. Townsend and the gathering here last evening. Now I need to speak to you all about Mme. Schiafino and her relationship with M. Townsend. I am sure you understand. I want to do this privately, and you are all advised to consider if you would like to have a legal representative present when we speak. This is now a formal investigation into murder and you will all be required to make a sworn statement at the end of our interview. To this end, I must ask you all to accompany me to the police station. I have several cars waiting to take you all there, and, when we have completed the process, you will be driven to wherever you wish—either back here to the Palais, or to your hotel, Professor Morgan, or your home, Doctor Brunetti."

Tamsin let out a little scream. "Oh no! Not a police station! I don't want to go to a police station! Captain Moreau—it's so late . . . Can't this wait until tomorrow? Can't you question me here? I don't want to go to a police station. I'm sure it's not very nice there!" Even in French, it was still all about the Widow Tamsin!

"*Yes*, it must be done tonight," replied Moreau, firmly. "Mme. Townsend—this is your husband's murder that we are investigating! Do you not care that the culprit might flee?"

"You think it was one of us?" asked Beni, his voice booming, maybe more loudly than he had intended.

Moreau smiled with his teeth, not his eyes. "This is still something we are investigating. There are many avenues for us to follow. You are the people who were with M. Townsend at his time of death and so, of course, are of interest to my investigation. As the people who were with Mme. Schiafino last night, and the people who found her body, again, you are of interest. In fact, you are *very* interesting people." He smirked. It wasn't a comforting expression.

"*I* didn't find her body," bleated Tamsin. "I've never been in her stinky little apartment. I don't know why I can't have a good night's sleep in my own bed. I didn't kill Ally and I didn't kill Madelaine . . . and I certainly didn't steal my own necklace. So why can't I do this tomorrow? Besides," she added quite slyly, "if you're interviewing us all, one at a time, it'll take hours . . . If you started with her," she pointed that finger at me again, "and went all night with the others, you might be ready for me in the morning, then you could come here and we could have breakfast together." It seemed that Tamsin had come up with the perfect plan—for Tamsin.

"Mme. Townsend, I must speak with you at the police station because we have special equipment there—cameras and recorders—in our interview rooms. It is not like the old days when a policemen and a suspect had a conversation, one to one, and then everyone accepted the policeman's version. No, no, it is not like that at all!"

"So we are all suspects?" asked Beni.

"Yes," replied Moreau.

There it was, finally out in the open. We were all suspects in one confirmed murder, an unexpected death and two robberies . . . or even three, if you were to count Mme. Schiafino's portrait.

It was at that dramatic moment that my handbag started to perform . . . playing the annoying tune I'd foolishly set as my ring-tone, which drove me mad the second it started. I apologized profusely as I scrabbled around trying to locate my phone, but by the time I triumphantly plucked it from the black hole that was my handbag, it had stopped ringing. Typical! I knew that wasn't the moment to find out who had called. I stuffed the phone back into the abyss; I'd check to see if anyone had left a message the next chance I had. I hoped it was Bud returning my call, and I also hoped that I wasn't going to get caught in a game of voice mail tag. I really wanted to be able to talk this all through with Bud. I was beginning to feel as though I was overboard and drifting from the ship—and Bud was the last chance I had for anyone to throw me a lifeline. I can't swim, so this mental image had me panicking, big time.

Apart from Tamsin's protestations, we were all quiet. Too tired to argue, I guess. And full. Well, I was, anyway. I was glad I'd eaten heartily. Who knew how long the night would be?

"I will take M. Fontainbleu with me to the station," said Moreau, standing. "He will be glad to be back at home and asleep, I am sure. I believe he knew Mme. Schiafino the best among you?" His quizzical expression drew nods from us all.

"That is a good idea, Captain," said Beni. "I am sure we are all happy for you to speak with Gerard first. We will wait our turn." I was pretty sure Tamsin wasn't happy that the aged gardener would be the first one to be heading for his bed, but then, frankly, I didn't care. I suspected that she'd be dealt with before me, in deference to her tragic loss, but I hoped that French gallantry would at least allow me to be interviewed before Chuck and Beni. Especially Chuck—it sounded like he'd just been relaxing all day—not dealing with a large lunch and a robbery.

"Captain Moreau, would it be alright with you if the rest of us spent a little time clearing up here?" I wanted to add, *Except Tamsin, of course, who probably won't lift a finger,* but I resisted.

Moreau looked around and nodded. "Yes, I will take M. Fontainbleu, and there are two more cars. Ladies in one, gentlemen in the other. Ladies first, of course," and he smiled that shark-like smile again and nodded to Tamsin and me. She looked at me as though I were something on the bottom of her shoe. Nice!

Late Saturday Night

IT TOOK BENI, CHUCK, AND me a little while to clear the detritus from Tamsin's balcony. I grappled with my conscience as we tipped unfinished food into plastic bags and then sent them hurtling down the garbage chute in the kitchen. I could almost hear my mother saying, "Waste not, want not, Caitlin." She always used my full name when she was trying to impress something upon me . . . or tell me off about something. Now no one calls me Caitlin except my doctor and my dentist.

The truth of it was, only the cheese was worth keeping for the next day. When we had begun clearing, Tamsin announced that she had to go and change her clothes for an ensemble more suited to attending an interview at a police station—*shocker, right?*—so the two men and I were left alone to do the best we could. Beni and I managed to drink coffee and smoke as we cleared. Chuck did most of the carrying to and fro, but all the conversation was what you might call "small talk" because none of us were discussing dead bodies or priceless jewelry . . . for a change.

I managed to duck out to the bathroom. I sometimes take advantage of the fact that men seem to think that all women have bladders the size of a walnut. I checked my phone and could see that whoever had called me earlier on had an 'unknown number', and was, therefore, not Bud. There was nothing I could do about that—it might just have been someone mis-dialling, after all. I called Bud's cell—voice mail; then his office—voice mail; then the Anderson apartment—again, voice mail. I finally tried Jan's cell phone. I know that calling the wife of someone you want to talk to is not really the "done" thing, but—needs must! I even got voice mail there, too.

It gave me a funny feeling, as though something was wrong. It's weird, isn't it? We're so used to being able to reach people exactly when we want

them these days that *not* being able to get hold of them makes you feel as though they've fallen off the face of the planet. I didn't leave a message at any of Bud's possible locations on the first try and decided to do something I'm not really good at. I laboriously typed a text message that simply read "Call me?" then sent it to Bud's cell phone. That would be where it would be most likely to reach him quickly. Where was he? The grow-op bust in Chilliwack couldn't have taken that long, surely? Usually, they take about an hour, tops, to get in, get the people out, and then it's all down to clearing the property and getting rid of the drugs. Then it's all back to the station and get the paperwork done . . . Bud would have been finished hours earlier.

It occurred to me that maybe something had gone wrong, and I didn't like that thought. Not one little bit. I remembered the big grow-op they'd found in the Okanagan region. The guys who'd set up the operation had trained bears, by feeding them dog food, to protect the site. Now, although this might be unlikely in Chilliwack, there was always the chance complex security measures had to be overcome. Bud would have gone out in his Kevlar, he always did, but what if the operation had gone sideways? If someone had been hurt? Or killed? What if Bud . . . no, I couldn't go there. I was beginning to feel panic in the pit of my stomach, so I looked at myself in the mirror and gave myself a talking to. I was in enough trouble as it was, and I couldn't go worrying about what was probably nothing at all back home in Vancouver. I had to use my energy to make sure I didn't continue as chief suspect in a double homicide and triple theft.

That got me focused. I emerged feeling mentally realigned, physically relieved and refreshed, and ready to face Moreau.

What I wasn't quite prepared for was Tamsin's interpretation of how it was best for a new widow to present herself for a police interview. Apparently, it involved a long black velvet dress, alarmingly high-heeled black leather boots, a black wrap edged with fur, a large black Kelly bag, and a pair of "Jackie O" sunglasses. It was eleven o'clock at night, for goodness sake!

"I'm ready now; we should leave," was all she said. Well, at least it wasn't "I'm ready for my close-up, Mr. DeMille," which it might just as well have been.

Luckily, I was ready too. Tamsin gave her keys to Chuck so he could lock up when he and Beni left. She and I took the elevator to the ground floor, which was still abuzz with people coming and going from Madelaine's apartment, and we made our way to the front door. Pierre Bertrand, the young policeman who'd translated for me at the police station that morning—my God, was it only twelve hours since I'd been there the last time—was waiting in the residents' parking area of the Palais, smoking and looking a bit bored. He brightened at the sight of us descending the steps.

"Ah, Professor Morgan, you are ready, good. I am to take you to Captain Moreau," he called as we approached him.

"Yes, young man," replied Tamsin, "we're ready. You can drive us now." As we moved away from the lights of the building and toward the parked cars, I half expected her to fall flat on her face in those sunglasses and stiletto heels. She couldn't have been able to see where she was going at all!

Bertrand smiled, and even bowed a little as he opened the rear door of the police car for Tamsin. He rolled his eyes as I got in. I winked back and smiled. He was sweet, and it was nice to see a familiar and friendly face among all the others that were scurrying about looking worried and pinched.

The drive to the police station was uneventful, with Tamsin's face turned away from me the whole time. She didn't speak at all. I wondered what thoughts might be rattling around in that head of hers. I reminded myself that she might be a cunning killer, pulling the wool over all our eyes. Then I reminded myself that I didn't have time to be wondering what *she* was thinking, and that I'd better start working out what *I* was going to say to Moreau when I saw him.

Bertrand's driving was all that Beni's wasn't—in other words, smooth and calm and involving no swear words at all, in any language. As we wound down the now familiar road from Cimiez through Carabacel to the area behind the Promenade des Anglais, I tried to not worry about Bud and to focus on my more immediate problems. It wasn't easy, because I was beginning to realize just how much alcohol I'd consumed that day and the effect it was having on me—a headache beginning behind my eyes. Tamsin's overwhelming and sickly perfume wasn't helping.

"Could you crack a window open, please?" I asked Bertrand, and he obliged, with some relief it seemed. Tamsin glared at me as though I'd just asked him to spray us with hydrochloric acid.

"Don't do that," she snapped at Bertrand, as though he were simply a chauffeur, "it'll mess up my hair!"

The policeman closed the window and shrugged, catching my rolling eyes in his rear view mirror, no doubt. Thankfully, I didn't have to sit there gagging for much longer, as we soon drew up to what appeared to be the rear entrance of the police station. This part of the building was more modern than the elaborate front entrance that I'd used earlier, and the interior matched the exterior: no fancy moldings and high ceilings here. Here it was all business and just a bit grubby and knocked around its edges.

Bertrand showed us to a waiting area, then disappeared. He returned before I had a chance to decide which of the dog-eared French magazines I would pretend to read. He announced that Captain Moreau would like to see Mme. Townsend. Tamsin shot me a look of superior satisfaction as she tottered away with Bertrand, and I felt like poking my tongue out at her receding figure. At least I was free of that dreadful perfume, though it hung in the air after she left, like a little waft of poisoned gas. I was waggling my arm about, trying to disperse it more quickly, when Bertrand reappeared and asked if he could sit next to me. Of course I said yes. I wondered why he wanted to sit—it didn't seem like a normal thing for a junior police officer to do.

"Captain Moreau has asked me to remind you that you are able to bring a lawyer with you to this meeting. We know you are a visitor, so I have the names of some people you might like to call. They are all lawyers of the correct experience, and they all speak English."

I'd forgotten about that.

"Tamsin didn't have a lawyer with her," I observed.

"Yes, Mme. Townsend has a lawyer. He was here before you arrived. Apparently, she called him before she left the Palais and told him to meet her here."

So the Widow Tamsin hadn't just been dolling herself up—she'd been arranging legal representation as well. Maybe she had a bit more sense than I'd given her credit for.

"Do *you* think I need a lawyer?" I was beginning to get a bit alarmed. "Is it normal for this sort of circumstance?"

Bertrand thought for a moment before he replied, "It is your right, at this time, to have a legal representative who can explain the law to you and can advise you what to say and what not to say. This is a serious case: two people are dead. Do you know anything about French law?"

I wondered how different it could be from British or Canadian law, both of which I had a working knowledge of, especially when it came to murder. I had to admit to myself that I really didn't know. So, what to do?

"I understand what you are saying, Pierre," I dared to use his first name in the hope that it would help us connect better—you never know when you're going to need a policeman on your side. He smiled. "But I have a strong belief that any investigation that is about finding out the truth will achieve just that. I have no intention of telling anything but the truth, so I think I'll be alright, thank you. I realize that I am in what might look like a difficult situation, being a stranger and all, but Captain Moreau strikes me as a very capable man, and I believe that he will be reasonable when he hears my story."

Bertrand chewed his lip as he thought for a moment, then said, "It is difficult for me to say more than this. It is your right to have someone who will speak for you, and you *are* a stranger, and two people have died since your arrival in their circle. The other people in that circle are well known in the city, they have a history here that is respectable and known. You do not. Maybe some things that have happened to you in the past might make even a good policeman think that your arrival and the deaths are connected."

Well, if I'd needed a wake-up call, *that* was it. I could only imagine the poor chap was trying to let me know, without saying it, that Moreau had investigated my background and had discovered I'd been arrested on suspicion of murdering my boyfriend fifteen years earlier. Of course, he'd have also discovered that I'd been completely cleared and that, although the case remained unsolved, it was evident I'd had nothing to do with it at all.

I reached out and patted Bertrand on the hand. "Thanks, I understand," I said, quietly, "but I'll be fine. I've worked with the police in Vancouver quite often, and I know that if I only tell the truth, it cannot hurt me. But I'll take the list, in case at any point I feel as though I should shut up and get myself a lawyer."

He smiled at me and got up to leave.

"By the way," I asked, "do you know any of these people? Are any of them better than the others? Or worse?" I grinned, the best I could.

Bertrand looked around somewhat furtively, then said, very quietly, "Laurent . . . he is my mother's brother." He winked, then walked away. I was left to contemplate my decision to go ahead without any representation. I hoped that my faith in the police was well founded, and that I wouldn't regret it. Pondering this kept me busy for a few minutes until Bertrand popped his head around the door to the waiting room and announced that Moreau was ready for me.

"That was quick," I said, bearing in mind what I knew about police interviews. They could sometimes go on for hours.

"Her lawyer didn't let her say much," whispered Bertrand as I walked beside him toward a corridor lined with doors, one of which he opened. He stood back for me to enter.

The room was a starkly lit cream-painted box, furnished with a desk and four chairs. Microphones on stands perched on each side of the table. Moreau was in one seat, and gesturing for me to sit opposite him. Before anyone spoke he turned on the recording device, then stated, in French of course, his own name, the date and time, and then invited me to state my full name, my temporary address in Nice, my home address, my date of birth, my occupation, and my nationality. I was surprised that I wasn't asked for my shoe size or my vital statistics. He stated, for the record, that Officer Bertrand would be present to act as a translator, then told me, once again, that I had the right to legal representation—a right which I then formally declined.

And then he was off. This time he made no attempt to speak slowly, and I had a real problem keeping up with him. Bertrand translated, which helped move things along.

"The deaths of M. Alistair Townsend and Mme. Madelaine Schiafino are being investigated. You are here to answer questions relating to these matters, and any other matters I believe might be connected, in any way, to those deaths. Do you understand?"

"Yes, I understand."

"We have already had an informal conversation about the events of Friday evening: your memories of them and your part in them."

"Yes."

"I will now ask you make a formal statement about these events, which will become the legal record. I will then ask further questions. Do you understand?"

"Yes." I was being incredibly positive so far.

"Please begin," added Moreau.

I began to recount my meeting with Alistair in the Cours Saleya on Friday, the events of the evening, that night and the following morning, up to and including my meeting with Moreau at the station. It didn't really take long.

When I'd reached the point of my leaving the police station, Moreau interrupted my flow. "Good, this is all as I have it in my notes. There is nothing you would like to add at this time? Nothing else you have remembered?"

I shook my head.

He continued, "Now, if you will please tell me, for the record, what has happened since then."

"Certainly, but before I begin, may I ask if you have been contacted by Commander Bud Anderson from Vancouver?" I wanted to know so that I could decide how best it was to continue.

Moreau looked puzzled and responded, "No, I have never heard of this man. Who is he, and why should I have heard from him?"

"Bud Anderson ran the British Columbia Integrated Homicide Investigation team for a couple of years. During that time he used me as a consultant on many cases. As you know, I'm a criminologist. I specialize in criminal psychology, with an emphasis on victim profiling—or victimology. This is what Bud used me for. To be able to work with his team, I had to gain some pretty high level security clearances from all the branches of the local, provincial, and federal law enforcement bodies in Canada. Now, I suspect you've been checking my background since we last met, and I am assuming you've discovered that, about fifteen years ago, I was held for questioning about the death of my boyfriend, but was cleared. Completely. I spoke with Bud earlier today and he said he would contact you to make sure that you understood my role with his team, and, to be frank, to tell you that you could trust me to not be the perpetrator in this case."

"That is for me to decide, Professor, as I would have explained to your 'friend' if he had contacted me." I felt a bit of a chill. I wondered if it would help if I used another approach.

"Captain Moreau, I have declined legal representation at this time because I honestly believe that the truth cannot hurt me. I can only assure you that I am blameless in all of the matters that are being investigated . . . but I realize that, of course, you only have my word for this."

He nodded. He didn't smile. I plowed on.

"I'm going to tell you what's happened to me since I left this police station this morning, but I'd also like to share some of my thoughts with you—because it's not just what's happened that's important, but what I have learned. I think it might have a bearing on this case that's vital."

Just as I was drawing breath to continue, Moreau held up his hand to stop me.

"Professor Morgan—I am the investigator here, not you. Your interpretation of facts is irrelevant. I want you to tell me simply the events that have occurred, and not your whimsical inferences." Bertrand had a bit of a problem translating this last bit, but I got the gist of it. Moreau was telling me to stick to the facts and not embellish.

I was beginning to feel a bit of pressure from Captain Moreau. I *knew* I could help. I had to work out a way of doing so without appearing to step away from a recounting of "the facts." I took the deep breath I'd been about to take when he'd stopped me and got on with it. I did my best and, because I didn't include anything judgemental, or about food, or anything like that, I felt I'd done a pretty good job of telling him what had happened. Needless to say, it took a while as I'd had a busy day.

He asked no questions, but he did take notes. I tried to not let the note taking throw me off course. When I'd finished I signified that I'd done so by describing my entrance into his office, about an hour earlier and rounded it all off with "There." I felt like saying "Ta-Daaaa!" but I thought that would be a bit much.

"That is your statement, Professor Morgan?" he asked dryly, taking the wind out of my sails. He sounded skeptical.

"Ummm . . . yes," I answered, unsure of what else he might have expected.

He looked at me very seriously as he said, "You have used no notes, and yet you have given me a *very* detailed explanation of your day. Much more detailed than most people are able to offer. How do you do this?" It was a barbed question. He sounded almost cross with me.

I sighed, knowing that the only way to proceed was to explain my "special gifts" to him, which wasn't going to be fun, but which was clearly necessary. It would have all been so much easier if Bud had called him; then I wondered why he hadn't. If Bud hadn't offered, I would never have asked, and he'd been so insistent. Why hadn't he done it? Bugger! I let out a sigh as I began, but begin I did.

"Captain Moreau, when I was a child I thought I was developing like all my peers. I thought in a certain way, I saw things a certain way and I recalled things in a certain way—ways that, for me, were natural. It wasn't until I hit my teen years that I realized I wasn't normal . . . at least, not in certain ways. As I grew older, studied psychology at university, I realized that I have some abilities that are unusual, and which have not yet either been explained, or even agreed upon as existing, by scientists. I have what is called by some a 'photographic memory.'" Moreau and Bertrand raised their eyebrows at this, but I kept going. "I don't have autism or ADHD, but I can see and make sense of collections of things very quickly. I also have the ability to recall multi-sensory memories at will. These are skills I seem to have been born with, but which, having noted them, I have also worked to train in my adult life. I have not been investigated nor tested by anyone in a laboratory, so there is no *evidence* that I have these abilities, which I keep to myself. But I use them for my work."

Moreau shrugged, and moved in his seat. He didn't seem to be sure about how to proceed. "Can you give me an example of what you mean?"

I thought for a moment, then said, "When Tamsin emptied her handbag onto the back seat of Beni's car, I couldn't help myself, I 'saw' what was there. For the record it was five lipsticks, six wads of used paper towels, a dozen pens and pencils, two notebooks, a purse, a credit card wallet, two sets of keys, a bottle of water, and what looked like a handkerchief tied at one end to form a little bag. I saw the contents for about five seconds. If I close my eyes a little, and hum to myself—I'm sorry, I don't know why it helps to do that—I can see them all again now. I can do this to be able to revisit places I have been. I have been through this process for my own satisfaction re-thinking the events of last night and our discovery of Madelaine Schiafino's body. I find it very useful. It helps me to see things I might have missed at the time—except, of course, I didn't miss them because I must have encoded them to be able to recall them, if you see what I mean." I got a bit carried away with the explanation, but it made sense to me. I wondered if it made sense to Moreau. It certainly seemed to have Bertrand intrigued.

"This is interesting," said Moreau slowly. "Do it for me now. Tell me about my office—the one where we met this morning. I know that room very well." If he'd had a gauntlet about his person, he'd have been flapping it in my face.

I hate it, absolutely *hate* it when people want me to perform like a trained bloody seal. It's exactly why I don't tell people all this stuff. It's not a party trick. I did understand why Moreau wanted me to do it: he wanted to see if I was talking rubbish. And, to be fair, he'd come up with a good way of judging me. So I agreed, settled myself in my chair, screwed up my eyes and started to hum. Of course, I had to stop humming to be able to tell him what I was "seeing," which threw me off a bit, but I did my best.

"Your office smells of tobacco and lemon-scented polish. You don't smoke in there now, but it has been smoked in for some time since the draperies, or furnishings, were cleaned. Otherwise it has a faint scent of—" I sniffed the air and said, surprised, "oh, it's you! Lavender, rose, neroli. It's not your cologne or after shave though. I think it's a body lotion. The carpet in your office is fitted and relatively old. It is greasy in spots and your desk used to be in a different position—either that or there was another desk in the room as well for some time: there are marks on the carpet near the window on the far left where the other, or your, desk used to sit. Someone in there used to smoke a pipe—I can smell it as I walk toward your desk, though not at your desk. Maybe you used to have your desk elsewhere and you smoked a pipe then, or, more likely, your predecessor in the office had his desk in a different place, under the window, and he smoked a pipe. That's more likely because, psychologically speaking, the new inhabitant of an office likes to move things around to put their own stamp on the place. I suggest that the office is always used by the person of your rank, and you took it over from your old boss, who you probably didn't like very much." Bertrand cleared his throat politely when I said this bit.

"Your desk is old, and, again, I suspect it has been in that particular room since it was new and it has been used by all your predecessors. You are shorter than the man you took over from, who was quite tall. I know this because the feet of the desk used to have round pads on them, and they left round indentations in the carpet, but now they are square and have been trimmed down. The desk was too high for you. The seat upon which you now sit allows you to have your feet on the floor, but scuff marks to the right and left of the opening for your feet show me that, for some time, your feet dangled, and you knocked the wood quite often—"

"Very good ... stop!" called Moreau, again holding up his hand. I opened my eyes and met his. It was a pity he'd stopped me—I was just getting going. "This is very interesting. It is clear that you can do what you claim," he stated bluntly. His manner was beginning to get to me. He was so absolutely without any human connection. He was all business, and grim with it.

"Yes, I can," I replied as level-headedly as possible. *Naa-naa-na-naa-na!* rang in my head.

"I should use this talent of yours, like your Bud Anderson does in Vancouver. You have told me the facts of your day; now tell me what you have learned, and what you think it means. I admire your trust in us, and I will be pleased to be taken into your confidence when it comes to your thoughts on the case."

Despite his words, his demeanor didn't convey a hint of admiration or pleasure. He was either playing me, or I'd passed a test that meant I was no longer a suspect. I suspected the former, but I acted as though it were the latter. After all, I wasn't in Vancouver, Bud wasn't there to hold my hand, so I'd have to put my faith in my own abilities and hope that, eventually, I could really win Moreau over.

"Thank you, Captain Moreau, I'd welcome the chance to do that. I think there are two possible reasons for the murder of Alistair Townsend: the necklace that is missing from his apartment, or the fact that he was pushing for a swimming pool to be built into the gardens at the Palais du Belle France. Let's start with the necklace, because that's what I know most about. Beni thinks that Alistair had somehow acquired a museum-quality, Welsh-gold Druidic necklace, dating from the first century AD, that became the property of a Roman family living in Cimiez; Chuck seems to think that Alistair had managed to get hold of something called the Collar of Death, which was a piece of jewelry used by the Gestapo and SS as a part of their adornment of young girls plucked from the locale and subjected to God only knows what before, presumably, being killed. Now, apparently only Alistair and Tamsin had seen the necklace before its theft, and Alistair had promised to tell everyone the story of his find after he had presented it to Tamsin at her party. I think I can do that now, because I believe I can put the pieces together, thanks to something that Gerard told me . . . albeit unwittingly. I believe that the necklace Beni is talking about and the necklace Chuck is talking about are one and the same. Both the theft of a Roman family archive from the museum at Cimiez and the photographic portrait of Madelaine taken from her apartment are connected to its disappearance. I need to explain a bit of background to help you understand why that is."

"Please do," said Moreau, quite graciously, *for him*.

"Beni told me about the ancient history of a gold necklace—it was taken from the dead body of a Celt by a Roman soldier. It was inherited by his family, which moved from Rome to Cimiez. Later there was an unsolved missing persons case, presumed to be a multiple murder. All this is recorded in the archive of the family in question—the archive was one of the items stolen from Beni's museum. Next, when the foundations for the Palais were being dug, bones were found by the workmen. One of the skeletons was bedecked with 'jewels.' I believe that the bones were those of the Roman murder victims, probably buried in a shallow grave at the time of their demise, and that the Celtic necklace was one of these pieces. I further believe that the wife of the architect of the Palais took it to Germany when she ran off with her young lover, who was German. This brings the story of the necklace up to the late eighteen-hundreds. I cannot tell you exactly what happened to it then, but it must have found its way—maybe through simple inheritance or maybe more nefarious or unpleasant means—into the hands of one of the high-ranking officers based here in Nice, during the Vichy years, when the Palais was Gestapo HQ. He brought it with him, and when the Germans left, it was assumed to have gone with him. If the stolen photograph of Madelaine Schiafino showed her wearing the necklace, then it might just be possible that it was something she was somehow able to hang on to when the Germans fled. Having seen her apartment, which is full of old items that were originally expensive, I'm going to guess that Madelaine's bank balance was pretty small. She was a very old woman, whose life had possibly exceeded the savings she had set aside for her retirement. Schiafino had some expensive *new* appliances there too, so I'm further going to suggest that you found a large amount of cash somewhere in her place, and that she did in fact keep the necklace, which Alistair bought from her for a very large sum of money. I believe that Alistair pieced the story of the necklace together in much the same way that I have—by talking to Beni, Gerard, and Chuck, and by finally confronting

Madelaine. Something you might not know about Alistair is how *very* good he was at getting people to confide in him. It was his trademark. He could talk you into telling him anything—about anyone, your own darkest secrets included. If he managed to get everyone to talk, and he had found out about Madelaine's past, he would have been well placed to get her to sell, *and* to keep quiet about it."

"If what you say is true, then who do you think had a motive to steal the necklace?" asked Moreau bluntly. It was an obvious question.

"Well, that's the trouble, you see!" I know I almost shouted, but I was frustrated, and tired and, believe it or not, hungry. I carried on. "Beni would have wanted it because he thought it was the Celtic necklace . . . indeed, that's what Tamsin herself referred to it as, so I think that is pretty well established. Chuck would have wanted it because, whatever he might say about being anti-Nazi and his grandfather being instrumental in the Nuremberg trials, he is infatuated with that era. I can quite imagine him wanting to possess something that was so viscerally connected with the Gestapo. Then there's Gerard. If his sister was one of the Gestapo's Collar of Death victims, I can quite imagine him wanting it as a remembrance of her, however terrible. And if we assume that Madelaine had sold the necklace to Alistair, I suppose there's an outside possibility she might have wanted to have her cake and eat it too. She could take the money *and* steal the necklace back, as a mark of her youthful beauty and, who knows, maybe also of her triumph at having survived what must have been a horrendous time in her life, but I have to say that seems unlikely.

"Whichever one of them did it would also have to have known about both the Roman archive and the photographic portrait of Madelaine. Obviously, they were both stolen to hide the identity of the necklace and to provide provenance should it be sold. To be honest, I don't believe that selling the necklace was the reason for its theft—I believe that whoever stole it wanted it for themselves. They also took the evidence of its appearance to cover their tracks. The only person I *can't* imagine wanting to, or needing to, steal it is Tamsin herself—I mean, it would have been officially hers in just a few hours, so what would have been the point? I do have a question which I am hoping you asked her during her interview: how did she know so quickly after Alistair's death that the necklace was missing? If we assume that Alistair had hidden it from her as a birthday 'surprise,' how could she know it wasn't simply hidden rather than stolen? That occurred to me when I re-thought the evening, and I guess I should mention it, in the spirit of openness."

I smiled as sweetly as I could, and waited for Moreau's response. I didn't have to wait long.

"What about you, Professor Morgan? Why might you have wanted to steal this necklace?"

I forced another smile. "Oh yes, let's not forget me . . . Well, I didn't know anything about the necklace until Alistair was dead, and it had, apparently, gone by then. So that's me out. Does that make it clearer?" I really hoped it did, because I was getting more tired by the minute.

Moreau sucked on the end of a pen and stared at me intently. The man hardly ever blinked, I noticed. It was very off-putting. He put down the pen.

"It makes a very interesting story, about a very interesting necklace. Do I take it that you think that Alistair Townsend was killed to accommodate the theft of the necklace? And that Madelaine Schiafino was killed to allow for the theft of the photograph of her wearing it?"

"Ah . . . now that's what I haven't made up my mind about yet," I answered, quite lamely.

"This is a pity, because then the whole case would be solved," replied Moreau patronizingly. The bugger! I did not say this aloud, because I was, after all, on the record. What I *wanted* to say was—*Oh, so you already knew all this then? Well, I'm sorry I took up your precious time.* I shut my mouth and waited for him to say something constructive.

He didn't speak, but burst out laughing instead. A big laugh, from deep inside him. I also noticed, for the first time, a smile in his eyes as well as on his face. His laughter stopped abruptly, but when he spoke he still had a genuine smile on his face.

"I am sorry. I am playing with you a little, Professor Morgan. It is my way—" Well, you could have fooled me—I thought you were a dry old bugger, "as the people who know me would understand. Seriously, you *have* given me new insights. I, too, am not sure how this connects with the two deaths, but it is a beginning. Now, you also mentioned a swimming pool?"

He *had* been listening—good. "Yes," I replied, "but I don't know much about it. All I know is that Alistair and Tamsin were for it; Chuck, Gerard, and Madelaine were against it. The local authorities had given the go-ahead for excavations to take place in the gardens, and the Syndic was going to vote on whether to go ahead or not. As I've said, knowing Alistair's track record in his business life, I would think that he'd have been able to talk most of the apartment owners into agreeing with his point of view—that was his strength. Also, having thought about his desire to find dirt on people, then hold it over them, I did wonder if he might have found out something about someone else in the apartments that they couldn't afford to let him make public, and they decided that killing him would be best all round? Alistair was not a well liked man when I knew him. No one had a good word to say about him—in fact, most had quite a few nasty ones to say behind his back. That's a dangerous quality to have—the ability to make people hate you."

"I agree, it is a very dangerous quality," responded Moreau. He fell silent.

I had a question that I was burning to ask, though I suspected he wouldn't answer it. "Captain, I wondered if you've received any toxicology reports back on Madelaine yet? I know she looked very peaceful, and she'd obviously had a bit of a shock to her heart the night before . . . but I thought there might be an outside chance that she'd been poisoned, though I couldn't see anything obvious at the scene . . ." I let the question hang in the air.

"A very interesting observation, Professor, but, of course, I cannot tell you any of the findings of our investigation because you are a suspect and a witness. I can tell you that the sad death of Mme. Schiafino was not the result of natural causes. That is all. Is there anything else you would like to share at this time?"

I gave it some thought, but decided to keep a few things to myself until I was sure. "I don't know what else to say, really," I said apologetically. "I cannot work out how the necklace was stolen. I'm assuming that everyone was searched at the hospital, like I was?" Moreau nodded. "If no one had it on their person, then I don't know where it could have gone . . . unless it wasn't there when we arrived, and it had been stolen earlier in the afternoon. I suppose no one's saying they knew where Alistair hid it?"

Moreau shook his head this time. Clearly he didn't want any of his "answers" being recorded by the microphones.

"So I suppose all I've done is float a possible theory for a motive that could still apply to three out of four people, for a theft that may, or may not, be connected to the murders?"

"It is as you say," he replied. "But I am sure that you will continue to think about possible methods, and how people might have had the means to commit the crimes, as you appear to be a *natural* investigator. I would, of course, prefer it if you would leave the investigating to us, the police. You are *not* working with the Vancouver police force. You are *not* a consultant to the police in this case. You have no standing, and we cannot offer you our protection. You are, I repeat, a witness and, until we close the case, a suspect. And I should warn you, Professor Morgan, that you must be very careful if you choose to continue to 'investigate.' I think that maybe you see this as an academic exercise—a chance to use your brain in a creative way. Two people are dead. We *don't* want it to become three, do we?"

"Oh, good grief, no we do *not*!" I replied quickly, "and I promise that I'll be a good girl and not stick my nose in . . . too far!" I risked a smile, and I got one back.

"I am now concluding this interview," said Moreau. He made some parting comments for the record and switched off all the devices in the room. Then he pushed back his chair, stood, and stretched. I took my cue from him and did the same.

He looked as tired as I felt, and I realized he still had Chuck and Beni to interview before his night was over. *Poor guy.*

As he guided me toward the door he explained that Bertrand would take me out and make sure I got back to my hotel safely. As I was leaving, he put his hand gently on my arm and said in a quiet voice, "Tell me, when you said that I had taken over the office I use from my old boss, and that I didn't like him . . . why did you say that?" He looked a little concerned.

I had to come clean. "One of the skills I have is reading people. I use it a lot. When I mentioned that your desk had been moved I saw a change in your expression: you knew the person who had used it in its old position, and you felt anger at the thought of that person. Now, most people feel anger toward those who have, at some point, made them feel powerless— so the man was likely your boss. I'm afraid your dislike of him was very apparent—he didn't just make you angry; you also felt indignant that he had held the post. I suspect that you felt he wasn't up to the job, eh?"

"Ah," was all that Moreau would say, and he winked at me. "You see much," he added.

"Yes, I do," I replied, and I dared a wink back at him. I followed Bertrand to a waiting police car, to be ferried back to my hotel and, oh please, please, please, a comfortable night's sleep. I was knackered.

The Early Hours of Sunday Morning

THE SAME GUY WHO HAD been at the reception desk at my hotel when I'd arrived back from the hospital was there again when I dragged myself out of the police car at two o'clock in the morning. As I smiled weakly at him I wondered if he thought I'd been there all day... and night, given that he was the one who'd given me the directions to the police station that morning. He looked surprised and puzzled, but I decided to say nothing and to retain an air of mystery!

I finally got to my room and flopped onto the bed, face first, just glad to be someplace where I could relax. It had been a hell of a day. I had to tell myself quite firmly that I couldn't just lie there like that all night—I had to get myself undressed, into the bathroom and into the bed to try to make sure I slept properly. For once, I listened to myself, and also took the time to remove my makeup and brush my hair. When I got under the covers, I couldn't get my mind to slow down. I lay there staring at the ceiling, wishing I could switch off.

You know what it's like when you can't sleep; it doesn't matter what you do, you just can't get comfy. I'd almost beaten my pillows to a pulp trying to get them to allow my head to nestle just so, but I still felt as though I was lying on a couple of bricks. Eventually, I sat up, turned on the bedside lamp, and reached for my pen. I hoped that doing a "brain dump" would let me wind down a bit.

I scribbled some notes on various bits of paper before I realized that, if I wanted to be able to read what I was writing at some future point, I'd better just open up my laptop and type. You'd be excused for inferring from my handwriting that I was a doctor of medicine, not a doctor of psychology.

Having pulled out all the paraphernalia that I'd managed to stuff into my little laptop case, and having managed to hook everything together, I sat and typed. I was hoping that the process would help me to organize my thoughts, but all it resulted in was a very long list of all the things I didn't know, or things about which I knew a little and wished I knew more. The whole process was rather frustrating.

I looked at my watch—it was three o'clock, so six in the evening in Vancouver. I was pretty sure that Bud would be home, so I called the Anderson apartment, his cell phone, Jan's cell phone, then the apartment again . . . nothing. Still just voice mail. Where the hell was he? For that matter, where was Jan? Again I was struck by the idea that maybe something bad had happened out at Bud's Chilliwack drug-bust operation.

This time, rather than panic, I decided I'd use the "Free Wi-Fi in Every Room" the sign in the hotel lobby promised. I checked the Global TV News website for anything about trouble in the Fraser Valley. There was nothing. I was relieved. I was pretty sure that if anything *had* happened it would have made it onto the news page.

Still not able to sleep, I let my eyes run over the rest of Global's headlines. The area's "Most Searched" stories, sorted by popularity: record amounts of rain had fallen on the Lower Mainland, and areas of Coquitlam and White Rock had flooded—no news there; those areas always flood when it rains heavily; gas had hit record high prices in Downtown Vancouver for the second day running—again, not really news; and a South Surrey woman had been the victim of a targeted shooting. I sat in amazement for a moment—I mean, how can people be more interested in the weather and gas prices than in a fatal shooting? A "targeted killing" *always* means a gang was involved. What *are* these women thinking who marry or go out with gangsters? This victim wasn't the first partner of a gang member to be shot that way; nor, probably, would she be the last. A year earlier a woman had been shot while her two-year-old son was sitting in the child-seat in the back of the car—just to send a message to her drug-runner husband. Terrible, yes, but hardly unpredictable.

I realized as I read the headline that maybe *that* was what had got Bud caught up at the office, or maybe even at the scene of the shooting, and the grip on my stomach stood down from red to amber alert. I was still a bit miffed that he hadn't followed through on his offer to contact Moreau.

With one concern slightly alleviated I decided I'd better try to give some more thought to *how* the necklace might have been stolen from the Townsends' apartment, rather *why*. If three people had a "why," then if I spent time working out the "how," maybe I could narrow things down a bit. I'm good with the "why" because it's what I do—I work out why people do what they do, but I don't usually get involved with how they do it. That's where Bud's lot always took over. I didn't have "Bud's lot," and Moreau had made it clear that I wasn't going to get any inside information from him, so I made a few notes and came up with some questions that needed answering.

#1 If the necklace was stolen before the party, who could have stolen it? Where were Beni, Chuck, and Gerard on Friday afternoon? Tamsin was out when Beni arrived with the bread, so the apartment was empty—a good time for theft.

#2 If the necklace was stolen at the party, how did the thief get it out of apartment?

#3 Who knew where the necklace was hidden?

#4 Was it even hidden—am I assuming this because it wasn't in view when I arrived, and no one said it was missing then?

#5 How did Tamsin know it was missing? She must have known where it was supposed to be. Why did she bother to check for the necklace when her husband had just died?

I was happy with that list—well, as happy as you can be when you've just written down a bunch of questions that you don't know the answers to. At least my thoughts were a bit clearer, so I followed the same process for the deaths of Alistair and Madelaine.

#1 How did digitalis get onto snails?

I stopped there. With internet access freely available there was no reason why I couldn't bone up on snail rearing and digitalis. It helped a great deal, because suddenly I understood why Alistair had been hosing down the snails he'd had delivered to the apartment days before the party. The snails would have arrived in boxes. Internet photos showed them to be large boxes, with holes in the bottom and the top. You keep the little creatures in the boxes for a few days before they're on the menu so you can purge them of all the nasty stuff that hangs around in their digestive tracts. Yuk—I saw the sense in that! If he'd been feeding them, which Tamsin said he had, it was likely that he'd been giving them dill: I could recall they had indeed been dill flavored. Apparently, snails' bodies *intensify* whatever they ingest. That was interesting.

I moved onto reading about digitalis, which is derived from foxgloves. I love their jolly spikes—they are so common in and around Vancouver, where there are lots of damp spots. I was surprised to find that the whole plant is toxic, not just the flowers. I tried finding out if one could make a toxic substance by drying foxglove leaves then grinding them into some sort of powder. I thought maybe someone could have sprinkled a powder onto the snails after they were cooked. It seemed that all the sources agreed that you'd need a lot of the stuff to make people as ill as we had all been, and a huge quantity to kill someone—and I was pretty sure we hadn't all been eating foxglove leaves in the salad! I couldn't envisage foxgloves even growing in Nice: bougainvillea, yes; mimosa, yes; foxgloves, no. It's just a bit too bright and arid on the Cote d'Azur for foxgloves. It was much more likely that Alistair's stash of digitalis-based pills had been employed.

I wasn't sure *how* the digitalis might have got onto the snails, but I was pretty sure it must have done so sometime between their preparation and their arrival at the table. According to several websites, the correct way to cook snails once they are out of their shells is by simmering them, something I was sure Alistair would have done because he was always one to do things the "correct" way. But even this would not have reduced the toxicity of the digitalis.

So my notes to myself ended up being just a list of words: cleansing, dill, digitalis, pills, simmering.

#2 How did the murderer know that Alistair would take/had taken extra pills?

Now that was a tough one. Either the murderer had depended on Alistair's apparently erratic dosing habits, which seemed unlikely, or they had somehow actively encouraged him to take more pills than usual that particular day. The second option seemed much more plausible. And it meant the murderer must have spent time with the victim on the day he died. I wrote down all the suspects' names, then thought about each of their whereabouts on Friday. As I worked through what I already knew, which wasn't much, something else suddenly dawned on me. I needed to find out where everyone had been on Friday after lunch, not only to know if they'd been in contact with Alistair, but also to determine whether they might have had access to the Townsends' apartment, giving them time to steal the necklace before the party.

I went back to my list. Tamsin, of course, would have had any number of chances to urge Alistair to take his pills, but I was still wondering why she'd want to steal a necklace that was going to be hers anyway. Beni had told me he'd been to the Townsends' apartment some time after four o'clock but no one was home. Presumably, he'd been at the museum before that, and he'd told me he'd gone back there between delivering the bread and catching a cab to the party. He'd seen Gerard at the apartment when he'd left the bread with him—so had Gerard been at the Palais all day? Had he seen Alistair later on, after Alistair left me? Where was Chuck all day? I assumed he worked from home, but I guessed writers do more than just write. At certain points in their creative cycle they must do other things, like carrying out research or checking drafts of their manuscripts. So maybe he'd been elsewhere that day. Madelaine—what about her? I knew as much about her whereabouts as I did of Tamsin's—nothing.

Yes, I decided I'd do some research when I'd had some sleep. But, how?

How was I going to come up with a reason to talk to any of these people ever again? They weren't my friends or anything. We'd been brought together originally by Alistair, and now thrown back together because of the horrible occurrences since my arrival at Tamsin's birthday party. I'd somehow have to come up with an excuse to talk to them all.

I finally realized I was getting sleepy. I hoped that if I made a quick dive into the bed, I might actually drift off for a few hours. I powered down the laptop, unhooked all the leads, and clambered in between the sheets, where I lay for a few moments fantasizing about something sweet to nibble on, before finally drifting off to sleep. Dreams about giant snails chasing me through skyscraper-high grass didn't wake me, though I was briefly roused by the noise of the garbage collectors outside my window at about four-thirty. I managed to slip back to my dreams, which were now populated by foxglove flowers eating pasta . . . in the way they can when you're asleep and dream-logic rules.

When my bedside telephone rang at nine o'clock, I awoke with a start to discover that the birthday cake I thought I'd been munching was, in fact, my pillow, and it didn't taste at all good. A dry mouth was the least of my problems. When I picked up the phone I heard sobbing, followed by Tamsin's high-pitched whine. "Oh, Cait—I'm so glad I got hold of you . . . Please come, come quick . . . It's Gerard, something terrible has happened . . ." And with that, she hung up.

Oh, whoop de bloody doo!

Good morning, Cait Morgan—this is your wake-up call . . . and off we go again!

Sunday Morning

I WASN'T REALLY WITH IT for a moment or two, which was understandable given that I'd had less than six hours' sleep, and none of those hours seemed to have been particularly reviving. I forced myself to the bathroom, where I showered, washed my hair, dried it, and put on my makeup—all of which gave me the chance to gather my wits about me to face whatever the day might hold.

Remembering that Tamsin was nothing if not a drama queen, I tried to find her phone number and call her back before I went storming up to Cimiez again, maybe on a fool's errand, or maybe to be confronted by yet another dead body. It was a fifty-fifty chance, I reckoned. My room didn't have a telephone directory, so I went down to the hotel lobby to be greeted by the now familiar face of the receptionist, who pulled a tired old book from under the desk and handed it to me with a suspicious look. I rustled through the pages until I got to the "T's," but there were no listings at all for "Townsend." Of course not. I tried "Damcott"—nothing—then finally "Fontainbleu." Of course, there were dozens! I finally found Gerard's number and entered it into my cell phone. On a final whim, I tried "Brunetti": there were a few, but only one with the initial "B," so I saved what I hoped was Beni's number and gave the receptionist back his book. He looked relieved. Maybe he thought I was some weird type of criminal who would have made off with it given half a chance.

I walked out of my hotel to be greeted by a beautiful morning. There literally wasn't a cloud in the magnificent blue sky; it wasn't just the color of the sea that had caused this area to be named "azur." My hotel was adjacent to the *zone piétonne*, so I walked the pedestrianized streets until one particular coffee shop smelled too good to pass by. I sat and ordered a double espresso, a bottle of Perrier water, and two croissants.

As I waited for my order to arrive I lit a cigarette, just to fit in, and decided to brave it and call Gerard's number. Uncomfortably, all I got was the ring tone, not even a chance to leave voice mail. I became rather more worried about what might have happened to the old man, which spurred me on to dare to dial the number that I hoped was Beni's.

A deep-voiced "*Pronto*," was the sharp reply.

"Is that you, Beni?"

"Yes—ah it is Cait, I think?" came Beni's welcome response.

"Yes, it is—I hope you don't mind me calling you?" It was a concern for me, on several levels. "You must have been with Moreau until all hours, and it's not ten o'clock yet."

"No, do not worry, it is a good surprise. How did you get my number? Did I give it to you?"

"No—but you're in the phone book. I looked you up." Was I beginning to sound like a stalker?

"This is good! Would you like to meet for breakfast? I would enjoy your company. We seem to eat together a great deal, you and I. It is very pleasant."

I'll be honest, my heart fluttered a little. Well, whose wouldn't? I've never been the sort of girl, or woman for that matter, that men take out on dates. I've always just sort of drifted into relationships. I know some women who are showered with flowers and gifts, collected in cars at an appointed time, taken out for nice dinners or even to the theatre or art galleries—all of which I would enjoy very much. But that hasn't been me. I'm "The life and soul of the party, Cait," or "You're always happier down the pub, aren't you, Cait." Here was a handsome man telling me that he enjoyed eating with me, and inviting me to do so again. It sounded pretty damned perfect! How I wanted to say yes, but instead, I did what I knew I *should* do.

"I'd love to, Beni—but I actually called you about Tamsin." *What a way to put a damper on things, Caitlin Morgan! When a man you fancy asks you to join him for a meal, tell him you'd rather talk about a young blond who's "got the hots" for him instead!*

"Tamsin? What is wrong now?" Beni sounded apprehensive, and as though he dreaded my answer.

I took a deep breath. "She rang me at my hotel telling me I 'had to come' because something dreadful has happened to Gerard. Please don't think I'm heartless, Beni; I think Gerard is very sweet and I'm very worried about him, especially given . . . well, you know." I didn't want to discuss dead bodies in front of a full café at breakfast time. "But I knew that if I was going to have to face another day like yesterday, I had to take the time to get myself cleaned up, and now I'm just about to grab a coffee and a croissant. I called the number I found for Gerard, but there's no answer, and Tamsin isn't listed in the telephone directory, so I couldn't call her back to get the full story. *You* were listed, so I thought you might be able to get in touch with her to find out what on earth is going on."

"It might be something very bad, or it might be nothing at all," said Beni, echoing my own initial thoughts. It was nice to know I wasn't alone in my assessment of Tamsin. "I will call Tamsin and will telephone you on this number when I have more information." He sounded very businesslike, then he hung up.

There went my chance to dine with the divine Beni. I comforted myself with the flaky, buttery croissants I'd ordered, and put my phone on the table so I could answer it quickly when it rang. My phone bill was going to be horrendous!

I'd just finished brushing crumbs from my blouse when my phone sprang to life. It wasn't Beni's number.

"Hello?" I replied hesitantly.

"Hi, Cait?" It was Bud. I was delighted to hear his voice—relieved too.

"Bud—yes, it's me! It's great to hear your voice. I was worried about you. Where are you calling from? Are you okay?"

"Cait, shh—listen, I've got to be quick. I can't talk for long, but I had to call you quickly to tell you I'll be out of touch over the next few days. I've got something to deal with here that has to have my full attention, and I won't have time to help you out at all. Sorry, but there it is." His voice sounded . . . I couldn't quite put my finger on it . . . defeated, yet still angry? He was almost whispering.

Instinctively, I knew that whatever it was he had to focus on, it was serious. My mind flew to the shooting I'd read about on the internet.

"Are you in South Surrey?" I couldn't help but ask.

"How do you know about it?" snapped Bud. It wasn't like him.

"I read about it on the internet," I replied, guardedly.

"I didn't know the news was out yet. At least, not all of it. Damn! Anyway, Cait—it's nothing you can do anything about. The whole team's on it, and we're pretty much sure we know who we're looking for, and where we'll find him. It looks like the idiot used his own SUV to drive away from the hit, and a witness got his plate number. He's holed up at a house that belongs to a known associate of his in Delta. I have to go now. I'm sorry I can't be there for you, but this has to take precedence. I'm sure you understand."

"Of course, I understand, Bud. Will it be . . . dangerous?" Again, I couldn't stop myself asking.

"It's always dangerous with these guys, we all know that—and this one, more than most. This is a new low, even for him. Dangerous or not, we'll get the bastard, you can be sure of that. If it's the last thing I do—I'll get him!" He sounded desperate, a man on a meaningful mission.

"Okay Bud—just go. All the best. Thanks for calling, it means a lot. I'll be fine. And give my love to Jan . . ." but he'd gone before I'd finished speaking. It had to be something big if he was still working on it at past two in the morning. Poor bugger—it looked as if he was having as bad and as long a Saturday as I'd had!

I'd hardly had time to begin to feel sorry for Bud, and Jan, who had presumably already spent half of her weekend on her own rather than with her beloved husband, before my phone rang again. This time I recognized the number as Beni's.

"Hello Beni—so what's up?" I asked, almost casually.

"It is very sad," he replied grimly.

"Oh my God—what now?" My heart sank as I thought of all the things that might have happened to poor old Gerard—and there I'd been sipping coffee and stuffing my face with pastries!

Beni's voice was strong and controlled. "When Gerard was dropped off at the Palais after Moreau interviewed him last night, he fell on the front steps and broke his hip. The police were still there, so they took him straight to the hospital, where they operated last night. He is doing well, but he is likely to be in hospital for some time. He needed supplies—clothes and so on, so he called Daphne, whom we met last night, because she has a key to his apartment. She then called on Tamsin at her apartment, because she knew that she and Gerard were friends. This is what set Tamsin off."

I could imagine it had. I was sure that, somehow, Gerard's unfortunate accident had immediately been interpreted by Tamsin as relating to her in some way, shape or form.

"So are you going to see Tamsin—or Gerard in hospital?" To me the answer seemed simple.

"First I will collect you," replied Beni, giving me a nice, warm feeling, "then we will see Tamsin, and we will gather some items for Gerard from Daphne, and take them to him in hospital. He is the one who needs us the most, but Tamsin must be dealt with first. I thought I might call Chuck and ask him to meet us as Tamsin's. What do you think?"

"I'm in the *zone piétonne* right now. How about I walk down to the Meridien hotel on the sea-front and I can meet you there?"

"Yes. Good. I will be there in twenty minutes—it is a date!" replied Beni, and he hung up.

I'll admit I was smiling as I finished my coffee and water. I suspect that I over-tipped quite a bit, but, in my own defense, I was feeling rather pleased with myself. I wanted to get going quickly so I could make full use of the Four Star public facilities at Le Meridien before Beni arrived to whisk me away in his flash car. I trotted off toward the glittering sea, knowing that I was going on a date . . . even if it had taken an octogenarian getting a broken hip to make it happen. Yes, I know it was a bit "Tamsin-y" of me—but a girl's got to make the most of the opportunities that present themselves.

Seventeen minutes later—yes, I was clock-watching—I stood outside the swanky entrance to the glamorous hotel that my university couldn't have afforded for me to stay at for half an hour, let alone five nights. Beni arrived in his magnificent convertible, its roof down, his sunglasses glinting with gold embellishments, dark hair blowing in the breeze, shirt collar open wide and showing off his perfect tan. He screeched to a halt, leapt out of the car, and opened the passenger door for me, then closed it carefully, as though as though I were a precious cargo. *I could get used to this*, I thought. I smiled and buckled up. His driving, as well as the law, made this a necessity.

As we pulled away, I knew I would remember that moment forever. It was one of those feelings you get only ever get a few times in your life. Something has allowed you an insight into another world not as an outsider, or an observer, but as a participant. It was heady stuff, and I could feel the excitement in the pit of my stomach as Beni Brunetti and I swept toward the Palais on that stunning May morning.

When we squealed to a halt at the giant black gates, Beni hopped out to press the buttons for Tamsin's apartment. She buzzed us in. Instead of pulling up in front of the main entrance to the beautiful old building, Beni swung to the right, along the driveway heading back down the hill, but now inside the walls of the gardens surrounding the apartment building. He took it slowly, which was a relief, giving me a chance to look around as we descended. I hadn't had an opportunity until then to see the gardens that were Gerard's life's work. Soon we were parked, and Beni rushed to open my door once more. *Yes, I waited for him to do it—well, it was such a treat!* We began the walk back up the hill toward the front entrance to the building.

"Is this where you had to park last night?" I asked to get the conversation started.

"No, farther on. It goes all the way around the bottom of the gardens, but it is one way only, so it can take a while," he replied, seemingly lost in thought.

About a quarter of the way up, Beni placed his hand lightly on my arm and said, "Come this way. Let us walk through the gardens, then you can see how beautiful they are, how lush and how well tended." I was surprised to hear him speak with such interest of something other than an ancient relic. I'm pretty interested in gardening, but in the passive sense. I like to see them and visit them, rather than work in them. I thought I might be in for a treat, in more ways than one.

We stepped over a low wall that ran between the driveway and the garden proper. We were transported from a world of grey stone walls, brown pea-gravel, and blue sky into a green cocoon that immediately felt cooler and gentler. Huge palms towered above us, and at our feet was a surprise—grass. All around us were beds demarcated by low, well-trimmed box hedges, and inside each bed was a mass-planting of one species, some of which I recognized. Roses, some sort of Shasta daisy, and bougainvillea occupied sunny beds, while shadier beds housed red and apricot astilbe and—good grief . . .

"Look—foxgloves!" I cried involuntarily.

Beni jumped. I apologized and took his arm.

"I'm sorry—it's just that I thought it would be too dry and too sunny to grow foxgloves in this climate."

"You are correct. I know that Gerard has tried very hard to grow these flowers. He tends them with much care. Do you like foxgloves?"

"Why, yes, they're a favorite of mine. They seem to be blooming much earlier here than they do in the area where I live," I remarked.

"It is warm here through the winter. I think they awake more quickly and grow more vigorously here." He smiled back at me. "I, too, like these. Farther up Gerard has some yellow ones. Shall we look?"

I was intrigued. "I didn't know there *were* yellow foxgloves. Yes, I'd love to see them." We moved off at a slightly quicker pace.

As we walked, the thought occurred to me that maybe a killer trying to find digitalis didn't have too far to look after all. I managed to put aside that macabre thought for a moment or two and was able to enjoy the buds that were just bursting open on a bed of yellow foxgloves. I wondered if I'd be able to find them back in Vancouver—I made a mental note to check. In the meantime, I allowed myself a moment or two to turn and look back down onto the whole canvas of the gardens. My word, Gerard had done a good job! It was true that now he was aided by a group of much younger men, but the vision had been his, the planning was still his and—oh, the poor man. I could imagine how he must have felt about the big hulk of a swimming pool being sunk into this wonderful creation.

"Do you know where they plan to build the pool?" I asked Beni, not expecting him to know much about it.

"But yes," he replied. "You see the beds near the bottom corners that have the olive trees in them?" I nodded. "You see the beds about half way up with, on the right, the red roses and on the left, the white roses?" Again, I nodded. "Those would be the four corners of the pool. A retaining wall would be built on this, the higher side, and the pool will be sunk into the cellars that are below the gardens."

"Why are there cellars down there?" I couldn't imagine.

"When the Palais was built it was as a hotel. The guests would demand the finest wines, so they built a web of cellars to keep large amounts of wines at the right temperatures. They built the cellars out of stone blocks above the ground, before they built the Palais, then they covered the tunnels they had built with the soil they removed when they dug the foundations for the hotel itself."

"What a clever idea," I commented. "It seems it was all very well planned."

"Yes, the architect of this building was a very clever man, and he had used this method in other places before he did it here."

As we turned our backs on the main gardens and continued through a couple of cool arbors quite close to the residents' parking area at the front of the building, I observed, "You seem to know a lot about the history of this building. Why is that?"

"Ah, it is old, and I like old things. And it is beautiful, and I very much like beautiful things." His words seemed to be laden with hidden meaning: I was hoping his emphasis was on "beautiful," not "old"; and maybe, even if he meant *both*, then I was in with a chance!

"It's not really your era, Beni, surely . . ." *I couldn't shut up, could I?*

"No, this is true. At one time I thought I might come here to live, so I read about the place, and spoke to a few of the older residents about it."

"Did you know about the remains that were found when they were digging the foundations for the building?" Had Beni made the connection between the different phases of the life of the stolen necklace?

"I have heard some rumors, but I think that this is all. Often there are rumors about buildings such as this one—of how many men died building them, or of things that were found at the time. I do not believe everything I hear," he replied quite jovially. I wondered if that joviality was just a bit forced, or if his eyes were creasing up because we were back in the sunshine again. I gave him the benefit of the doubt, but the magical walk through the greenery was over, and we had to face the obnoxious Tamsin.

Ah well—I told myself that into every life a little rain must fall. It had been a very informative morning, and fun too, with Beni playing his part of the dashing Italian romancer to the hilt, and me getting all googly in the car. I had to put my game face on and get ready to take another chance to poke around the apartment where Alistair had died—I knew I hadn't seen it all. I wondered how I could convince Tamsin to give me a guided tour. It might not be easy, but I was ready to give it a go.

As we mounted the steps to the imposing front door, I couldn't help but imagine poor old Gerard tumbling down them in the early hours of the morning. They were good, solid, wide steps, and I wondered how he'd managed it. He'd had a poor night's sleep the night before, and a long day, and it was very late at night, so maybe he'd just lost his balance and slipped on the edge of a step ... those steps he'd been climbing his whole life. Maybe I was beginning to see crimes where none existed, so I told myself to concentrate on the crimes I knew were real enough.

"You do not speak much, Cait, but I believe you think a great deal," observed Beni as Tamsin buzzed us into the building.

"If you keep your mouth closed, people might *think* you're a fool, but if you open it, they might *know* you are," I replied, quoting my mother. I even used her voice—we'd always sounded alike, and the words echoed in the voluminous hallway. It freaked me out a little.

"Ha! This is very true," replied Beni, laughing, his booming voice overwhelming the echoes of my mother's warning.

His laughter carried us up in the elevator to the third floor, where we were met by Tamsin's pinched little face peering around her own front door. She motioned to us to come quickly, and we reluctantly did so. She stood there in her bare feet, wearing more black garb of some soft: maybe she was going to take a Victorian stance on mourning dress, and wear nothing but black, ever again. She slammed the door behind us, dragged us into the kitchen and finally spoke.

"I'm sure I'm next! They'll get *me* next, I know it!" She looked terrified.

Ah, so *that* was it. Tamsin had decided that there was a "they" and that "they" were out to get her.

Beni took a deep breath and adopted his "uncle full of bonhomie and comfort" voice. He reassured Tamsin that she would be just fine, that no one was out to get her, and reminded her that while there had indeed been two murders, Gerard's misfortune was just that—an accident, and she wasn't to let it upset her. I was gobsmacked that it took a slip-and-fall to reduce her to a gibbering wreck, as opposed to her husband's cold-blooded murder but was probably just me being "judgmental" again.

"Have you eaten today?" asked Beni solicitously.

"I ate bread. With Alistair gone there didn't seem to be any point making toast, so I just ate bread . . ." Her whiny voice trailed off pathetically. *Good grief—is it such an effort to put bread into a toaster and push a button?*

"I will make you food," said Beni, taking control. He moved Tamsin to one side and pulled open the door to the refrigerator.

"There's not much there, I checked yesterday," I commented. "There's enough cheese in there to probably feed the entire building, and there were eggs. I'm assuming it's all still there." I couldn't imagine that Tamsin would know what to do with an egg, other than eat it once it had been prepared for her.

"I don't know what's there, and I don't care . . . What's the point of it all? He's gone, and I'm all alone. I don't think I can go on . . ." Again, she did that trailing off thing with her voice. I ground my teeth. It was safer than letting my mouth form words.

"It is noon already—we will all have lunch," declared Beni, as though Tamsin and I were in the apartment next door. "I shall cook. You ladies, you will let me do this!"

I wasn't going to object, nor, clearly, was Tamsin. I saw a chance and jumped at it.

"Hey, Tamsin—if we're banished from the kitchen, what if you show me around the apartment? I'd love to see it all. I bet it's pretty special upstairs, eh?" I tried to jolly her along. It was hard work, and I wasn't sure I was that good an actress, but she bought it—or else she too was gritting her teeth and just being polite to me in front of Beni. Either way, I didn't care, so long as I got to see the rest of the place. I wanted to see what hiding places there might have been for that necklace, and I wasn't going to achieve that by only ever seeing the kitchen, balcony, downstairs, and bathroom. I'd already laboriously recalled those areas in my mind's eye to establish where the wretched thing might have been secreted, with no luck.

"Oh, alright," Tamsin replied, very quietly for her.

I walked out of the kitchen and asked, "Is it okay if we go upstairs?"

"Yes, feel free, but it's just the TV room, and our bedroom and bathroom. It's not very exciting, you know."

The sight that met my eyes at the top of the stairs might not have been very exciting, but it wasn't something I had expected. I took a moment to take it all in. The rooms looked as though a bomb had exploded in the back of a truck full of clothes, which had been left to lie where they fell. I *swear* every surface was littered with clothing of one type or another. The floor, the sofa in the TV room, the TV itself, the bed and the chairs in the bedroom, the floor of the bathroom, the bath, and even the toilet—all covered in skirts and pants and blouses and shirts, scarves and tops and sweaters and dresses and more skirts. If you could wear it, it was there.

Shoes, sandals, and boots, either singly or in pairs, were dotted in among all the clothes, making crossing the floor something of a challenge.

As I walked I picked up and gathered a pile. Tamsin, proceeding beside me, opted for the "kick it to one side" routine. I wondered if that was how this mess had started, and pondered how long it might have been there. I figured that Alistair probably wouldn't have stood for it, so maybe she'd managed to create all this chaos since his death. If it hadn't been so frightening, it would have been impressive.

The only reason I wanted to see upstairs was to evaluate possible hiding places. Given that I could only see Tamsin's detritus, I realized pretty quickly that I wasn't going to get much out of this particular foray. Just as I was planning a strategic retreat, Tamsin called to me from the bedroom, asking me to come to look at something. Dreading what it might be, I entered the room reluctantly, cautiously navigating through the mess on the floor, to find her holding a silver-framed photograph of her and Alistair. It looked like it had been taken on their wedding day. He was smiling like the cat that's got the cream, and she was gazing winsomely at the camera, with a circle of flowers in her hair and a rock the size of Gibraltar on a heavy chain around her neck. I didn't dare think it was a diamond, but it certainly looked like it.

Tamsin was looking at the photograph with what I could only describe as true love in her eyes. She said, "Ally liked giving me necklaces—he said I had a pretty neck. He got that one from a man in South Africa and gave it to me for our wedding. It's in the bank now. He never let me wear it. I might get it out and wear it to his funeral. It's so pretty."

As I looked at her I knew that the love on her face and the wistfulness in her voice weren't for Alistair—they were for the jewelry.

"Do you know how he gave it to me?" she asked.

"No," I said sweetly, shaking my head with disbelief. She seemed to think I was encouraging her.

"He had the caterer make a raspberry jelly for me—or do you call it 'Jell-O' because you're a Canadian now? You're weird, you know, sometimes you sound Welsh and sometimes you sound ... well, almost American ... It's like you're a fake—you know, what Ally would have called 'jumped up' ... Why do you talk like that? Is it so you sound more clever?"

Good grief, this woman didn't need anyone or anything else to distract her—she could do it to herself, very easily.

I replied as calmly as possible. "I guess it's because I can't quite shake off my Welsh accent, or the British words I grew up using, but sometimes, having lived in Canada for more than ten years, my new vocabulary and accent kick in. It's not something I'm conscious of—it just happens. I suppose that sometimes it depends on who I'm speaking to: you're English so I suppose I might use the word 'suppose' instead of 'I guess' . . . or maybe not. Does that help?"

Tamsin thought for a moment, then replied, "No, not really. I don't understand. Anyway, like I was saying, raspberry is my favorite flavor, and it was a 'very special' dessert for the feast we had the night before our wedding. At least, that's what Alistair called it . . . and he hid the necklace in the jelly, so it *was* very special . . . I found it with my spoon! Oh, it was fun! It was a bit messy too, of course, but Ally cleaned it all off for me and then put it around my neck. I wore it for the wedding. After that he made me put it in the bank. I've got another one—look!"

Out of a drawer in her bedside table, Tamsin pulled what looked like the necklace in the photograph. "Ally said he'd spent a small fortune on the real thing so it was worth spending a few bob on a fake that was good enough to fool pretty much everyone. Wasn't he clever! I feel different when I know I'm wearing the real one. And the pearls too." With that, she pulled a jumble of strands from the same drawer. "*And* the black pearls." I suspected that she could have gone on for a while: Alistair might, for all I knew, have been some weird sort of fetishist, considering what a fuss he'd clearly liked to make of his wife's neck.

"He *loved* my neck," cooed Tamsin, cupping tangled jewelry in her tiny little hands and sliding them over her aforementioned body part.

"Lunch!" called Beni from below us, and she dropped the lot on the bed and took off. My God, her attention span lasted about as long as that of a two-year-old.

I looked at what she'd carelessly discarded and wondered how much of it was real and how much was fake. It started me thinking about Alistair and his patterns of behavior. I was sure I'd just learned something very useful—and it wasn't that Tamsin was disorganized, messy, or easily distracted—because I'd known all that before we'd come up to see her boudoir.

Sunday Lunchtime

AS I FOLLOWED TAMSIN OUT onto her balcony, it was a joy to see the beautiful city below us, and the sea beyond, spread out in the midday sun. I couldn't imagine it was a view of which one would ever, *could* ever, tire. I'll admit I felt a pang of jealousy that Tamsin saw it every day, and I didn't. At least one of the good things about my type of memory is that I can always sit and hum myself back to a place or a time that I have especially loved, and it's real to me once again. I suspected I'd be revisiting this particular scene on quite a few winter nights in years to come.

Beni jarred me out of my thoughts by shouting "Lunch!" quite close to my ear.

"Yes, we're all here!" I replied, probably quite snappily.

"I am calling Chuck—he said to call when the food was ready," Beni replied, smiling at my scowl.

I was mystified. "Don't you think he meant for you to call him on the *phone*?" I thought it was a perfectly reasonable question.

I'd hardly managed to finish my pithy observation before Chuck's head popped out between the open shutters a couple of floors above the balcony. He called down to us, "Won't be a minute! And I'll bring the bread."

Asking a question whose answer was probably perfectly obvious, I said, "Is that where Chuck lives? Right there?"

"Of course," replied Tamsin, as though I were a complete idiot. To be fair, she had a point. It hadn't occurred to me that when Chuck had said he "lived upstairs," he had meant it literally: his apartment was directly above the Townsends'.

"Oh, handy," I said. "It must save a lot of phone calls when you can just speak to a neighbor like that."

"Yes," replied Tamsin, who like a greedy child had already set upon the scrambled eggs that Beni had prepared. "He and Ally used to chatter like that for ages, until the mean old woman in the apartment between us complained. She said she didn't want to know all our comings and goings and we should be more thoughtful about who we disturbed out here. She even had a go at Ally when he was hosing down those boxes of snails—she said it was unhealthy for him to put them underneath her window. Silly woman! I mean, it's not like she even speaks much English, so I don't know what she had to complain about." Tamsin seemed unable to comprehend that having to hear people talk loudly to each other could be annoying in whatever language they might choose to communicate.

"Well, maybe she saw it as a bit of an imposition on her peace and quiet," I suggested.

"I don't see how—she's old and deaf, like half the people who live here," was Tamsin's sulky reply. She sighed through a mouthful of eggs. "I wish there were more young people living here like me. We could have lovely parties. I like parties."

Chuck rang the doorbell and Beni let him in. Chuck popped on his sunglasses and handed the sticks of bread to Beni as he walked out to greet Tamsin and me, and Beni let him take a seat before presenting him with his plate.

"*Bon appétit,*" said Chuck in his best French accent as he picked up a fork, and we all dug in. It was a quick meal to eat, but it hit the spot: scrambled eggs, cheeses, fresh bread . . . all simple, delicious, and sort of comforting.

"You make great eggs," I told Beni when my plate looked as though it had already been through the dishwasher.

"And you enjoy your food with real enthusiasm," replied Beni, smiling. I took it as a compliment.

"You eat very fast," observed Tamsin, who, despite her quick start, was now just picking at the middle of a piece of bread, rolling it into little balls and piling them along the side of her plate. I felt as though she was accusing me of some terrible crime.

Beni leapt to my defense. "Cait eats at a normal pace; Tamsin. You are very slow."

"It sure is a nice day," commented Chuck, finally entering the conversation on a neutral note. We all agreed that the day was wonderful.

"I didn't realize that you live so close—vertically speaking, Chuck," I said.

"Yes, it's a great view from up there, and with my desk at the window it's almost as though I'm outside all day. Great place to work." He nodded and smiled. "Very inspiring."

"Have you read any of Chuck's books?" asked Beni.

Oh dear—the answer was "yes," but I hadn't enjoyed them. They weren't my sort of thing, really. I like a good, old-fashioned murder-mystery, rather than those complicated spy books, where everyone's running around shooting at people and blowing things up, but not knowing who to trust. *Clue: the answer is always "no one."*

"Yes, I have," I answered honestly enough. "I read a couple when I was on holiday a while back." It had been years earlier and I couldn't find anything else on the paperback-swap shelves in the hotel. "They're really interesting—" confusing? "and full of action—" for the boys who read them, "and gosh, there are some untrustworthy people in them. How do you come up with your stories and your characters, Chuck? It must take forever!" I thought I'd navigated the treacherous waters pretty well—*and* I'd managed to hit the ball into Chuck's court.

Chuck rocked back in his chair and said, "Oh, I don't know—it's a mixture of research and just thinking hard about things, really. Sometimes I'll read something, a fact maybe, that sets me off."

"Was that what happened with those guns in the baskets in *The Democratic Despot*?" I asked, appearing interested.

Chuck beamed. "Oh, you've read that one. That's the one they've just made into a movie, you know?"

I didn't, but it made sense. The book had one main character, two supplementary ones, and just one location—they could have saved up most of the budget for all the explosions at the end.

"It's been a great experience adapting it for the screen. Quite the learning curve." He seemed excited. "And, yes, to answer your question, the idea of putting guns in a basket and lowering and raising them was something that really happened during the Second World War in several locations where someone was held prisoner high up in a building, and they were able to get help from outside. Well spotted!"

He seemed genuinely delighted that I'd remembered the detail. *Little did he know!* I thought I'd take one more opportunity to please the man who, frankly, other than the conversation at the party, I'd hardly got to know at all, so I added, "What about that device in *The Fledgling Fugitive*? You know, where Dana, the female spy, pours poison down a wire into Dimitri's ear while he's sleeping? Did you get that idea from Shakespeare?"

"Hey—she's good!" laughed Chuck. "Boy, you sure know your English literature! What's with the names of my characters? How'd you remember them so clearly?"

"She's weird," replied Tamsin, still sulking and being bitchy.

I shot Tamsin what I hoped was a withering look, but I let it go. "Oh, I read it quite recently," I lied, "and you write your characters so well, I guess they just stuck. As for the poison, well, I was lucky enough to get to 'do' *Hamlet* in school, so I remember that Claudius poured poison into old King Hamlet's ear . . . And, of course, it was a common theme for Shakespeare— he liked the idea of ear-poisoning, either with actual poison, or with words, as in *Othello*." I realized I was letting this all get away from me a bit, but it had started me thinking.

"Well, you say very kind things, Cait," continued Chuck, "and I'm sure pleased to meet a fan. Hey, how'd you like me to sign some books for you? I have a bunch of them upstairs."

Well, what could I say?

"Oh Chuck, you're too kind, thank you!" I wondered how much they'd weigh and if they'd take my suitcase over the limit—assuming I ever managed to get on an airplane to fly home at all, that is.

"Why don't we do it now? You're finished here, right?" He was all action, like his books.

I'd been planning on enjoying a cigarette, but I had to agree, and pushed myself out of my chair.

"I will make coffee while you are gone," said Beni, also rising because, after all, a lady was leaving the table.

I glanced back at him as Chuck led the way, "That would be great," I called. Meaning it. I dutifully followed Chuck past the elevator to the stairs.

"It's not far," he said, then bounded up the stone steps two at a time, his slim frame making easy work of the climb. I labored up behind him. Every time I climb stairs I promise myself I'll stop smoking, and lose weight, and get more exercise, and just generally be a much better person . . . Then I get to the top, recover, and throw all my promises out of the window. I finally met Chuck outside his apartment, where he'd left his front door open behind him. As I entered I could see that the floor plan of his home was pretty much exactly the same as the Townsends', except that, of course, he didn't have the balcony. His apartment was much more masculine in its furnishings and its atmosphere. Lots of bookshelves lined the walls between the tall windows, as one might have expected. Most of the books, I noted quickly, were about the Second World War, and the wood of his furniture matched the wood of the floor, making it almost disappear. The room looked quite spartan, without much adornment upon the walls except several frames filled with wartime German medals. There was one jarring note, however. In a corner there was a strange contraption that looked like an orange plastic fishing rod, broken into in sections, but without the reel attachment. I couldn't begin to imagine what it was, so I asked.

"What's that?" I pointed at the plastic tubes.

Chuck looked in the direction I was indicating and smiled. "Ah, one of the 'research' parts of my work. It might feature in my next book. Or maybe not . . . I'm not quite sure yet."

Ah well, I wouldn't hold my breath!

As he had mentioned, Chuck's desk was beside the window which overlooked the balcony below. He sat down at it, pulled a few volumes off the shelves beside him, carefully removed the gold cap from a beautiful fountain pen and started to write inside their covers. He was giving me hardbacks—even heavier!

"Is there anything special you'd like me to write? It's K-A-T-E, right?"

I shook my head. "No, it's C-A-I-T. It's short for Caitlin. I always use Cait. Please, write what you think is appropriate . . . but maybe don't mention the murders. I might want to forget them!" I smiled. I'm sure that irony was playing about my lips somewhere.

"Is that a Welsh name?" he asked politely. "I remember you saying you were Welsh, right?"

"Yes, I am, but the name's more Gaelic than Welsh. My mum liked it. It means 'pure,' the same as 'Catherine,' which was a very popular name when I was born. She wanted something a bit different, so 'Caitlin' it was."

"Wasn't Dylan Thomas's wife named Caitlin? He was from the same place as you, right? Swansea?" Chuck asked.

I was impressed. He'd obviously been paying attention to our conversation at dinner.

"Yes, he was from Swansea, and his wife's name was Caitlin. I don't think she lived up to the meaning if it," and I laughed.

"And do *you*, Cait? Are *you* 'pure'? Or are you something different—something you pretend not to be?"

What *very* strange questions, and the way Chuck asked them gave me the creeps. There was something menacing in his voice and his eyes. He smiled quickly, as if he was trying to imply that he was being cheeky. I'd read him quicker than he'd been able to change his expression, though, and cheeky wasn't what he was being. Not at all. I decided to play along.

"Oh, Chuck," I patted him as he resumed writing, "you *are* naughty! Of *course* I'm pure. As the driven snow." I laughed—probably too operatically.

"Hey," I could hear Beni, below us, "don't have too much fun up there! I am feeling left out. Besides, the coffee is almost ready."

I walked around behind Chuck and peered out of the window, to see Beni about thirty feet below me. I spoke in my normal voice when I replied, "We'll be right down."

Beni also used his normal voice to reply, "Very good," and he disappeared back into the Townsends' kitchen. It was interesting that Chuck could have communicated so easily with anyone on the balcony below.

"Beni said that the coffee's ready," I said, turning to Chuck.

"Yeah, I heard him," replied Chuck casually, finishing his final signature with a flourish, then passing three fat books to me. I looked inside them, one at a time. They were all signed and dated, but beside his signature he'd written three different notes: one said "To Cait . . . a very clever woman"; the second read "To Cait—I've enjoyed our time together"; the third simply said "To Cait—a true fan." I felt bad about that one, and I could feel myself blush. Luckily, Chuck misinterpreted my reaction. He reached up and put his arm around my waist and said, "Don't blush, Cait, it's true, you really *are* a clever woman."

I laughed, nervously no doubt, as I slid myself from his embrace and moved toward the door, which was still open. "We'd better get back down," I called, trying to get away as quickly as I could. I looked back to see Chuck carefully stowing his fountain pen back in its proper place. I held the door open, waiting for him. A woman in her sixties came down the stairs ahead of me, walking past Chuck's front door before turning toward the next flight down. She looked at me with some curiosity, smiled politely, and nodded a greeting, then caught sight of Chuck inside his apartment and her face brightened.

"*Ah, Monsieur Damcott, une femme! Quelle surprise agréable! Bonne journée!*" She waved at him cheerily.

Chuck waved back as he walked toward me and replied, "Ah, Madame Blanche—*bonjour* to you too!" As he locked his door he whispered to me, "I don't know why she always talks to me in French like that—she has a very strong accent—she knows I don't speak French very well!"

Ah, but I caught it, and I bet you have no idea she just said that it makes a nice change to see you with a woman! I thought, but I decided to keep that to myself and make my way back to Beni . . . and the coffee. As I walked down the stairs I wondered about Chuck and the comment his neighbor had made. Was he gay? He certainly gave off an aura of hiding something about himself. Maybe that was it. Luckily there's not the stigma attached to homosexuality that there used to be—if it even *had* existed that way in literary circles at any time. I wondered how a gay spy novelist would fare, given the demographic of his target market. If his upstairs neighbor had formed an impression about his possible sexuality, then what about his downstairs neighbor? Interesting. Boy, sometimes you can learn a lot in a short time!

Back at Tamsin's front door, Beni let us in, and we all trooped to the balcony for coffee. I couldn't help noting that Beni was a natural host, whereas Tamsin, our *real* hostess, didn't seem to give a hoot if we lived or died.

I settled to my coffee and pulled out my cigarettes. "Is there anything sweet to eat?" I asked Beni, then I realized what a faux pas I'd made. My mother would have "crowned me," as she used to say. Not only had I asked for something I hadn't been offered, but I'd asked the wrong person.

"There is nothing sweet here," replied Beni apologetically. "I checked. I too have the sweet tooth sometimes." He smiled. I couldn't imagine a single cavity daring to form in that perfect mouth.

"Ah well," I said, and lit my cigarette. "Never mind. Though I would kill for a nice big piece of cake, or something like it . . ."

Tamsin let out a squeal, slammed her coffee onto the table, got up, and ran, sobbing, to the kitchen.

What on earth had I said to set her off like that? *Maybe mentioning "killing"?* Both Beni and Chuck shrugged, looking mystified.

"Ah, poor Tamsin, she is very . . . nervous," observed Beni. I wasn't sure that, on this occasion, he'd chosen the right word: I'd have gone with "melodramatic." But there, that's me.

"Someone should go to her," said Chuck, looking at me.

I sighed, stubbed out my cigarette, and stood. "I'll do it," I said. I knew I should. I followed Tamsin into the apartment and found her lying on a couch, sobbing into a pillow. *Lovely.*

"Come on, Tamsin. There, there." I patted her back. "I'm sorry if I said something that upset you. I didn't mean to. I know it must be a very difficult time for you." I was being as sympathetic as I could be, given that I don't think it's really in my nature. And while Tamsin hadn't exactly endeared herself to me since we'd met, it was true enough that she *had* just lost her husband.

"Oh, don't patronize me," she hissed at me as she looked around, her face tear stained and angry. Her reaction took me by surprise. "You think you're so clever, so much better than me. Well, I don't want your sympathy. I don't want people thinking you're nice because you're kind to me. You're not nice. You think I'm a fool. You're always showing off how clever you are—how much you know. I think you're stuck up and weird, like Ally said. If it hadn't been for all this, I'd never have had to see you again!"

I was shocked. "You phoned me and asked me to come here!" I replied.

"Well, I made a mistake," she snapped back. She was still glaring at me with her angry little eyes when Beni came into the room, and I saw her expression soften into helplessness again. She began to sob pathetically. So that was her game. I refused to play.

I sighed and turned to Beni. "I don't think we can be of much use here. Let's leave Tamsin to sort herself out for a few minutes. Let's wait on the balcony." I got up, smoothed my pants, and whispered to Tamsin, "You won't get him that way, dear. He's not that kind of man." I was gloating, and being a little cruel.

Tamsin looked at me with a queer smile on her face and whispered back, "Oh, Cait, you're really *not* that clever, are you? They're *all* that sort of man," and she wiped at her eyes, which were almost dry in any case.

It looked as though the battle lines had been drawn for a fight I hadn't even planned to take part in, and, as I walked back out onto the balcony, it seemed that another confrontation was in progress.

"I tell you, I saw no such thing," Beni was saying.

"You're a liar and I know it. You must have seen it when you left the table . . ." replied Chuck.

They both shut up as soon as they saw me, and I was left to wonder what they might have been talking about. It could have been anything, but I had a nagging suspicion that it was something important.

I sat, lit another cigarette, which I hoped I was actually going to be able to smoke, and picked up the coffee pot to top up my cup. It was empty.

"More coffee, anyone?"

Both men rumbled a sulky "no" in my general direction, and Beni sucked hard on a cheroot. I decided to not bother with more coffee.

"Any news from the police on the break-in at the museum yet, Beni?" I asked, innocently enough.

"No. Nothing." He sounded morose.

"Have you heard any more about Madelaine's death through the grape-vine here?" I asked Chuck.

"Nothing." He sounded just as grumpy.

Oh great, I was stuck with two miserable men and a woman who had the knives out for me—fantastic! I got up and walked to the balustrade that surrounded the balcony, letting the breeze blow away the feeling that invisible walls were beginning to close in on me. I wanted to run away from it all, back to Vancouver, to my little home, and to my friends—well, okay then, to Bud and Jan who are about the only friends I've got—and to a place where everything was clean and fresh . . . not full of people who were wearing masks to hide their true selves. Then I remembered that even in paradise there's danger, as poor old Bud knew only too well. Even amid the wonders of nature, I'd helped him on so many cases where hiding the truth was what had got people into trouble—killed, even.

I finished my smoke and walked back to the ashtray on the table to stub it out. Tamsin re-emerged and floated across the balcony, smiling weakly.

"Oh Beni," she whispered huskily as she sat down beside him, "I wanted to ask if you'd come with me to the funeral? I've arranged everything for Tuesday morning."

Well, that was news to me, and Beni and Chuck, too, by the looks of it.

"How have you done this?" asked Beni, puzzled. "Have the police said that you can?"

"Have they released Alistair's body?" echoed Chuck.

Tamsin looked quietly pleased with herself. "Oh yes, they called this morning, so I made all the arrangements. I had to ring and ring before that vicar-man at the church answered, but I got him in the end and he said that ten o'clock on Tuesday would be fine."

"I guess the rector was quite busy, today being Sunday," I observed, as wryly as I could.

"Oh, is it?" replied Tamsin, airily. "One loses track of time when one is grieving," she added, looking suitably tragic. "One" this and "one" that—who did she think she was—Lady Bountiful?! She was really laying it on thick. Surely Beni would see through it?

It seemed he didn't.

"But Tamsin, *of course* I will escort you. You must not worry, I will be there to support you, as you wish." Beni smiled kindly at Tamsin as he replied, then looked at me and added, "Will you still be here then, Cait? You will come to Alistair's funeral, of course?"

Instead of replying that I'd rather be on a plane back to Canada, I said, "Of course." I used my most gracious voice. But I couldn't just leave it there, could I? "It will be an odd experience for you, Tamsin, I'm sure," I said, looking directly at the woman, almost daring her to answer, "because you don't believe, do you? I mean, you're not a Christian, right? That twig waggling and chanting that you did when Alistair died—that all seemed to be . . . well, not Christian anyway. What was it exactly?"

Tamsin smiled a happy little smile and replied brightly, "Oh, that's something I was reading about in a book." I tried not to let my shock show. "It's very interesting. Chuck loaned it to me, didn't you Chuck?"

Chuck looked vague as he replied, "Which book was that?" I wondered how many books he'd ever loaned to Tamsin.

"Oh, you *know*, the one about that place in Germany where all the Knights of the Round Table used to meet . . . you know, like King Arthur. It's got that funny name . . . Wewy-something. You *know*! Where they had all those big ceremonies and all those important relics—like in *Raiders of the Lost Ark*. It was ever so good! Oh—what was it *called*?" She was wailing like a child.

"Do you mean Wewelsburg Castle?" I asked.

Tamsin looked surprised. "How do *you* know about it?" she snapped. I suspected that what I was about to say would fall under Tamsin's heading of "showing off."

"Oh, I guess I read about it, too, someplace," I replied as casually as I could. "It was the Nazi's 'Camelot' wasn't it, Chuck? Himmler's spiritual home for the SS once they'd achieved the perfect balance of race and power they were striving for in Europe? I think they just opened it up to the public. It was pretty controversial, I remember. Have you been yet? I should think it's just your cup of tea." I recalled the medals that adorned his walls upstairs.

"Oh, why would Chuck want to go to a nasty place like that?" asked Tamsin, annoyed. "In the pictures in the book it wasn't even pretty on the outside, so it can't have been pretty on the inside. They used to have some interesting secret ceremonies there. Like back in the olden times. I thought it couldn't *hurt* to do that when Ally died. If his spirit was passing right by us, which it must have been, it was my duty to help it on its way. Even if I didn't want him to go. So that's what I was doing. But, no, you're right, I'm not really into church, or spirity things. It's all a bit much for me, kneeling and bowing and singing. I like the old stuff better. Lots of love potions and spells and gallantry and horses. I like the idea of having an 'eternal flame.' The rector at the church said I couldn't have one for Ally. They don't do that there. Maybe they'd do it in that castle place."

Tamsin's interpretation of the bizarre occultism that had been practiced by Himmler's Grail Order, the SS, was not only frighteningly naive, but also sadly familiar. We humans often fill our spiritual void with all sorts of rubbish that we half understand, then hang onto as though our lives, or our souls, depended upon it. Funnily enough, she'd alighted upon a particular area of fascination for me: how man, as an animal, is differentiated from all other animals by his desire to worship something bigger than himself— something mysterious, and just beyond his grasp. It was clear that this wasn't the place for a metaphysical or spiritual conversation, so I just sat there and pondered poor Tamsin . . . and wondered to what extent Chuck might be interested in this field.

"I doubt they'd do anything like that there," replied Chuck to Tamsin's comment. "I should imagine they'd be over-run with such requests if they did." It was an interesting comment, and one I couldn't let pass.

"Do you mean there are lots of people who'd like to be remembered with their own eternal flame at the place that was built by concentration camp inmates and prisoners—people used as slave labor so that Heinrich Himmler could practice his own unique form of religion at 'The Center of the World'? Surely not."

"There's a surprising number of neo-Nazi groups all around the world these days, and some are very big, and powerful," replied Chuck gravely, "and many of them think of Wewelsburg as a shrine. They hope, one day, to see the Spear of Destiny in its appointed place there. But I'm pretty sure that the German government wouldn't allow personal memorials to be placed at the site. As you said, Cait, renovating the place and opening it to the public was pretty controversial in its own right."

Somewhere in my head a picture was forming. Ideas and thoughts were shifting and resettling. I was still at sea. I lit another cigarette and drew on it, hard.

"We should collect some clothes for Gerard and take them to him at the hospital, as he asked," said Beni, his practical tones cutting across the suddenly heavy atmosphere, restoring a sense of time and place.

I looked up and said, in a chorus with Tamsin, "We should."

The widow and I looked at each other, then she said, sharply, "I *know* Gerard, you don't. *I* should be helping him, not you. He's *my* friend. You'll be leaving as soon as you can. I'll still be *here*. With my *friends*." She was looking at Beni as she spoke. It was clear that she wasn't just talking about Gerard. I got it.

She was right. I was just passing through . . . at least, if I could work out what had happened to Alistair, Madelaine, and the necklace I was. In that instant, I sighed and faced the facts. I'd have to take the moments of flirtation and flattery and put them into my memory banks . . . and get on with the job of working everything out, so I could go home.

Beni said he'd get Gerard's key from Daphne to collect some things for the old man. Tamsin offered to help him. Chuck said he had a few things to sort out at his place before he could leave. I offered to stay behind and, once again, clear away the remains of our meal. We all agreed with the plan of action. After lots of cheek kissing, everyone headed off in their various directions.

I carried a few plates into the kitchen, put them down, and found a beer on the counter, freshly poured into a lovely cut crystal glass. I wondered who had poured it—and for whom? Beni, Tamsin, and Chuck had all just gone out through the kitchen, one after the other. Surely no one would mind if I drank it? It looked very inviting.

"Fancy a cold one, Cait?" I asked myself.

"Don't mind if I do," I replied to myself. I picked up the glass and let the cool bubbles wash the back of my throat. It was a beautiful day, and pretty soon we'd all be on our way to visit poor old Gerard in hospital, with his much needed supplies. Until then, there wasn't *that* much to clear . . . so I couldn't see the harm.

Sunday Night

I WOKE WITH A SPLITTING headache, and knowing that I'd had some pretty wild dreams. Everything was black. I had no idea where I was. I rubbed my forehead. It was damp . . . or was that blood? I couldn't even see my hand in front of my eyes. I realized I was sitting against a wall made of big, rough blocks of stone. I knew this because their lumps were digging into the base of my spine. Beneath me the floor was slightly less bumpy, but stone nonetheless. Everything was cold, me especially.

What the hell was going on? Where was I? Why was I there? How had I got there—wherever *there* was?

Not being able to see anything, I felt my body parts, just to make sure that everything was where it should be, and that it was all still working. It was. Nothing broken, or twisted. Well, that was a relief. I felt about me and located my handbag on the floor a few feet away. I scrabbled about inside it until I found a lighter, which I flicked into life. Its brightness blinded me, so I let it go out, then waited a moment and lit it again, this time away from my eyes.

In front of me was another wall just like the one I was leaning against. To my right and left the two walls continued into blackness. Okay, so I was in a tunnel.

I let the flame go out and listened. Could I hear anything? Only my own breathing. Could I smell anything? Not much—but there was something . . . what was it? It wasn't dampness, and it wasn't soil. I couldn't put my finger on it—though I *knew* that I knew what it was. I let it go. It would come to me.

I pushed myself up the wall until I was standing. My whole body ached. How long had I been there? I couldn't see my watch, so, again, I scrabbled around in my purse and found my phone. It told me that it was 10:09. I assumed it was Sunday—though, frankly, I could have been there for more than a day and I'd have been none the wiser. I checked my phone again, but there was no signal. I guessed that would have been too much to hope for, and further surmised that whoever had dumped me here had left my bag with me because they knew it wouldn't help me. And they must have been familiar enough with my location to know that there was no phone signal.

I tried to kick my brain into a higher gear. What was the last thing I remembered?

Drinking a beer in Tamsin's kitchen after lunch on Sunday.

Okay.

Did I feel hungry?

Yes, but not ravenously so. Okay, I was more certain that this was the same day as the day I had drunk the beer, because otherwise my tummy would have been telling me otherwise.

Was my headache the result of having been hit on the head? Or not?

I felt all over my head and I couldn't pinpoint any part that was more tender than any other. I'd probably been drugged, not hit. It must have been the beer.

I was good so far.

There was something on my neck—a wide, flat, metal hoop, with lumps on it. I didn't own anything like it. I felt it a bit more carefully and tried to unhook it behind my neck. I couldn't work out the way the clasp worked, and I couldn't turn the thing around either. What on earth was it? I felt it again, then I knew. I had never seen it, and I'd only heard a vague description of it, but I knew it was the Collar of Death.

Wonderful! I was wearing the necklace that had always been the harbinger of doom. That cheered me up no end. Why the hell was it on *me*? I resigned myself to the fact I could do nothing about it. I was only making my neck and my arms sore, so I stopped. I was *not* happy. But I had to apply my energy to what really mattered. Getting out!

Where was I? I told myself to not waste the lighter fuel, but to use my brain.

If someone had drugged me, then I'd have likely collapsed. If I'd been drugged to the point of collapse, I had to admit it would have taken someone with a lot of strength to move me—I'd have been a dead weight. It would have been a big job to move me far. Or maybe not. Quite a few modern drugs allow the person who's taken them to move about, albeit with help, and then remember nothing about it. Maybe I'd been "roofied." If so, then I'd have needed support and steering, not carrying, and I could have been moved quite a long way—by car even. I could have been taken anywhere, then drugged again, so that I'd become unconscious.

What is it they say? Three minutes, three days, three weeks.

A person can survive for three minutes without air. There seemed to be lots of that, and I was pretty sure I'd been conscious for more than three minutes already. Three days without water? I supposed I'd be able to manage that, if I had to, but I was already very dry and thirsty. Three weeks without food—the thought horrified me! I had quite a while to find my way out of wherever I was without expiring. Good.

I shouted for help as loud as I could. My voice reverberated off the stone walls around me. I thought I might as well keep trying, but I suspected I was wasting my time. Given the stone walls, the funny smell—*what the hell was it*—the dryness of the air, and the coolness of the temperature, I must be underground. As the thought came to me another one occurred: what if I was in the cellars underneath the gardens of the Palais? They'd been built out of stone, then covered over with tons of earth. That could be it.

What had Beni said? Ah yes, "they built a web of cellars." I wondered if he'd meant that literally—an actual web-shaped set of cellars, all converging on a central point. I felt along the wall behind me, and I could sense a slight concave curve. I pulled out my lighter again and held it up: I could just make out both walls and, sure enough, they had mirror curves. The one in front of me was the inner wall of the curve. I decided to feel my way along that one. Surely I could manage in the dark, and I let the lighter go out.

I took my time because the ground was uneven. I felt as though I was inching my way along, but I supposed I was making progress. Nothing around me changed, not the light, not the sounds, and not the smell or the airflow, so I just kept going. I didn't think about crying out again, as it didn't seem to make sense. As I felt my way along, I kept thinking about who might have put me there, but I knew the only way I'd work that out was to work out who had killed Alistair and Madelaine, and who'd stolen the necklace. I was now convinced that it was all the work of one person. Otherwise, *why* would I be wearing the precious necklace?

The wall was my main focus, and that was a good thing because it abruptly stopped. It disappeared around a corner. I almost fell forward, but managed to stop myself. I used the lighter to establish that, while the wall behind me continued around, the one in front of me now turned left, and was faced by another wall—yes, it was like the spoke of a wheel running away from the wall behind me . . . maybe a spider's web *was* the pattern they'd adopted after all. I had a choice to make: stick to the outside wall, and hope to eventually come to an exit, or head off to the center of the web.

I sat down, carefully, to think. If *I'd* been dumping someone, I wouldn't leave them anywhere near an exit, would I? No, of course not, because then they'd be likely to find the way out—or maybe make themselves heard. Would I have the time and energy to take them as far as possible from the entrance? Maybe, maybe not—it all depended on who'd been doing the dumping and how long they'd had to do it. If I *was* in the cellars for the Palais, which had been built to house the wine when the place was a hotel, it would make sense that there'd be an entrance to them inside the building itself—they wouldn't want to send people outside in order to get wine, would they? No, of course not. Such an entrance would have to have a tunnel from the Palais to the actual cellars because they didn't connect with the place itself, and the Palais was higher than the cellars, so there'd either be steps or a sloping exit.

Having worked through this, I decided that my only course of action was to follow the outside wall, and to not be tempted to try to walk through the center of the web. It might well be a shorter route, but I was, quite literally, in the dark, and I didn't want to misjudge things and inadvertently get side-tracked. I stood up, pulled my bag back onto my shoulder—checked my cell phone again just in case there was a signal. There wasn't, and the battery was getting pretty low—why the hell hadn't I charged it up before I went to bed the night before? I pushed myself over to the outer wall and carried on going, hoping that I hadn't already missed the vital tunnel away from the web . . . if that was, in fact, where I was.

As I moved slowly along, I had hoped that my eyes would become acclimatized to the darkness. Maybe they had, but it made no difference—I couldn't see a damned thing! I was beginning to feel a bit hopeless, and to wonder if my bright ideas about where I was were just stupid, because I didn't seem to be getting anywhere, other than farther forward. I couldn't feel *any* change in the angle of the ground below my feet, and, for all I knew, I was walking along a tunnel that was miles long and wasn't the cellars at the Palais at all!

I looked at my phone again. It was 10:52. My God, was that all the time I'd been at it? It felt like much longer. I sat down, with my back against the wall again, pulled out my packet of cigarettes, and lit one. I reflected on how strange it was that I was sitting God only knew where, smoking a cigarette as though I was relaxing. The red tip hissed as I sucked in the smoke, which hit my dry throat and made me cough. Well, it served me right, I supposed.

I could see the smoke as it left the glowing tip, before it disappeared into the darkness. I held my breath . . . was it me doing that, or was it being wafted toward my left, the direction from which I'd come? I sat and watched the smoke intently. I moved the cigarette from position to position.

Yes! The smoke was *always* moving toward my left! Yeah! I felt immediately revived. Air was definitely coming from the right. Maybe there was a way out not much farther along. I got up and held the cigarette in front of me, like a tiny little torch, and moved onward, using one hand to feel along the wall.

Suddenly I tripped over something, fell forward, and almost broke my ankle and my wrist at the same time. The cigarette fell from my hand. I reached down to hold my ankle, and my hand found something cold, smooth, and hard. It rolled as I touched it, and it sounded like . . . glass. Yes, it was a glass bottle. *Yes!* Another victory—you find bottles in a cellar, don't you?

As soon as I felt the bottle I knew what I'd been smelling since I'd opened my eyes—the lingering aroma of wine that had been spilled a very long time ago—almost a metallic smell. I grabbed hold of the bottle and felt it all over: yes, wine. I was so thirsty I'd have given anything for a drink right about then, but what was I going to do about opening it? I knew I didn't have a corkscrew in my bag, and I couldn't convince myself that trying to break the bottle's neck against the wall would result in anything but a bloody mess—with *my* blood being involved.

I pulled out my lighter again and held it up. Along the wall I'd been following stood floor to ceiling racks containing a lot of bottles—the racks weren't full, and they looked as though they were in use because while the bottles were dusty, they certainly didn't look as though they'd been there since the war. I took this as a good sign.

I realized I'd have to keep using the lighter because I couldn't really follow my wall anymore, and didn't dare lean into the bottles to support myself. I kept my eyes peeled and followed along the racks, hoping that their presence meant I was getting closer to the parts of the cellars that were more accessible from the Palais. Eventually, I came across a whole stack of bottles with gold foil tops.

Oh goody—champagne! Yes, I can guess what you're thinking, but what *I* was thinking was that here, finally, was something I could drink because I could *open* it! I pulled out a bottle and removed the cork. It really did open with a sigh, not a pop, which I know champagne is supposed to do. I swigged from the bottle . . . and it was *bliss*. I'm going to say it was the best champagne I'd ever tasted, but, frankly, a bottle of water would have been just as welcome at that point. I stood for a moment, greedily slaking my thirst and enjoying the taste.

The bottle was heavy, so I sat myself down again and lit another cigarette. I felt almost festive. That lightness of spirit, or maybe it was lightness of head, set me to thinking . . . Five minutes probably wouldn't make much difference in the whole scheme of things—what if I just gave myself a few moments to think about the whole thing . . . try to get the "big picture" sorted out in my mind?

I couldn't make notes, and, frankly, I didn't feel particularly able to organize my thoughts. I decided to try another technique that can sometimes be helpful for problem solving. I closed my eyes—not that there was any real need to do that, but it's what you're supposed to do—and I opened my mind to allow visual images to form, almost as though in a dream. It's called "wakeful dreaming." It wasn't something I'd done often in the past for myself, but I'd helped others to do it.

The first thing I had to do was to concentrate on each of the people involved in this in turn. I had to allow each person to "gather about them" things that my mind somehow related to them. It sounds odd, but it's one of those techniques that allows the mind to do what it *wants* to do, rather than having your consciousness imposing order upon things. It encourages subliminal connections to be made. It's pretty much the same process as when we are dreaming, when our brains take the opportunity to sort through things that have made an impression upon us and file them away.

First I saw Tamsin. She was wailing, waggling smoking sticks, and wearing dozens of huge necklaces, all of which were dripping with blood; she was standing in a pile of clothing that was heaped about her, then she threw a big bunch of keys at me and shouted "You'll never find it! They're all the same."

Next I saw Beni looking handsome and well groomed as usual, except that he was wearing a toga, rather than his normal clothes; he smiled as he held open his car door for me; when I got into the car I could see that ancient scrolls were strewn all over the floor, along with loaves of bread and broken glass. He leaned toward me and, very close to my ear, he whispered, "They'll never find us here," then he kissed me.

I tried to drag my mind from Beni and focus instead on Chuck. He was suddenly very blond-haired, and he was goose-stepping down the front steps of the Palais, followed by a troop of young men all doing the same thing. He carried a long orange wand that dripped blood, and a basket full of guns; he was laughing and whispering something, in German, that nonetheless echoed aloud, as though he had shouted.

I saw Gerard crying like a baby and floating in a swimming pool full of flowers that now sat at the foot of the Palais steps; the pool was overflowing, its waters washing away the gardens that lay beyond; he held a small, dark-haired girl in his arms, and he was stroking her hair.

Madelaine came to mind. She was alive, and singing Edith Piaf songs in a smoke-filled bar, dressed as Mata Hari. She held a miniature version of the photograph of herself that had been stolen from her apartment, but in it she was dead.

Alistair popped up, laughing and looking rosily healthy. He carried a giant birthday cake in one hand and a giant snail in the other; the snail was without its shell, but alive and slimy. "Which one do you want, Cait?" he was asking me, pushing them both toward me. I could feel myself backing away from him, then the snail started to eat the birthday cake.

There was Moreau was sitting in a tiny version of his office, standing behind a tiny version of his desk and shouting at me that I had to leave Nice—now; he was red in the face, a mass of emotion and anger. Bertrand was beside him, laughing at me and speaking gibberish.

Next, I unexpectedly saw Bud standing in his flak jacket, which was covered with blood, and pointing at a street sign that said "Beautiful Beaches of South Surrey"—it was riddled with bullet holes. He was screaming something at me—I could see his mouth moving, but he was making no sound.

Marty, the Andersons' tubby black lab, bounded toward me, covered in sand and soaking wet; his tail was wagging, and he had something in his mouth . . . it was a gun, but it was made out of orange plastic, like a toy. Jan joined him, again, covered in sand and dripping wet. She was holding Marty's leash and calling for him to find Bud.

Finally, there was me. In the picture of myself—I'd knocked off about forty pounds, but that's allowed—I was clearing Tamsin's kitchen of plates and food and bottles and glasses and knives and forks and spoons . . . stuffing everything directly into the garbage chute. Then I jumped into it myself and wound up on a pile of moldering scraps and black plastic bags in a small dirty room that smelled of old wine, but I knew I was fine because I had two sets of keys and five lipsticks in my pocket and all I had to do was find the key that opened the door.

I let all of this float about in my head, as it would have done if I was asleep. I didn't force it, I didn't even try to make sense of it. Parts of the images fell away, and parts of the images became sharpened . . . then it all clicked into place. It all made sense. It was amazing.

I had a moment of total clarity, and I knew exactly who had stolen the necklace, and when, and how, and why . . . *and* how they'd killed Alistair, *and* Madelaine. I couldn't believe I'd been so stupid!

I also realized that I was in great danger, and I could suddenly hear my heart pulsing in my ears. If I was right, I had to get out of the cellars and call Moreau, fast—because, otherwise, someone else might die soon, and it could well be me!

Very Late Sunday night

WHILE IT HAD DAWNED ON me that my quick escape was imperative, knowing I was in danger didn't help me get out of it. I took a final big swig of champagne (oops . . . it was half empty!) and set the bottle down. I picked up a full one, acknowledging that you never know when you might need a bottle of champagne, ignited the lighter once more and decided that I had to try to move ahead more quickly. But I was now concerned that I might, literally, run into someone who meant me harm. Before I moved, I listened carefully. It was so quiet that I could actually hear the bubbles effervescing in the champagne bottle at my feet.

Moving toward what I *hoped* was a way out felt even more painfully slow than before. I was buoyed by the fact that the wall was continuously lined with racks, because I felt that, maybe, I was getting closer to the tunnel that would eventually take me back to the Palais. My thumb was getting very hot keeping the lighter going, so I had to keep switching hands, and the little flame reflected off the bottles in the racks as I moved along. Here and there were spaces, then I came to a wide gap in the racks and . . . yes! A door!

My heart raced as I moved the lighter around looking for some sort of handle. It was an old wooden door with a heavy metal latch. I tried it, but it was stuck. I could see rust. I tried knocking the latch upward with the cork end of the champagne bottle that I had stuffed into my handbag—they're pretty sturdy things, champagne bottles, and, after a few knocks, the latch opened easily. The excitement rose in my stomach. I pushed the heavy door, daring to let the lighter flame die for a moment. Was this my way out? Or did a rusted latch mean it was a door that hadn't been used for some time?

The air did not rush toward me, nor was there any change in the light, so my heart sank a little. I re-lit the lighter and saw I was in a tiny room—it couldn't have been more than five feet square—lined with bricks, rather than the large stones from which the tunnels had been constructed. It was clear that it wasn't going to provide me with an exit, so I let the door close and moved on. There were no more racks in this stretch of the cellar. I soon found another door and used the same method to open the latch, only to be confronted with yet another little cell . . . of *course* . . . *that* was what these little rooms were—cells! Maybe they'd been built into the tunnels during the war. I hated the idea, but I could see that it would make sense for the Gestapo to have somewhere "convenient" to imprison those they wanted to question . . . and who knew *what* else. After opening a third door I was beginning to find the whole thing very depressing, and wondered about the wisdom of continuing to look for a way out within rooms that more than likely offered none.

Something drew me to the fourth room . . . a smell that I recognized . . . and it was not stale wine. I opened the door easily, without the aid of the champagne bottle, and looked inside. This room was different: the smell was of decay, and the floor was covered with bunches and bunches of dead flowers. That was the smell. A bunch of roses, fresh white ones tied with a big white bow, lay against the far wall of the cell, nestled among a collection of crucifixes. I confirmed that the latch would allow me to open the door from the inside, and pushed the door all the way open so that it sat back on its hinges. I made sure it wouldn't swing closed by using the bottle of champagne as a door-stop. I knelt to pick up a large card that sat beside the white roses.

A trembling hand had written, "*À ma soeur—aimée pour toujours, G.*" The only "sister" I could think of who would be loved always was Gerard's. "G." The bouquet couldn't have been more than a few days old. Behind it, and behind all the crucifixes, was a large hole in the brick wall. I replaced the card and pushed my lighter into the hole, then my arm, my shoulder, and my head. Something was glowing in the flame . . . I could see something white, and something ragged. My brain tried to make sense of it. Leg bones and ragged cloth. I realized with a start that I was looking at human remains, and I bumped my head hard as I recoiled. Bugger!

I rubbed my head. It didn't help.

I had to be sure, so I looked into the hole again, being careful not to knock my head. This time I craned my neck around to try to see more. I saw the bones of a foot, of two feet . . . then of three, four, five. So there was clearly more than one body bricked up in there. I wondered whose bodies they were, and my mind flew to Gerard's story about the women who had disappeared from the Palais—his sister among them. That *had* to be it. This was where the missing women had been hidden. I wondered about the other cells: had they also been used to hide the remains of those killed by the Gestapo and the SS?

Suddenly, Gerard's attachment to the gardens became more understandable: the bricks that had been chipped away had not been removed as the result of recent effort—the hole had been there for some time. He must have known about it for years. The gardens were his memorial to his sister, and to all those other women. No wonder he'd been so set against the building of the swimming pool: Alistair's plan would have despoiled his sister's grave.

I sighed. How terribly, terribly sad. I stood alone, in the dark, surrounded by death and decay, and couldn't help but feel my own mortality. Would I ever escape this place? Or would I end up—I jumped. In the absolute silence I had heard something.

What was it?

It was the sound of someone walking along the tunnel in hard-soled shoes. I moved quickly to the door and listened. The sounds were coming from the direction in which I'd been heading. I could see a yellow light reflecting off the tunnel's walls.

I had to act quickly. I pulled the champagne door-stop away and closed the door as quietly as I could. Before it closed completely I heard a voice say, "I wonder how far in they took her? It can't have been too far, she was too big to carry for long . . ." I knew I'd never heard that person speak before. I closed the door and allowed the latch to fall silently.

I guessed that the young man with the incredibly posh English accent was referring to me. I felt wounded. I rationalized that maybe, for once, my weight had helped me—if I'd been lighter I might have ended up much farther away from the exit, which I now assumed was quite close by.

I couldn't hear anything except my own breathing, which seemed to echo in the tiny room. I hoped they couldn't hear it through the door. Through a tiny crack between the door and the uneven stone floor, I watched their light pass by. It seemed they were continuing on in the direction from which I had come. I wondered how long I should wait before daring to open the door. I counted ten steamboats, then moved the latch as slowly and quietly as I could. Gradually, I opened the door. Once it was open a little I stopped and listened. Nothing. That could be good or bad. I opened it farther and stuck out my head. Still no light, no sounds. I could feel air moving. I hoped they'd left a door open, somewhere.

I told myself that I wouldn't know for sure if I didn't move, but I felt loathe to leave that little space. Finally, I stepped into the corridor. No more racks leaned against the wall, so I could move faster by just running my hands along the flat of the wall itself. I took the chance of using the lighter, and it was only moments before I saw the most wonderful, beautiful sight ahead . . . a half open door, and electric light beyond. *Yes! Yes!*

I stuffed the lighter back into my bag and ran on tiptoe to the door. I peeped through a small panel of wrought ironwork to see what was on the other side: a well-lit staircase. *Fantastic!* I managed to squeeze through the door without having to push it open farther. I checked to see if I could lock or bolt it behind me, to keep whoever it was trapped inside the tunnels— but it clearly needed a key, and a big one at that.

Ahead of me was the staircase—wide, shallow, stone steps swinging off to the right. Bare lightbulbs were strung along the ceiling, which arched above me. I began to climb as quickly and as quietly as I could. It wasn't long before I was breathing heavily. I tried to keep the heaving silent—after all, I didn't know what was ahead of me, except more steps, because I couldn't see around the sweep of the arc. I kept going, telling myself that my life depended on it, and got into a bit of a rhythm. The stairs seemed to go on forever, but, finally, another door appeared above me—a twin of the one below. It was closed. I approached it as stealthily as I could, gulping in air as quietly as possible. I got to the final step and peered through the metal grill. Nothing. Everything beyond was in darkness, but I could have sworn that I could hear someone snoring in the distance. I told myself I was imagining it.

I put my hand on the lever handle, and pushed. *Please let it be unlocked . . . please let it be unlocked . . .* The mantra kept pace with my breathing. Finally the lever was fully depressed and I pushed the door gently. Nothing happened. *Oh no! It's locked!* I couldn't accept that, so I pushed down a little harder on the lever and more forcefully against the door. I lurched forward, and the door creaked open.

I was *out*, but where *was* I?

I looked around me—everything was dark, and I really *could* hear snoring. Suddenly I knew exactly where I was. I was in the basement of the Palais, looking along the corridor where the rental apartments were located—where Gerard lived. I was *so close* to being safe. I pushed the door closed behind me, released the handle, and ran along the corridor as quietly as possible. I had no idea how long it would take the people in the tunnel to discover that I wasn't there any longer—hopefully quite some time, since they didn't seem to know how far away I might have been left. I knew they could be back at any moment, so I couldn't hang about.

But what should I do, exactly? Where should I go? Run out of the front of the Palais, out onto those deserted streets in the middle of the night and hope to . . . what? Find a cab just waiting for someone to need them? What if the people from the tunnel came after me? They'd be bound to start looking for me in the area—and they'd probably find me!

I had to come up with an alternative plan.

I couldn't go to anyone other than Moreau—it was far too risky. I had to get hold of him on the phone and ask him to come and get me—that was it. I shoved my hand into my handbag to find my cell phone. Once I'd navigated around the bottle of champagne, I found something small and cold. I pulled it out. It was a single key.

Of course! It was the spare key to Madelaine's apartment that we had got from Daphne, the cleaning lady. I must have automatically dropped it into my purse after I'd unlocked Madelaine's door. I recalled that her apartment number was eleven, though the police notice and the wax seal on the door announcing that it was a crime scene and not to be entered by unauthorized persons was a bit of a give-away too.

I ignored the notice, broke the seal, put the key into the lock, and entered the apartment of the late Madelaine Schiafino. I closed the door behind me and dared to let out a deep sigh of relief, though I didn't turn on a light. Luckily, having been there before and remembering the layout of the apartment, I was able to do what I needed to do most at that point—find the bathroom! With the bathroom door shut tight, and feeling pretty secure, I flicked on the lights. I managed to not let the sight of myself in the mirror frighten me.

I pulled out my phone and the card that Moreau had given me, and dialed his number. I could picture the phone sitting on his desk, in a dark room, ringing out for all it was worth. I hoped that if he wasn't there in person at—I glanced quickly at my phone's glowing panel—a quarter to twelve on a Sunday night, there would be some system in place for his calls to be forwarded to a human being. It seemed that there wasn't, because all I got was the chance to leave a message.

"Captain Moreau—it's Cait Morgan. It's almost midnight on Sunday. I need your help. I know who killed Alistair and Madelaine, and I believe they would now like to kill me. It is too difficult for me to explain in French. You have my number. My battery is low. I am hiding in Madelaine Schiafino's apartment. Please come and get me." I hung up. Should I dial the emergency number and ask for help? I wondered what I would say? How I'd explain myself? Then I had a thought.

I turned out the lights, crept out of the bathroom, and emerged into the main sitting room. Moonlight streamed through the window in front me, showing me the way to the laptop in the corner. I figured that, if I shuttered the window and kept the screen facing the wall, I'd be able to use it without any light being visible from outside the apartment. I rearranged the room a little, got myself settled, turned everything on, worked out how to create a document, and began to type.

I type quite fast for someone who never had a typing lesson in her life. I attended a school for girls where they seemed to assume that useful life-skills, like typing, cooking, and sewing, needed to be taught to only those who weren't up to Latin, physics, and chemistry. I was self-taught when it came to computers, and while I might have been able to read and memorize all the manuals ever written, it didn't mean that I was a whizz with a keyboard.

After about half an hour, I'd written a fair summary of what I'd seen, heard, and worked out. I saved the document, then opened the internet browser and accessed my own e-mail at the university. I carefully typed in Moreau's e-mail address, attached the document, and sent it. I did the same to myself, and, for good measure, Bud. It couldn't hurt. When I pressed the Send button I felt a tremendous release: I still wasn't sure how I was going to keep myself safe until I was rescued by Moreau and his men, but at least I'd told my story, in full. Writing it down had helped me confirm my thinking. I *knew* I was right about it all. I realized I was by no means out of danger, but I felt relieved, as though I'd achieved something very important.

Just before I exited the internet I thought I'd quickly check to see if there was any news about a big police operation in Delta: maybe I could put my mind at rest about Bud.

I opened the news page and there it was: a photograph of two guys flat on the ground, their hands cuffed behind their backs, and masked men in Kevlar police vests standing over them, holding semi-automatic weapons.

"Gang Busters Swoop Down on Suspects," read the headline. Good, Bud had got them! Had there been trouble? Was he okay? The full story wasn't likely to mention him by name (all the guys on his operations tried to keep their identities secure), but they would be unable to keep any injuries a secret.

I scrolled down to read the full story, eager to know what had happened:

Residents of a quiet Delta neighborhood woke in the early hours of Sunday morning to hear shots ringing out, as the BC Gang Investigation Team arrested two men suspected of the targeted shooting of a woman at Crescent Beach, South Surrey, some eighteen hours earlier. No one was injured during the take-down, though the suspects were attended to by paramedics before being taken into custody.

The suspects' names have not yet been released, but neighbors say that they were used to seeing the police in attendance at the property. One local man claimed that the house was a center for gang activity.

This action follows on the heels of the release of the name of Saturday's shooting victim. Jan Anderson, 54, was the wife of the newly appointed head of the BC Gang Investigation Team, Bud Anderson. The couple had been married for eleven years. They had no children, but the family dog was also injured in the attack on his owner. Commander Anderson was not available for comment, and it is not known if he was personally involved in the operation that led to the capture of the two men suspected of killing his wife.

I was looking at a picture of Jan. She was smiling. At me. I'd taken the picture. Last summer. In my kitchen.

I felt giddy. I couldn't focus on the screen in front of me because my eyes were welling up. I held onto the table to steady myself. Hot tears rolled down my cheeks and plopped onto the keyboard.

I didn't want to believe it—but it was there in front of me.

Why hadn't Bud said anything? Wait—what *had* he said? I ran through our last conversation in my head. This time it meant something very different to me: of course, he *thought* I'd read the news releasing Jan's name . . . he *thought* I knew. I'd only read the headline. I hadn't put Crescent Beach and South Surrey together . . . except, maybe, in my wakeful dreaming exercise, which also suddenly made sense. What had Bud thought I'd meant when I'd asked him to give my love to Jan? Or maybe he'd hung up by then? My God, he'd taken the time to phone me to say he couldn't help *me* when he was on his way to try to find the men who had killed his *wife*. Oh, bless him! What the *hell* was he thinking!?

I wiped my eyes and sniffed. Oh, bugger—I'd just sent him that e-mail about all this necklace stuff. What would he think? I could have kicked myself! "Selfish cow" was what he'd think—and he'd be right. I mean, *Jan* was dead. *Dead.* I still couldn't really wrap my head around it.

I had to e-mail Bud again—or call him...No, not call him—he wouldn't want to be bothered with me. Yes, e-mail was best. What if he wasn't bothering to check e-mail? Oh good grief—I didn't know what to do for the best. In an ideal world I'd have been able to run up to Bud and give him a big hug and hold him and let him cry, if he wanted to. Well, no, in an ideal world Jan would be fine...but...oh, you know...

I decided that an e-mail was best, but when I reached the empty Subject field, I ran out of steam. I didn't know what to write. What *do* you write at a time like that?

In the end, following the title, "I'm so sorry," I typed,

> Bud, I don't know how it feels for you. I don't have any words that will help. I don't know *how* to help you. I don't know when I'll be there. I don't know if you'll have time for me when I am. I do know that I loved Jan and I will miss her. Everyone who knew her loved Jan—she was a truly unique woman. Have the strength to trust those around you who love you. All my love and sympathy, Cait.

Once again I pushed the Send button. This time there was no sense of elation. Just misery, a sense of inadequacy and loss, and more tears.

I held my head in my hands. Oh Bud...poor, poor Bud. What would he do without her? They'd been real soulmates. He'd be devastated. I knew *I* was, and she was only my friend, not my spouse. I wanted to sob. I wanted...Oh, I wanted everything to be back the way it was before I'd come to this wretched place...I wanted Jan and Bud to be fine—and poor Marty too—and I wanted *me* to be fine...and I wasn't. I was alone, and sad, and frightened, when I wanted to be at home, safe and warm and with the people I loved.

I suppose I might have stayed there until Moreau came to get me, but before I'd even had a chance to turn off the laptop, I heard a voice outside the window.

"I tell you, she's gone! Why on earth would she hang around here? She's probably in a taxi on her way to the police station right now. It wouldn't have taken her long to get to the taxi rank at the bottom of the gardens, and there are always taxis there—it's where they all hang about to smoke and chat until the clubs turn out." It was the same voice that I had heard in the cellars. I shut the laptop and tried not to breathe, or sniff, or sob.

I could hear a mumbled reply, but couldn't catch what the other person said. All I could hear was the posh English voice replying, "I say, you're not serious, are you? I mean, that wouldn't be sporting!" It seemed to be an odd comment, but I was glad he'd made it because it gave me a chance to hear that his voice was moving farther along the back of the building. He and whoever was with him were walking away. I didn't dare move. I sat still for what must have been five minutes, gathering my thoughts, trying to decide what to do.

Should I wait where I was or risk trying to get a taxi to the police station? Would I get through the gardens, undetected? I might run into the very people I was desperate to avoid.

Suddenly I felt my telephone jiggle in my pocket: at least I'd had the sense to set it to vibrate and put it somewhere I could feel it do just that. I moved quickly into the bathroom again. Without bothering to check the display, I answered the phone in a whisper.

"Hello, Moreau?" I hoped it was him.

"Cait—it's me, Bud. What the hell is going on?"

I felt myself suck in my breath—and then I just fell apart. Crying and sobbing, I tried to tell Bud how sorry I was about Jan, but I could hardly form the words for lack of oxygen. I kept repeating "I'm sorry . . . I'm so sorry, Bud . . ."

Eventually Bud told me I had to put down the phone, blow my nose, and pull myself together. I did as I was told. When I picked up the phone again, I managed to form a sentence, though my hands were shaking.

"Oh Bud—I just read the news about Jan. I am so, so sorry. How are you doing?"

Using his "calming" voice, which I'd heard on many occasions before, Bud replied, "Cait—believe it or not, I'm fine. I've done everything I can at this stage for Jan. I can't bring her back. My life has changed forever. I know that. But I don't know how, yet. I read your e-mail—too fast to get all the details, but I *do* know you're in real trouble, and that maybe I can help *you*. Have you reached Moreau yet? Are you with the police? Where are you, and what's happening, Cait?"

I decided that, rather than rant on about Jan, I'd answer his questions. "I'm hiding in the apartment of the dead woman, Madelaine. I heard the voice of the man from the cellars outside the window here a few moments ago, but I think he's gone. I really don't think it'll occur to them to look for me here. I haven't been able to reach Moreau. I've been wondering if I should just call the police and get them up here to bring me in. What do you think?"

"Cait—listen. When I go, you call the police and get them, somehow, to come to you with a fast car and get you out of there. Give them a password to use when they arrive, and do not open the door to anyone who doesn't use that password. In the meantime, I'll get hold of Moreau. You call me back as soon as you're in the protection of the police—right?"

"Yes, Bud, right. And Bud?"

"Yes?"

"Thank you . . . and I'm so sorry."

"Shut up, hang up, and dial, *now*—there's plenty of time to be thankful and sorry when you're safe!" And he was gone.

I punched 112 into my phone. As soon as I heard a voice I began my request in my best French. I finally ended up speaking to Bertrand. What a relief. I explained that I was in danger, where I was, and that I needed help. He promised to be with me as soon as possible, and we agreed on the password "Laurent," as he was unlikely to forget his mother's maiden name.

I hung up. There was nothing to do but wait, and I'm not very good at that, so I tried to tidy myself up a bit: I didn't think of it as vanity, but as a politeness to those who would have to see me.

I brushed the muck from the cellar off my clothes, combed and re-tied my hair, wiped my face with a wet wipe I'd picked up at the restaurant where I'd eaten the *moules* with Beni, and blew my nose a few times. Then I took my first real chance to examine the infamous Collar of Death that was clamped around my neck. Even in the stark bathroom lights the gold from which it had been fashioned all those centuries ago had a deep, warm glow. I'd expected the workmanship of such an ancient relic to be rudimentary, but it was finely chased with raised oak leaves, mistletoe berries, and vines. It was beautiful. And, apparently, to be feared. I pushed such silly ideas aside and had one last go at trying to get the thing off my neck, but gave it up as a bad job.

Now all I could do was sit and wait. And wait. I checked my phone. It had been twenty minutes. Where the *hell* was Bertrand? Finally I heard a knock at the door of the apartment. I turned off the bathroom light and opened the door, listening intently. What if it wasn't Bertrand?

Immediately my heart began to pound loudly, and I strained my hearing to its limits. Again, there was a gentle knocking at the door. Damn—I should have agreed on a secret knock with him, not a password. That would have been easier to hear.

Why was he knocking so quietly? Why not just knock away and risk disturbing the neighbors? He knew I was fearing for my life, after all!

I pulled the champagne I'd carried up from the cellars from my bag and held its neck, like a club. I crept toward the door, trying to make no noise. I put my ear up against it. Nothing. What the hell was Bertrand playing at? I pulled back and examined the door. There was no spy-hole to look through. If it *wasn't* Bertrand and his colleagues out there, who might it be? I didn't like any of the answers I came up with.

Once again I leaned forward to listen for the password. As I did so, the door splintered, and I was hurled into the large entry-way mirror behind me. A looming silhouette came toward me and I heard a voice say, "It's her—quick, grab her!" Then I lost consciousness.

Monday Afternoon

I WOKE WITH A SPLITTING headache. Everything was black. I didn't know where I was—again. I began to panic. My torso seemed to be pinned down. I couldn't move my arms. I couldn't even move the fingers on my left hand. I could feel my heart pound in my chest. Everything hurt. I felt dizzy. And sick. I realized my eyes were still closed, so I opened them slowly, terrified of what I might see. Everything was white. Blinding lights blazed down on me.

"*Elle est réveillée!*" said someone. I had no idea what that meant.

I blinked until my eyes became accustomed to the brightness. I saw Bertrand sitting beside me. I tried to say his name, but he immediately "Shh'd" me. Besides, my lips were too dry for me to move them properly.

"*Attention—elle est réveillée. Venez vite!*" he called.

Suddenly there were faces above me: two women I didn't know, and Bertrand.

I licked my lips, and rolled them together.

"Thirsty," I managed to croak.

One of the women held a straw to my lips.

"Okay, okay," she said.

I sucked. It helped. I cleared my throat. She smiled at me.

"You are safe," said Bertrand.

That was all I needed to know. I closed my eyes and let my head relax back into the pillows upon which I was propped up. I gave myself a moment to collect my thoughts.

The last thing I remembered was the noise of bone against glass. The pain in my head reminded me that it had been my skull hitting the mirror in Madelaine's entry hall. I opened my eyes again. Clearly, I was lying in a hospital bed. The smell of the place alone signified as much. I looked down at my body. I was tucked tightly into a bed, both arms had drips attached to them and my left wrist was in a plaster cast. I wiggled my toes. They seemed to be functioning okay. Turning my neck sent pain shooting into my head.

"You must not move," said Bertrand. "The doctor will be here in a moment. Try to be still."

"Did you get . . . ?"

Again Bertrand "Ssh'd" me and nodded. "Everything is taken care of. The captain will be here after the doctor. You can speak to him. They said I could wait here with you. I did not want you to wake alone. It is my fault, this. I tried to get to you, but I am a junior officer. I could not act without the approval of my superior. If I had been faster, this would not have happened. I am very sorry, Professor Morgan. I did my best."

I managed a smile. He was sweet. "It's Cait. And I'm *here*, aren't I? I might be sore, but I'm not dead. I think that's what they had planned for me."

Bertrand nodded. "I think so too," he replied gravely. "I think that is why they will not charge you," he added.

I was puzzled. "Charge me? With what?" I really couldn't imagine. I hadn't done anything wrong.

"The doctor is here. I will be back when he is finished," he said quietly, and he stood to leave.

"Bertrand—before you go . . . can you ask Moreau if he has told Bud Anderson that I'm safe? It's important. Please?"

"Commander Anderson knows," he replied, nodding. He threw a very odd smile my way, then left.

The doctor appeared, looked down at me, a chart in his hand, and smiled. "Glad to see you're back with us," he said.

"I'm glad you speak English," I replied. "I don't think my French is up to much right now . . . I'm sorry . . ."

"That's alright, don't say you are sorry. You have been saying this all night. What is it you are sorry for?"

Now that was a question and a half! I didn't even dare start to answer it, truthfully, so I just said, "Oh, I'm probably just feeling sorry for myself. How am I, by the way? My head hurts like hell."

"This is to be expected. You have ten stitches in the back of your head, but the scans suggest no concussion. So, no lasting effects, except the loss of a patch of hair which we had to shave, but the hair should grow back, in time, and cover the scar." He said should—good grief! "Your left wrist is broken, but it is a good break. Six weeks in this plaster and you will mend. You have some pulled muscles in your left shoulder, but it is not dislocated: you must have put out your left hand to try to stop your fall. Your right side? We cleaned up the blood. None of it was yours. No damage there."

"Who else's blood got on me? And how?"

The doctor looked at me with concern. "You do not remember?"

I thought for a moment, but nothing came back to me. "No—I can't remember anything after my head hit the mirror. What happened?" I was getting quite concerned, and the doctor's reply didn't help.

"I think it is better that you talk to the police about this. From a medical point of view I am not worried: I think it may be a normal reaction to the blow to the head and the . . . situation . . . that you do not remember. Maybe one day it will come back to you. I will tell this to the police captain when he comes. I think he will understand." He wrote something on my chart.

Well, that'll be more than I do, I thought to myself, but I decided to wait until Bertrand came back to ask what had happened, because, clearly, the doctor wasn't going to tell me.

"What about these?" I asked, nodding painfully at the needles in my arms.

"I think we can remove them now. You have been sedated. We can allow you to leave here later today, with some pain medication that you will find useful. Your vital signs are good, all your readings are normal. We have treated the traumatic injuries. You can be discharged."

"What day is it?" I asked. I had no idea.

"It is Monday." He looked at his watch. "It is two thirty. You were brought here about twelve hours ago."

"Can I fly?" I asked.

The doctor looked puzzled. "In an aeroplane?"

I smiled and said, "*Yes*, in an 'aeroplane.' I haven't gone mad, thank you." *Good grief!* "I'm due to fly back home to Canada tomorrow. Can I do that?"

The doctor gave it a moment's thought, then replied, "If the police allow it, yes. There is no medical reason to stop you. You must report to your doctor when you get there. I will make sure that all your records are ready for you to take when you go to the cashier."

The cashier? Oh bugger. Of course. I hoped that my travel insurance would cover all this. I saw mountains of paperwork in my future.

"Thank you," I replied absently, then I gave myself a mental poke. I added in a rather more sincere tone, "And thanks to you and all the team for looking after me and sorting me out. I really appreciate it. Thank you."

The doctor smiled at me and said, "You are welcome. Do you mind if I ask you something?"

"No, ask away."

"Who is this 'Bud'? You have been asking for him in the emergency room. You were very upset, crying. Is he your boyfriend?"

A wave of sadness flowed over me as I answered, quietly, "No, not my boyfriend. He is a good friend, a colleague. His wife . . . just died. She was my friend also. I miss them both."

I could feel a tear begin to spill from the side of my eye, and roll down my cheek.

"Ah," was all that the doctor said, as he left the room. His expression was enigmatic.

I managed to work out how to move my right arm without dislodging the needle poking out of it, and I wiped away my tears. I also tried moving around a little to see what hurt, and how much. I realized the doctor had been right—my left side had really taken the worst of it, but, thankfully, my right side wasn't too bad. Being a righty, not a lefty, that was a good thing.

Having established what was in working order and what wasn't, I looked around for Bertrand. I was alone in a little room whose half-glassed wall divided me from what sounded like a nurses' station beyond. I kept trying to remember what on earth had happened after I had hit the mirror, but I couldn't come up with anything: it was like trying to catch a cloud.

I was beginning to get a bit restless when Bertrand finally popped his head in and said, "The captain has arrived. Good luck!"

"Thanks," I replied, worried about why I'd need "luck." What the hell had happened? "Bertrand," I called before he'd left the room, "can you stay and translate? I don't think I'll be able to cope with the language right now." He looked hesitant. "Please?" I tried to make my most appealing face.

"I will ask the captain," replied Bertrand, and he disappeared.

I could hear Moreau and the doctor talking to each other outside my room. Then the captain appeared in the doorway. His expression was grim. I didn't like the look of that.

"*Professeur Morgan? Bon, vous êtes réveillée. Nous devons parler.*"

As he entered and sat beside me, I said, "Could Bertrand translate, please?"

Moreau didn't answer, but he turned his head and called Bertrand into the room.

"*Merci, Capitaine,*" I managed. I felt relieved. Bertrand hovered at Moreau's elbow, and filled his now usual role.

"You will be discharged today, Professor. That is good news." Moreau spoke gravely.

"Yes, I'm very pleased. I'm due to fly home tomorrow, and the doctor said that would be okay."

"We will see about that," replied Moreau. He looked at me intently, then said, "The doctor tells me you cannot remember what happened after you were knocked over at Mme. Schiafino's apartment. Is this correct? Nothing?"

I shook my head, carefully. "I've tried, Captain, but I can't remember anything. What happened? They said I had blood on me—someone else's blood. Was someone injured? Who?"

He didn't reply. He just looked at me. He sucked his teeth and said, "You do not recall beating anyone?"

"Beating someone? Me? Who? When? With what? Why?" The questions tumbled out of me. "I don't remember beating anyone. I'm not the beating type. What are you talking about?" I was nonplussed.

Again, Moreau didn't answer immediately. I could sense intense mental activity behind his cold, watchful eyes. He blinked, sighed, and said, "You battered a young man about the head with a champagne bottle last night. The bottle broke. You continued to beat him with the broken bottle. Bertrand here had to pull you off him. You would not stop."

I was shocked. "Me? I did? When?" I couldn't comprehend what he was saying. Moreau's face was grave. "Oh my God . . . he's not . . . ? I didn't . . . ?" I couldn't say it.

"He is alive, but in a critical condition. He might lose an eye."

I sat for a moment, struggling with what the captain was telling me. I could feel my heart pounding. The damned machine that I was hooked up to seemed to beep more loudly. I pushed myself to an upright position. I was struggling to make sense of it all.

"Captain—I've never hurt anyone in my life! I'm not a violent person. Who was he? Why would I do that? Oh my God, the poor man! I'm so sorry . . ." It seemed I had more reasons for apologies than I knew about. I held my head. Why couldn't I remember?

"The young man is called Henry. Henry Tyler-Whyte. He is English."

"I've never heard of him. Who is he? Oh, wait . . . was he the man who was looking for me in the cellars?"

"I believe so. He found you at Mme. Schiafino's apartment."

"The last thing I remember is hitting my head against the mirror there. The door flew open and I fell backward. Did I hit him after that? I know I had a bottle of champagne in my hand when I was at the door. But hitting him? I can't recall that . . ."

"For a woman with a photographic memory, that must be unusual," said Moreau, suspiciously. "This attack, it is serious, you know." It wasn't a question.

I realized I was in *big* trouble. Why couldn't I *think*? I can *always* think. It's the only thing I'm good at, after all.

I was babbling, but I didn't stop. "I didn't *mean* . . . well, I don't *know* what I meant to do . . . I *can't* have meant to . . . Oh, I don't *remember*! I *do* remember I was afraid. I'd heard knocking at the door, and I was trying to listen to find out who it was. It must have been him. He must have broken down the door. Maybe I didn't lose consciousness for long. I *must* have been defending myself. I *must* have been. You've got to believe me! But I don't even know what happened myself . . . so how can I ask you to believe me? Oh God. I'm so sorry . . ."

"Tell me exactly what happened, as you remember it, after you sent the e-mail to me. Take your time. This is important. Tell me everything." Both Moreau and Bertrand had pulled out notepads, and were poised to record my answers.

I calmed myself, as much as I could, the machine stopped beeping, and I began. "I sent the e-mail to you, then I sent the same e-mail to Bud Anderson, and myself . . . you know, just to be sure. I checked on news stories in Vancouver and, oh God," I took a big breath and said it fast, "I discovered that Bud's wife, Jan, had been killed. I didn't know until then. I felt badly about the e-mail I had sent Bud, so I sent another one, apologizing about the first one . . ."

"I know about Mme. Anderson's death. It is a terrible thing that the wife of a fellow officer would be killed just because she is his wife, and because people want him to stop hunting them down. I have told him this. He telephoned me at home, in my bed, to send me to bring you to safety. I have also spoken to him today."

"How is he?" I was anxious about Bud. I wanted Moreau to tell me he was fine.

"He is a strong man. I, too, am a strong man, and I do not know how it would be if my wife died this way. I think he has a difficult time ahead of him. He has asked me to keep him informed about you. He is concerned about you. He helped you a great deal last night, by contacting me. I was on the scene quickly because of his call. Please, continue with your story."

"It's not a 'story'—it's what happened," I snapped. He shrugged, and I carried on, regardless of the implication. "I heard voices outside Madelaine's window. One voice was definitely the man I had heard in the cellars, but the other voice was too muffled for me to know who it was, or even if it was a man or a woman. I thought that they must be the people who'd gone into the cellars to find me, that they'd discovered that I'd run off, and were searching the area around the Palais for me. I *thought* they'd gone away. Bud phoned me, and I went into the bathroom to talk to him—I thought I was safer in there. Then I called the police, and I finally got through to Bertrand, and he told me to wait, so I waited. When I heard a knock at the door I listened in case it was him. Like I said, the door burst open, I hit my head, and that's it. Nothing. Until I opened my eyes here, with Bertrand beside me."

"I saw you at the Palais before the ambulánce took you. Do you remember that?" asked Moreau, pointedly.

I shook my head. "Thanks for coming," I said, a bit sheepishly.

"Do you remember what you wrote in the e-mail you sent me?" he asked sharply.

This time I nodded. "Yes, of course. I can remember everything up to the blow to my head." It was time to ask the critical question. "Did it all make sense to you?"

Moreau nodded. "It did. And we have them. They did not try to flee. One is very sorry—knowing that wrong was done. The other? Pah—the other is very arrogant. They are not talking. They have lawyers."

"I'm glad you have them," I said. "Well, maybe *half* glad."

Bertrand was translating very quickly, but looking increasingly puzzled. I suspected that he didn't really know about everything that had been going on. I decided to try to help.

"Do you know who's been arrested, Bertrand?" I asked.

He shook his head.

"So Captain Moreau hasn't told you who the killer is?"

Again, he shook his head. "I have been here the whole night and day," he said. He looked tired.

"Why don't you tell him?" I asked Moreau.

"*You* tell him," he replied. "Tell him what you told me in that e-mail, which my wife very kindly translated for me on the telephone while I was driving to the Palais."

"Are you sure?" Was this a sign of trust on the part of Moreau? He nodded, then got up, offered Bertrand his seat, and motioned that he was going outside to make some phone calls. Bertrand didn't have to translate, so he just listened. He looked pleased to be sitting down.

I began.

"It was complicated, and I was stupid. It took me longer to put things together than it should have done. I think I was a bit distracted so I wasn't really focused, like I usually am on a 'real' case. What finally helped me was the birthday cake, the type of boxes the snails were kept in, and discovering that I could hear Chuck's voice from Alistair's balcony."

"What birthday cake?" asked Bertrand. "I do not remember any birthday cake."

"Exactly," I replied. "There wasn't one."

"I see," said Bertrand, but I could tell that he didn't.

I decided to try another approach. "You've heard everything I told the captain in my interviews, right?" He nodded. "You know how I bumped into Alistair, and he invited me to the party, and how he died, and about the break-in at the museum, and my theory that the necklace that disappeared was the Roman necklace that the archives mentioned, and that Madelaine was pictured wearing, and that Alistair was going to give to Tamsin?"

He nodded again.

"It was agreed that everyone, except maybe Tamsin, had a reason to want to steal the necklace." More nodding. "Okay, so I had to work out if the theft of the necklace was the reason for the deaths, but I realized I couldn't do that until I worked out *how* Alistair was killed. I eventually managed to put two and two together: I knew that snails would eat and intensify the taste of dill, which I believe Alistair was feeding them, but I also learned, or, rather, worked out, that snails' bodies would also intensify the toxic effects of the digitalis in foxglove leaves. There were foxglove leaves in the gardens at the Palais, so all someone had to do was to feed those leaves to the snails and they'd become quite poisonous. Knowing that Alistair often took extra pills when he wanted to feel at his best, they could be pretty sure that he'd be the only one who'd succumb to the total dose—though, to be honest, I don't think that the murderer cared if anyone else became seriously ill, or even died, so long as Alistair was killed."

"You could have all died?" asked Bertrand, wide-eyed. This time I was the one nodding, and, thankfully, it didn't seem to hurt quite as much. "You were *all* ill. Wasn't the murderer afraid they would die themselves?"

"Good question," I replied, "but the murderer just made sure they hardly ate any snails at all, so they only had *some* symptoms of digitalis poisoning—enough so that they didn't stand out from the rest of us. If the killer had poisoned the snails long before they were cooked, then I thought it didn't matter where everyone was the night of the party. It didn't matter who went to the kitchen. But it *did* matter. I realized, much later on, that access to the kitchen was *vital*, because that's how the necklace was stolen."

"So the necklace was in the kitchen?" Bertrand's eyes were even wider. "*Where?*"

"In the birthday cake."

"What birthday cake?"

"Exactly."

Bertrand threw up his hands. "I do not understand. Why was the necklace in the birthday cake? And where *was* this birthday cake? I was there when we searched the apartment. There *was no* birthday cake."

"*That* was what I missed. It was stupid of me. You see, when I saw Alistair in the Cours Saleya and he invited me to the party, he told me himself as he was leaving that he was off to collect a very special birthday cake. Later on, Tamsin told me that, on their wedding day, Alistair had hidden a gift for her in a dessert jelly, so I wondered if he'd maybe hidden the necklace he was giving her in her birthday cake. When I'd looked around the Townsends' kitchen, there *was* no birthday cake. Now, if there *had* been one, you guys wouldn't have taken it for testing, because we were all poisoned before we'd got to that part of the meal. So the cake *should* have been there but it wasn't. When I innocently said to Tamsin that I fancied some cake after our meal she got very upset. I always thought it odd that she'd *known* her necklace was gone, but I finally—*finally*—worked it out: Tamsin had guessed that her necklace was hidden in the cake, the cake had been placed in the kitchen—ready for presentation later on—and she'd noticed that the cake was missing when she came through the kitchen to the balcony after Alistair's death. That's how she knew that her necklace was gone. The murderer had also known of the necklace's hiding place and had stolen both the cake and the necklace, all in one go."

"What did they do with the cake? You cannot hide a cake!"

"Ah, you can if everyone thinks it is garbage. The killer simply tossed the cake into the garbage chute in the kitchen, knowing that they could retrieve it later on. If anyone saw the discarded cake in the garbage room before they had time to get to it, they'd just assume it was rubbish."

"Ah," said Bertrand, his eyes lighting up a little. "The killer went to the place where the chute deposits the garbage and collected the necklace from the cake later on? After they are out of the hospital?" I nodded. "Does everyone have access to this place?"

Again I nodded. "I'm going to guess it's locked, but that residents each have a key."

"That excludes Beni?" asked Bertrand.

I smiled. "I wish it did, but I suspect he could have got hold of a key if he'd wanted one," I replied, thinking of the two sets of keys I'd seen tossed out of Tamsin's purse onto the seat of Beni's car.

"What about Madelaine?" asked Bertrand.

"Her kitchen showed signs that she'd been entertaining someone—there were two of everything washed and wiped dry there. I believe the killer brought food containing a poison, maybe it was more digitalis. I don't know for sure because your boss refused to tell me what had been found in her system. He even ate with her. There was a smell of garlic in her living room, but not in her kitchen: I interpreted that to mean that the food was brought there, not prepared there. Maybe something like soup? There were bowls in her kitchen—they had been used but not put away. Lots of garlic would disguise many less pleasant flavors. I know that everyone had the opportunity to do this. Tamsin took the longest bath in history; Beni claimed to have parked far away; Chuck and Gerard had been at the Palais for hours. I believe that the only reason that Madelaine was killed was so that the portrait of her, a photograph of her wearing the Collar of Death, could be stolen. If the killer didn't have the portrait, they wouldn't be able to prove the necklace was what they claimed."

"So the museum break-in . . . ?"

"Ah, well, that was a tough one. Once I allowed myself to consider everything objectively, I realized that there *was* only one person who could have done it, and, I'm sorry to say, he did. Doctor Benigno Brunetti 'robbed' his own museum. He staged the whole thing himself. He removed something, some component, that the window installer needed to be able to finish his job. He didn't demand that an alarm be connected before 'leaving' the museum and then he broke a window that would have been too small for anyone but a child to crawl through. All to rather clumsily cover up the removal of the Roman family archive that, had Alistair had his way, would have proven the necklace was worth much more than anyone imagined.

"You see, while Alistair had put the whole thing about the necklace together, Beni hadn't. Beni believed the necklace to be the one mentioned in the archives, but knew nothing about its links with the Gestapo, Madelaine, or Gerard's sister. Even if he had, I don't think he'd have cared. I seriously think that anything less than seventeen hundred years old is of limited interest to Beni—except when it comes to women, of course. All he knew was that, if Alistair had the necklace, it wouldn't be long before he came calling on Beni's expert opinion to increase its value immensely. The 'theft' of the archive was the only way that Beni knew to prevent Alistair from profiting in a way that Beni thought was reprehensible. I think the archive will be found, safe and sound. Beni wouldn't damage or destroy it. He loves old things far too much to do that."

"So we have arrested Doctor Brunetti?" asked Bertrand.

"I believe so. I told Moreau about my theory in the e-mail I sent, and he said he acted upon it. I know it's not a big or important theft, and I'm not even sure what the charges will be, exactly. I can't imagine it will do Beni's professional career much good. We all have to live with the consequences of our actions. I suppose at least Beni will not be subjected to Tamsin's unwanted attentions anymore."

"What about the murderer? Was Beni the killer?" Bertrand couldn't wait.

"No, Beni wasn't the killer. I don't think he could harm a fly. I was unsure about which of the others might have done it: I honestly believed that Tamsin, Gerard, and Chuck all had the capability to kill someone. Tamsin Townsend isn't the dimwit she pretends to be. She's got a brain and a plan . . . and that plan involves separating rich men from their money. I could quite believe that she would have killed Alistair to get her hands on his estate, *and* the jewels that he wouldn't let her wear. Gerard was obsessively attached to his dead sister, the Palais, and the gardens. To be honest, I could imagine him killing to protect the Palais from the plans that Alistair had for a swimming pool—and, of course, he'd know all about foxgloves and digitalis. As far as I knew, Chuck, like Beni, had only ever been able to discover half the story of the necklace. Beni knew the Celtic, Druidic, and Roman parts of the story, but Chuck only knew about the Gestapo connections. Gerard never told anyone except Alistair about the architect's wife running off to Germany with the necklace that had been dug up at the Palais, nor had he told anyone but Alistair about Madelaine's time at the Palais during the war. Chuck might have wanted to own something that was a part of Gestapo history, but how would he have known about the portrait of Madelaine? Or the fact that this necklace was an ancient one, rather than just something that had been fashioned during the war years?"

Bertrand shrugged, looking at me attentively.

"I got my answer the moment Chuck popped his head out of his window. He could overhear every conversation on the Townsends' balcony, and possibly quite a few taking place inside. Chuck, the man obsessed by the Gestapo, the SS, and the occult mysteries of Wewelsburg Castle, and a man who would, no doubt, be desperate to own a necklace that had such an ancient history, and such a close association with the Gestapo. *He* could have heard all that Alistair had been told by Gerard and Beni and, like Alistair, *he* could have pieced together the whole history of the necklace. I suspect that Alistair managed to convince Madelaine to sell it to him quicker than Chuck could steal, or maybe buy, it from her. I also think that

Chuck had a plan to steal the archives from the museum, but hadn't managed to get around to that before Beni robbed him of his chance.

"You see, I understood that Chuck might have the strongest motive to steal the necklace, and to kill Alistair to prevent its whole history from becoming public, *and* to kill Madelaine so he would have the portrait showing her wearing the necklace—but I still couldn't work out how he'd poisoned the snails. Luckily for me he invited me into his apartment where I saw a strange telescopic pole. He could have attached foxglove leaves to the pole and simply popped the leaves into the snail boxes which were, after all, stored for days just thirty feet below his window. Not quite guns in a basket, but the same sort of idea."

"Guns in a basket?" repeated Bertrand quizzically.

I shook my head. "It's nothing, just something he'd written in a book once. It's not important—though it did get me going on a particular train of thought."

Bertrand still looked confused. "Then . . . what?"

"Yesterday afternoon he realized that I'd seen the telescopic rod in his apartment, and that I knew he could overhear conversations on the Townsends' balcony. When I mentioned that I wanted cake he thought I'd worked out that bit too—which I hadn't at that time—it took some wakeful dreaming for me to be able to put it all together. He made a quick decision that I was a danger to him, drugged me, and dumped me in the wine cellars."

I stopped and thought for a moment. "Now, this is where maybe *you* can help *me*, Bertrand, because that's where I get a bit lost."

"You do?" asked Bertrand, surprised.

"Well, yes, because in the wine cellars I heard that English man's voice—Henry Tyler-Whyte, according to Moreau—and he was talking to someone who might well have been Chuck. But he was referring to 'they.' He and the person with him weren't the ones who dumped me in the cellar. There *must* be more people involved. I honestly thought Chuck was acting alone. Do you know who 'they' are?"

"*Oui—I* know," said Moreau. He'd been standing just out of sight, beyond the doorway, and now stepped into the room. Bertrand shot up from his seat. Moreau motioned for him to sit again, which Bertrand was clearly not comfortable about. He did as he was told, and began to translate as Moreau spoke.

"The man Tyler-Whyte is a known neo-Nazi. Chuck Damcott, it seems, is a leader of such a movement here, in Nice. His home is a meeting place for the group, though everything is kept very quiet."

"Of course. He's *not* gay!" I exclaimed.

Both Bertrand and Moreau looked very puzzled. I thought I'd better explain. "A neighbor of Chuck's said that it made a change to see him with a woman. I thought at the time that might mean he was gay. Sometimes, if a man or a woman works very hard at hiding their sexuality, or any other aspect of their persona, they *are* able to build a wall that is difficult to read through, so to speak. I just assumed I'd misread him. If the neighbor was seeing men coming to his apartment all the time, maybe they were members of his neo-Nazi group."

"It is likely," replied Moreau. "I expect quite a few of them were called in to help when he decided you were a danger, Professor Morgan. They had melted away when we got to the Palais. Only Tyler-Whyte was left. He couldn't run. He was too badly injured. We are searching Chuck Damcott's apartment now. Of course, he is saying nothing—except to tell us that we are all stupid because we are 'inferior.' There are already some very interesting records that we have found hidden away at his place, which I believe will be of interest to many people outside Nice. There are also SS Death Head rings, swords, and medals—a whole array of things which are connected to his 'interest.'" He paused and frowned.

"Before the Nazis came, my family name was Morpurgo, a Jewish name. It was changed to protect my father. My family was not alone in doing this. Neo-Nazis will not find much sympathy in our courts."

Moreau brought his eyes back to me and continued. "Of course, we also have the telescopic pole for testing, as well as several possible sources of toxins in Damcott's apartment, and the necklace, traces of the birthday cake, and the photographic portrait of Mme. Schiafino. With respect to her death, I did not 'refuse' to tell you what killed her, Professor Morgan;

we simply do not know yet, though we have seen in the autopsy that an ingested poison attacked the central nervous system. As I am sure you know, toxicology reports take a little longer, especially when it is nothing we can guess at. With Alistair Townsend we knew he took digitalis, so it was checked during the first screening."

"Does Tamsin Townsend know about Chuck Damcott?" I asked. I wondered how she would have reacted to the news.

"Ah," said Moreau, smiling wryly. "She is a strange one, no? I interviewed her again this morning, with her lawyer present, of course, and I showed her the necklace that was stolen. She identified it as the one her husband had intended to present to her at the birthday party, but she seemed much more interested in how long it would be before she can have it back than in why Chuck Damcott killed her husband. Her focus in life seems to be *things*. Though I suspect she sees many people as merely things. She is young—and pretty—and I think she is much more focused than she allows people to think."

"I couldn't agree more," I replied. "I doubt she will be a widow for long," I added.

"Maybe she will be one more than once," observed Moreau wryly.

"And Gerard . . . how is he doing? Is he here, in this hospital?"

"Yes, he is just two floors below here. He is a fighter, that one. The surgeon told me he will take time to heal, but his new hip should last for many years. I confronted him with the information about the remains in the cellars, and he confirmed the old stories told of many people being buried there. He has made it his life's work to honor the dead there. I will do all that I can to ensure the local authorities protect those cellars and those gardens as a memorial to the people who silently gave their lives at the Palais during those terrible years. I do not think a swimming pool will be built, not while there are people alive who remember—or their children, or their children's children. Gerard can continue to oversee his gardens, when he is able. In the meantime, they make a beautiful picture for the news stories that are being filmed about the capture of M. Damcott."

He spat out the man's name with venom.

"I'm glad that you caught him, Captain," I said. "I think Chuck Damcott is a very dangerous man. People who are obsessive can lose all sense of perspective."

"He has done this already. All this for a necklace . . ."

"It wasn't for the necklace *itself*, Captain, but what it stood for. I'll bet he believes it connects him to a great power, a power that exists across time, and which will allow him, in turn, to exert power over others. Like Himmler and *his* obsession with Arthurian legend and the Druidic Merlin, Chuck Damcott, grandson of a man who prosecuted the Nazis at Nuremberg, will do anything to connect himself with what he sees as some grand vision of the world, where power comes from *things*, relics that must be preserved." I stopped as I suddenly remembered something.

"I can hardly believe that he put the Collar of Death on me. I can only imagine that he saw it as an act that would allow him to contribute to its history when he finally killed me. How did you get it off me? I hope the doctors didn't cut it off—it really is a museum piece, you know. Beni was right about that, at least."

"The necklace was not cut off you, though you were most keen for it to be taken away. You kept shouting that it would kill you—that you would die if it stayed on you. You seemed very sure of this at the time, which is understandable, given the history of the piece and the circumstances that brought you to be wearing it. It has a very intricate clasp device. I was there when it was removed. We are now holding it as evidence, of course," replied Moreau.

"Good," I replied. "Though I still cannot remember anything after the bang to my head. It's very odd that I was frightened that I was wearing the necklace. I don't believe in curses, and, even if I did, this one wouldn't have affected me."

"Why not?" asked both Moreau and Bertrand in unison, one in French, one in English.

"Well, I don't believe in curses because—well, I just *don't*! And when Beni told me what was written inside the necklace, I understood what it meant. He told me it said three things: 'Before Luentinum,' which I took to mean that the gold from which the necklace was made was taken from what is now called the Dolgellau Mine, before the Romans gave it a Latin name; it also had 'Arawn Sees' written on it—Arawn is a god from Welsh mythology—a Death Lord. Presumably, that meant that he'd be keeping an eye on any of the wearers."

"This does not sound good," commented Bertrand, looking worried.

"Don't worry, Bertand. The third inscription said 'True Blood or Spilled Blood.' Now, the curse that was supposedly uttered—anyone of non-Celtic blood would die if they wore or owned the necklace—leaves me out of the realm of being cursed. I am Welsh, through and through, on both sides of my family, for many, many generations. You don't get much more Welsh than me—so, you see, I had no need to be afraid of the collar. If I was ranting about you having to take it off me, I was clearly not acting logically."

"Had you been drinking?" asked Moreau, unexpectedly.

"It feels like I've hardly stopped since I got here." I smiled sheepishly. Then I added more seriously, "Yesterday I drank coffee, the beer that I'm assuming was drugged, and about half a bottle of champagne while in the wine cellars." Moreau raised his eyebrows in surprise. "It was all I could find, and I was *very* thirsty at the time. Why?"

Moreau stroked his chin. "It might be that there was a reaction between this alcohol and the drugs you were given. The doctor tells me that this is possible—that a violent reaction might occur. Perhaps this is why you were acting illogically. Maybe this is why you beat the man."

So, we were back to that. "Is there any news about him? Will he be alright?"

"The doctors tell me he will keep his eye, but he will be scarred. He will make a full recovery otherwise."

I was glad, but I knew I still wasn't out of the woods. "Will I be charged with assault?" I asked, unsure about the correct terminology in France for beating a man about the head with a broken bottle.

"It is for my office to decide if you committed a crime," replied Moreau, meaningfully. "I believe you were under the influence of drugs administered to you by the group to which Tyler-Whyte belonged, and that you believed yourself to be in mortal danger. I do not think charging you would be a good use of the Court's time. We have people to deal with whose intent was to kill. It is better we use our resources on them."

I felt a tidal wave of relief wash over me. Given what I'd been through, I knew tears wouldn't be far behind. "So am I allowed to fly home tomorrow?" I asked, with some trepidation.

"Yes. You may leave. You have a good friend in Vancouver who needs you now, I think. You should go to him."

He was right. How I wanted to see Bud. To comfort him, and to thank him for helping to save me, at what must have been the worst time of his life.

"Thank you, Captain. And thank you, Pierre Bertrand. You saved my life, young man. I will never forget that." I reached out and took his hand. "Let's keep in touch by e-mail when I'm gone. Okay?"

Bertrand smiled back at me and said, "I would like that very much. I have been pleased to meet you—though I wish the circumstances had been better."

"Me too," I replied. "And you, Captain Moreau. Will *we* be keeping in touch?"

"I think I might have some more questions for you, but this, too, we can tackle by e-mail. Please give my best to Commander Anderson. He speaks very highly of you, you know."

"Thanks," I replied quietly. "I think the world of him too."

"I can see that," said Moreau, as he walked out of the room.

Tuesday Evening

I'VE ALWAYS THOUGHT OF VANCOUVER International Airport as stunning. As I stood on the escalator carrying me down into the passport control area, I enjoyed the freshness of the air given off by the waterfalls, marvelling at how exhilarated I felt to be back home. It was hard for me to believe I'd been away for less than a week—though, to be honest, the flight I'd just got off had felt about that long. I couldn't wait to crawl into my own bed and feel the comfort that comes from being in familiar surroundings.

It's not easy flying with a broken wrist, but at least the sight of the plaster gets you sympathy. Of course, the big chunk of hair I had missing and the obvious wound on my scalp drew a few odd glances. It had been impossible for me to rest my head throughout the whole journey. I was exhausted. Totally drained, physically and mentally.

Of course three jam-packed international flights all landed within five minutes of each other, and the line ups ahead of me looked daunting. No sooner had I stepped off the escalators than a woman in uniform approached me.

I could feel my aching shoulders hunch as she asked, "Are you Professor Cait Morgan?"

"Yes," I answered hesitantly.

"Could I see your ID, please?" she asked politely.

I grappled with my handbag and finally managed to pull out my passport and my customs declaration form. She scrutinized both. Then she gave me a warm smile and said, "I'll hang onto these. Follow me, please. Can I give you a hand with that bag?"

I thanked her, then tried to keep up as she strode toward the "special line"—you know, the one for flight crews and people with those passes. She walked me to the front of the line, handed my documents to the officer in the booth, and that was it. I was through. It was like a little miracle!

"I'll come with you to collect your bags," she said. She pulled out a luggage cart and we waited for my suitcase to plop out onto the carousel.

"Umm . . . who are you, exactly?" I asked.

"I'm attached to the security services at the airport," she said. She was just stating the facts.

"I see," I said, even though I didn't. "Well . . . umm . . . although I'm very glad to have your help, of course, what have *I* done to deserve such special treatment?" I was puzzled.

"We were alerted to your arrival and told you needed some extra help," she said, smiling pleasantly.

"The airline alerted you?" I asked.

"No. VPD. They'll be waiting for you outside."

Ah. I was to be met by someone from the Vancouver Police Department. Initially, I wondered if I was to be arrested on sight at Moreau's bidding. Then I realized that couldn't be the case because if it was, the RCMP would be running me in. It must be something else. I didn't say any more. I thought it best not to.

My suitcase finally arrived—last off, of course—and my "helper"—I'll call her that, because "minder" sounds too menacing—placed it carefully onto the cart. She walked with me through the double doors that led into the arrivals hall. "You'll be alright from here?" she asked.

"I guess so." I wasn't in handcuffs yet, so that was a good sign.

"Bye then," she said cheerily, and she waved as she disappeared back into the baggage claim area.

I started to push the cart as best I could with one hand toward the exit. I didn't get very far before I was approached by two policemen in uniform.

"Professor Cait Morgan?"

I nodded. I was ready to surrender peacefully.

"Please come with us. We'll take that." One man pushed the cart and they escorted me to the main exit. Heads were turning. I must have been quite a sight. I was tired, and I was hungry, and I just wanted to get home. It seemed as though that might never happen.

Outside, to the left of the main exit, we headed toward a big black Suburban with tinted windows—like the ones the FBI uses. My heart sank. So many things were running through my head, but none of them made sense. Then the driver's door of the SUV opened, and out stepped Bud.

I had never, ever, been so happy to see someone in my entire life.

Of course, I immediately started to cry. *Idiot.* Relief. Sadness. Happiness. Tiredness. Pain medications. Everything hit at once.

"Bud!" I hobbled as fast as I could. He was smiling. Can you believe it—actually smiling! "Oh Bud . . . I'm so sorry . . . you poor thing . . . oh God, poor Jan . . ." I was blubbing so much that the hug I'd planned became him handing me a wad of paper tissues as he helped me into the passenger seat and got me buckled in. The two policemen tossed my stuff into the back of the truck. Bud thanked them, and a lot of back-slapping followed. Finally, he got in beside me and we were off.

"Home, I guess?" he asked.

I was rubbing my nose with a tissue as I answered. "Yes please. Home would be perfect."

We sat in silence as we moved slowly out of the airport. I had no idea what to say.

"You're quiet," said Bud, once we were out on the open road.

"I don't know what to say. Except, thank you for getting me through the airport so fast—I assume that was your doing?" He nodded. "And thank you for helping to save my life in Nice."

"You're welcome," he replied. "I'm assuming you'd do the same for me."

"Well, of course I would, but how could I . . . ever?"

"You never know, Cait. You never know."

"Well, *whatever* I can do to help. You know you've only got to ask." I meant it. "Oh Bud . . . I'm so sorry for you. Jan was just wonderful. I'm *so* sorry. So *sorry*. And I know you might not want to talk about, but I've got to ask . . . what happened? Are you able to tell me? Can you talk about it?"

Bud sighed.

"It looks like they thought she was me, Cait. The guy thought he was killing me." His voice was full of anguish.

"What do you mean? How could anyone think Jan was you?" I didn't understand at all—Bud's about five-ten and stocky, whereas Jan was about my height, and, unlike me, she was slim. It seemed impossible that anyone could mistake Jan for Bud.

"She was in my truck, wearing my big wet-weather jacket and hat. She was just a shape to him. It seems that the gangs had ID'd my vehicle a while back, and when this bastard saw it, he decided he'd be a 'hero' and take me out. But it wasn't me—it was Jan, ready to take Marty for a walk in the pounding rain."

I took a moment to let it sink in. I'd thought it couldn't be any worse for Bud, that losing Jan was as bad as it could get. Now I realized he'd have to live with the knowledge that he'd been the target. Poor Bud.

When I spoke next it wasn't about Jan, or Bud. I couldn't ask him to talk any more about that. "What about poor Marty? Is he doing okay?"

Bud smiled wryly. "The little guy's a hero, you know? He got a part of his ear shot off trying to grab the gun. Dumb dog. Anyway, the vet said it's a tough place for a wound to heal, but that he should be fine, in time. They operated to removed a bit more of the ear flap, just to make it less ragged, but they want to keep him in for one more day, just to make sure there's no infection. He's got a giant bandage on what's left of his ear and the biggest 'cone' you've ever seen—apparently he's an expert at pawing! He looks pathetic, and he's playing it for all he's worth."

I could imagine! I suspected that Marty would be getting lots of treats for a while to come. "Aww, I'm glad he'll be alright. He's a grand dog. Nuts, of course, but hey . . . look at his owners, right?"

Oh bugger! Oh damn! What had I said?! I could have kicked myself.

Bud must have seen the look of horror on my face.

"Hey—don't let it worry you," he said, kindly. "Even *I* keep saying 'we.' It'll happen. For a while I guess. I know people don't mean it, and I don't want them to feel bad about it. You shouldn't. I know what you meant."

"Thanks, Bud. I'm such an idiot."

"Yes," he nodded, "you certainly can be." He smiled.

"Again, thanks!" I dared a smile myself. "By the way," I added (I wondered if I could get myself out of the hole I'd been digging), "I know it might not help, but I'm glad you got the guys who did it."

"It helps a lot," replied Bud flatly. "You know I'm not the vengeful type, but I'm glad we've got the bastards, *and* with enough evidence that the judge won't be able to let them get away with it. We did everything by the book. Airtight case."

"Good for you, Bud."

Silence followed.

"The service is next week," said Bud. "Christ Church Cathedral, Downtown. Ten o'clock on Monday."

I almost said, *All the bells and whistles,* but I managed to stop myself in time.

"All the bells and whistles," said Bud. "She'd have hated it."

"Yep." I knew she would have. Jan disliked it if anyone made a fuss about her.

"So why there?" I asked.

"So many people want to attend, I don't have much choice. She had a lot of friends. Belonged to so many groups. They all want to say goodbye. And I have no right to say they can't. So it'll be a big do. Hundreds of people I've never met. Food afterward. It'll be a nightmare. I'm dreading it."

"But *you'll* have a lot of friends there too, Bud." I looked at his stern profile. He was concentrating intently on the road ahead. He looked older than when I'd last seen him. I guessed I looked a bit different, too.

"No. Not friends, Cait. I have colleagues. That's it." There was an edge to Bud's voice, a hardness I'd only ever heard when he'd been questioning suspects. "I didn't need anyone but Jan. And she . . . well, she used all that time we weren't together—those long days when I was at work catching bad guys, 'making a difference'—she used that time to build her own support network. I'm sure they're all great people. And I know they'll all want to support *me* now . . . but I'm just not that type, Cait. But, hey, I don't need to tell *you* that. We're neither of us the 'group' type, right?"

I, too, turned my attention to the road ahead, fresh tears streaming down my cheeks. Bud was right—I was the sort of person who never liked to join a group or hang out with a bunch of people. It just wasn't my sort of thing.

What he said deeply saddened me. I'd always thought of Bud as a friend. Apparently, he didn't think of me in the same way at all. I was just a colleague. It came as a shock.

The silence between us had felt comfortable, but it suddenly felt more tense.

At least, it did to me.

I wiped away my tears and told myself I was being stupid and selfish. That if I cared at all about Bud then I should think about *his* needs, not my own, and that, at this time, if ever, I should be as supportive a "colleague" as I could be for him.

We didn't talk again until we pulled up in front of my little house. I was so pleased to be there at last. Bud switched off the ignition and got out of the truck.

"Hang on a minute," he said, as I tried to reach my seat buckle. "I'll come and get that for you. Just stop wriggling. Give me a moment."

I sat still and he unbuckled me and helped me find my house key. He insisted I take his arm as we walked along the little pathway to my front door. He opened the door and threw it wide so I could enter, then he brought in my suitcase.

"Where do you want this?"

"Oh, just dump it there," I said, pointing at the floor in front of me. "I'll sort it out a bit at a time, then I'll just shove it in a corner until I can dump it in the basement."

"Okay," he replied, laying it on the floor with a look on his face that said, "On your own head be it."

And there we stood. Two colleagues with a battered suitcase on the floor between them.

"Thanks, Bud. I really appreciate all your help. I'll be just fine now. You get off. I guess you must have lots to do."

"Not really," he said. "What will you do about food? Have you got anything in?"

I suddenly thought about all the stuff that had probably gone off my fridge during the past week. I'd rushed to the airport so fast I'd forgotten to clear out the perishables before I'd left.

"I'll order a pizza," I said. I laughed aloud. I couldn't help myself.

"What's so funny?" asked Bud.

"Oh . . . it's a long story, Bud, and it's really not important—or even funny, really. It's just that the idea of ordering pizza . . . well . . . it involves fancy restaurants in the south of France delivering posh meals to the homes of women who can't even manage to boil an egg for themselves." It sounded so stupid, saying it aloud. How very far away the Townsends' balcony seemed: not just on a different continent, but in a different world. "Hey . . . it's not important. There's no need for you to hang about here with me. I *can* dial with one hand, you know, and I'll be all unpacked and tucking into a large, thin-crust pepperoni before you know it."

"With extra cheese?" asked Bud, smiling.

"How well you know me!" I replied. "With the hundreds of pizzas that have fuelled your investigations over the years, you must know *all* your colleagues' favorites, eh?"

A strange look clouded Bud's face. He looked hurt. Wounded. He scratched his head. His wedding band glinted in the lamplight.

"Cait, when I said in the truck that I only have colleagues . . . ?" I nodded. "I didn't mean *you*, Cait. *You're* a friend. You *know* that, right?"

I felt tears welling up inside me.

"Well . . ." I hesitated, "I've always thought of *you* as a friend, but . . ."

"Oh, come on, Cait! Jan always said that you and I were like male and female versions of the same person. How could we *not* be friends? We each know what the other one is thinking, and feeling, don't we?" I nodded. "We have our differences too. I guess that's why we get on. Jan never saw that—she could only see how similar we were, not how different." He seemed to lose himself in remembrance for a fleeting moment, then said, "So yes, I really only have colleagues because . . . well, that's just *me*. But you're a *friend* Cait Morgan. And don't you forget it."

I shook my head. "Never."

"Good. I'm glad we got that sorted out. So, shall I order, while you get yourself organized?" he asked.

"You want to stay and have something to eat?" I was surprised.

"Cait—they've sent me home from the office, Marty's still at the vet's, I need to eat . . . and the apartment . . . well . . ."

"Empty?"

"Like a vacuum. Every bit of air sucked out of it. Thanks for understanding, Cait. It's times like this that a person needs another person who understands them. And I might need that a fair bit over the . . . I don't know . . ."

"However long it takes," I said.

"It'll take forever, Cait. There's a whole part of me that's missing. It'll never be the same again."

"I'm sorry, Bud."

"I know."

And there we stood. Two friends with a battered suitcase on the floor between them.

Four Months Later

I WOKE WITH A SPLITTING headache. Everything was dark. I had no idea where I was. "Serves you right for opening that second bottle with dinner last night," I told myself. *Never again*. Yeah—sure!

I looked across the pillows at the new man in my life and smiled. "Good morning," I said quietly. His amber eyes gazed deeply into mine, then he planted a big, wet lick on my forehead.

"Marty—yuk! Stop it," I cried. I knew he wouldn't calm down until I'd let him out and fed him, which I did. Having showered and dressed, I gave Marty a good going over with his special comb. He loved it. His shiny black coat looked magnificent, and he was looking better for having lost the pounds that the vet had insisted he had to take off. Apparently, Marty hadn't been very keen on the first type of diet food he'd been given, then Bud had changed it to something else vet prescribed—it cost an arm and a leg and Marty loved it. So Marty had eaten himself thinner. I wondered if there was a human version.

"Bud will be here to collect you today, Marty," I told him. As he cocked his head, showing he'd understood every word I'd said, his wonky ear flopped about—too cute! I gave him a cuddle. He didn't object, though I got the distinct impression he was merely tolerating my attentions.

Marty had been my house guest for the past two weeks. Before he'd arrived, I couldn't have *imagined* how different a person's life would become simply because of the presence of a seventy-pound Labrador. Since Bud had brought him over—and the truckful of supplies to accompany him— I'd become completely captivated by this adorable, totally entertaining, and unquestioningly loving creature. I was going to miss him like hell. I'd even begun to contemplate getting a puppy myself, but in my heart of hearts I knew that while I could jiggle my schedule a bit for a couple of weeks, so that Marty wouldn't be alone for too long, there was no way I could ever spend the time I'd need to (or want to) with a puppy.

However, I wondered if Bud might let me 'borrow' Marty now and again . . . just so I could get my dog-petting fix. It's amazing how quickly I'd become addicted. I decided to ask him when he arrived. I looked at the kitchen clock. It was eight o'clock. Bud's flight was due to land at three. So I had lots of time.

I was hoping he'd had a good break, and a smooth journey home.

Frankly, I'd thought he'd been mad to go, but apparently he and Jan had been promising themselves they'd go to Egypt for years, and they'd booked this trip a month or so before Jan had been killed.

Initially, Bud had wanted to cancel the whole thing. Then he announced he'd decided to go after all. Alone. And would I look after Marty?

Me? The person who'd always found looking after a houseplant a challenge? Caring for a dog for two whole weeks?

Of course I'd said yes.

After that first night, when I'd ended up having to lift Marty onto my bed just so he'd stop whimpering, we'd really bonded. How can you *not* bond with a creature that eats all their meals with you, becomes your bedfellow, wants to follow you into the bathroom and even tells you when it's time to wake up? He was such a good boy.

It was Saturday, so I spent the day tidying up the house, clearing away the detritus that I feel it's only reasonable to allow to gather through a busy work week. I packed Marty's food, bed bags (day beds, of course), grooming kit, medications, and toys into the rubber bins Bud had used to deliver them. Everything was looking pretty good by the time Bud's taxi pulled up at the front of my house. Until Bud emerged.

Marty went berserk. I don't know how he knew that it was Bud out there on the street, but he did, and he ran around the house, upstairs and down, jumping up at me, pulling on my sweater, knocking over the little table inside the front door that had a very nice cactus on it (they really don't need much attention). By the time Bud was actually at the door, the whole place was a mess. I grabbed Marty's collar as I struggled to open the door. He didn't understand that to let Bud in, he'd have to get out of the way. The creature was frantic with excitement, and threw himself at Bud, almost knocking him over.

After a few minutes of frenzy, Bud said, "So, you haven't been feeding him, eh?"

"Yeah—right—he's a waif!" I replied, trying to gather up broken pot shards, soil, and the remains of a very spiny cactus. It wasn't easy, and I was worried about Marty's paws.

Bud tempted Marty away from the perilous cactus and into the kitchen with the promise of a treat that he magically produced from his jacket pocket. I wondered how long it might have been there and if it had made the journey to Egypt with him.

I dumped the contents of the dustpan into the bin beneath the kitchen sink and asked, "Coffee? Or do you just want to load up and be off?"

"Coffee'd be great—thanks," said Bud. Marty was gradually simmering down, but his tail was wagging so fast that I thought he might hurt himself. Bless him!

I didn't think asking "did you have a great time?" was the right way to go, so I stuck with something more neutral. "How was it?"

"It was tough," said Bud, petting Marty's head with vigor. "Amazing place. But tough. Jan would have loved it. It was everything we'd ever thought it would be. But bigger. It's *so* much bigger than it looks in the books or on TV. You get no sense of scale until you're there, standing next to something that was built with almost no tools, thousands of years ago. My God, it makes you think! We're nothing, aren't we? Just specks. Insignificant."

"Yes. That's how it made me feel when I was there."

"Did you prefer Cairo or Luxor?"

"Luxor, and the Valley of the Kings."

"Yep. Me too. I mean, the pyramids are incredible—but they're so . . ."

"Yep. They are."

"So, any news?"

"Bud, you're just back from an incredible trip almost half way around the world, and you're asking me if *I've* got any news?"

"Just normal stuff, you know? How's *this* fella been, eh?" Bud and Marty were smiling at each other—I swear.

"He's been a very good boy, haven't you?" Marty all but nodded. "And I shall miss him when he goes. If ever his Dad can bear to loan him out, he's got a taker, hasn't he?" Until then, the way that dog owners talked to their pets had always puzzled me, but now it seemed to make perfect sense.

"I'll bear that in mind," said Bud, smiling and petting. He was checking out Marty's wonky ear, which had now fully regrown its fur, like my injured head had regrown its hair—thankfully.

"Oh, I *have* got some news for you," I said, as I poured coffee and dared to put a few cookies on a plate within paw-reach of Marty. "You remember the Widow Tamsin, in Nice?" Bud nodded. "Well, I got an e-mail from Pierre Bertrand this past week."

"Ah, your little French boyfriend," teased Bud.

I gave him a suitably withering look. "Oh, come on, he's sweet—all enthusiasm and wide-eyed innocence . . . And he did save my life, after all. Well, he tells me that Tamsin is to marry a Polish count at Christmas. The ceremony will take place in Gerard's gardens at the Palais. He's off his crutches and will be giving the bride away."

"That'll be fun for them all," replied Bud. "Will she be going up the aisle with one octogenarian, and back down with another?" I swatted at him. "Well, come on, Cait, I know I never met the woman, but your descriptions of her have been . . . shall we say 'caustic'?"

I smiled. "Yeah, I haven't been too kind about her, have I? And I have to admit that when I read Pierre's e-mail, I couldn't help but conjure up a mental image of her swooshing up the aisle, bedecked with finery and jewels, on the arm of some rich, withered old guy. And I don't mean Gerard. Which might be doing her a terrible disservice, but I suspect it's not too far from the truth."

"What about Nazi-boy? Any news yet on when his trial is due to kick off?"

"Pierre said it would likely be in the new year."

"Yep. That's about as long as it takes here," noted Bud. But I knew there was a very different trial on his mind. I decided to carry on.

"Apparently, Beni Brunetti went off to Milan and is now back with his wife: they're making quite a splash in the fashion business there."

"Ah—Beni with the wonderful eyes, and the wonderful teeth, and the wonderful—"

"Bud—don't be mean! You're just making fun of me now. I told you it was just a passing thing. Honestly . . . I'm never going to tell you any secrets ever again if you're going to be like this."

"Yes, you will . . . Marty, down!" Marty's nose was poking above the table top sniffing out the exact location and recipe of the cookies.

"I guess. Unless I save them all up and tell them all to Marty instead. *He* won't make fun of me, will you Marty? No you won't. You're a good boy!" I got up and petted my new friend as I reopened the packet of cookies. A few more wouldn't hurt.

"*I* have a secret to tell Marty," said Bud.

"You can tell me too," I offered.

"Well, it won't be a secret for long, so I guess I might as well. You see, I've been thinking—"

"Don't strain yourself."

"Ha, ha—very funny. No, this is serious, Cait, I've had a lot of time to think over the past couple of weeks . . ."

I sat myself down. Bud deserved my full attention. "Go on," I said.

"Well, I know I had that couple of months off work, but there was such a lot going on that . . . well, I guess I was just doing stuff and not really thinking ahead. You know?" I nodded. I'd seen how he'd been: like an automaton, running at full speed, with no direction. "Well . . . I guess that I've finally had a chance to think about where I go from here. How I carry on without Jan. Not day to day. But for*ever*. You see, Jan was the planner. She was the one looking ahead and mapping out our future. And now . . . well, there's no Jan. So no future. At least, not with her. And being in Egypt really affected me. Like I said, it's all so old, so big . . . and so much about dead people. It made me think that I can probably go one of three ways: I could kill myself and be done with it all—and don't think I haven't thought about it."

"Oh Bud, don't talk like that," I said quietly.

"Don't panic," he replied with a weak smile. "I'm past that now. About three months past it. But you need to know I considered it. Seriously. But let's put it to one side. So, if I'm going to be around for a while, I could live my life as a memorial to Jan and keep on living the life that *we* were going to live, doing what *we* were going to do, alone. And that's what I was trying when I went to Egypt. It had been our dream. And being there without her was just awful. So I don't think that *that* option is going to work. So there's one more alternative, and that's what I've decided to do."

"And that is?"

"I can set about building a new life for myself. I've tried to think about what Jan would have wanted me to do, and I think I'm making the right decisions. They have to be decisions that *I* can live with—not what some-one who's not here might, or might not, agree with. Jan will always be a part of my life—but a part that's missing now. She's gone. So . . ." Bud took a big gulp of coffee and looked me straight in the eye. "I've made some pretty big decisions, Cait. It's time. First, I'm going to resign from the force."

"You're kidding!" It was out before I could stop it.

"No, I'm not. I've put in more than thirty years, and I'll never rise above my current rank. I'll get a good pension and there's Jan's life insurance. It sounds cold, but because of that I can manage to live the rest of my life without working. My heart's not in it any more. And that's not fair—to me, or my colleagues. It could even be dangerous. I could end up putting someone's life at risk."

I didn't know what to say, so I ate another cookie.

"I'm going to sell the apartment and buy some acreage somewhere out toward the Fraser Valley. Marty'll love it, and, who knows, he might even get a friend to play with—there are lots of dogs at the pound who'd like a few acres to run around and a good friend like this fella. Right?" He was talking to Marty again. "When I'm settled, I'd like you to marry me. How about that?"

"What?" I believed my ears, but my brain was telling me he must be speaking to the dog. He *must* be! He couldn't be talking to *me*!

"I want you to marry me, Cait. Do you want to marry me?"

"Me. Marry you? Don't be ridiculous! Of course I won't marry you. Are you mad?"

Bud looked taken aback. "Okay, okay, calm down. I didn't think I was *that* repulsive."

I stood to speak, then I sat down again. I reached for another cookie, but the plate was bare.

"Well, thank *you*!" I exploded at the plate.

I was shaking with anger. And terror. And confusion. Why had he said *that*?

I wasn't sure what I should say next, so I made sure I spoke straight from my heart. I tried to be calm, despite the mass of emotions that were welling up inside me and threatening to take over my tear ducts.

"Bud Anderson, you are *quite* something. First of all, you're not repulsive; that's not what I meant and you know it. You've had women of all sorts chasing after you your whole life because of those blue eyes of yours and that wicked sense of humor you've got, and don't shake your head like that because I know it's true—the guys you work with have *all* told me, so there! And, you know what? You might well be right to leave the force, and even sell the apartment and move on to, literally, pastures new. I'll do whatever I can to help with all that, and be as involved as you like, because we're friends. That's what we are, Bud. We're *friends*. We might be the only real friend the other one has, but that's not a reason to ask me to marry you. *It's not fair!* I'm not made of rubber, Bud. There are only so many times I can 'bounce back,' you know! Everyone seems to assume that 'Cait will always be fine,' but quite often, Cait isn't 'fine.' Quite often Cait puts her trust in people and they let her down. Or Cait lets someone into her life and they just use her. Or Cait falls for someone and they turn out to be a violent, alcoholic scumbag who knocks her around, then winds up dead and she gets the blame. I *cannot* allow myself to be used again, Bud. At some point I have to protect myself. I'm breakable, Bud. I'm more than the fat woman in the pub who's one of the boys. I'm more than a life support system for an intellect. I'm not going to step up and make everything lovely for you by replacing Jan."

"No, no . . . You've got it all wrong—I've said it all wrong. I don't want you to replace Jan!" cried Bud. He looked horrified.

"You might have *said* it all wrong, Bud, but that's not the problem. I've never allowed myself to think of you . . . that way. You were Jan's husband when we met. When Jan died, well, you've spent more time with Marty since then than with me—or anyone else for that matter. *You* might have been thinking about this for two weeks, but I still think of *you* as my *friend* Bud. *Jan's husband*, Bud. I mean, come on, we've never . . . well, we've never *anythinged*! We haven't dated, or held hands, or cuddled, we've never kissed—and we've *certainly* never you-know-what-ed. See? I can't even *say* it! How ridiculous is that? I'm a grown woman, for heaven's sake! A marriage has to be more than two friends settling down together. There have to be feelings, Bud. Feelings."

Bud looked hurt. "Don't you love me? I thought you loved me, Cait. You act as though you do."

And there it was, finally. The Question.

The one that really matters.

Not "Will you marry me?" but "Do you love me?"

It was the time for truth.

"Yes, I love you, Bud. I do. I'm not sure that you love me. No! Ssh. Please. Not in the *right way*. I think that you *believe* you love me. But I also think that there's so much upheaval in your heart and in your life right now that this is the worst possible time to say you're ready to make a commitment to another human being. I'm not even sure you should be getting another dog, let alone a new wife. So don't do this. Please? Don't pull me toward something I don't believe you're ready for. Give us time?"

Bud looked resigned but hopeful. "Okay, I'll give us time, but not too much. Life can be over a lot sooner than we think, as we both know."

I saw red. "That's a *terrible* thing to say! Don't *ever* do that again, Bud! Do *not* hold Jan's death over me, or over 'us' . . . or anyone else, for that matter. That'll never work. You need to cool off, Bud. You need to think about this—no, *we* need to think about this—for a hell of a lot longer than two weeks! It's . . . well, as you can tell . . . it's taken me by surprise." I was beginning to catch my breath, to calm down a little. "I tell you what, Bud: if you still want to, you can ask me to marry you again a year from now. Between now and then, you are absolutely *not* to mention it at all. Not to me, or anyone else. How about that?"

Bud nodded. "A year it is," he said. "And in the meantime . . . ?"

"In the meantime, we'll do . . . well, you know . . . ordinary stuff. We'll be friends, and we can see what feels natural as we go along. Okay?"

"Okay. So, can I kiss you now?" Bud asked very quietly. "Would that feel 'natural'?"

I couldn't help but smile. In fact, I know I was beaming, and almost in tears. And my tummy was churning. That wasn't because of all the cookies. Well, maybe it was a bit.

"I guess . . . I don't really know . . ." I replied.

So we stood, a bit awkwardly; and reached out to each other, quite timidly; and we held each other, for a long time; and then he kissed me.

"We're going to enjoy doing things together we've never done before," said Bud, eventually.

"As always, you're right."

Acknowledgments

MY IMMENSE THANKS TO THE following people: Martin Jarvis and Rosalind Ayres—if they hadn't produced my short story "Dear George" for BBC Radio 4 in 2007, it's unlikely that I'd have found the confidence to write the two volumes of short stories within which Cait was born and developed; Dr. G. Anderson, School of Criminology, Simon Fraser University, BC, who helped me understand the path Cait might have taken to build her career; my friends in the south of France—Monique and Jonas, who allowed me to "use" their apartment, and Anne, my "French connection"—they opened their hearts and homes to me, and showed me a Cote d'Azur I could never have discovered alone; Stephen Halford, BSC, a museum technician and "Victorian naturalist" at Simon Fraser University, BC, who took the time to talk to me about critical elements of my plot; Ruth Linka, and everyone at TouchWood, who gave Cait a chance to live her life and have her adventures; Frances Thorsen of Chronicles of Crime, my editor, who was very gentle with me; and my family and friends, who have supported and encouraged me in so many ways, especially when I have feared that this novel might never be realized.

Born and raised in South Wales, CATHY ACE moved to London after graduation to pursue a career in marketing communications. Since relocating to British Columbia in 2000, she has taught at various universities, and is currently lecturing at Simon Fraser University. Cathy's love of crime fiction began at an early age: she graduated from Nancy Drew to Agatha Christie when she was ten and has never looked back! Cathy makes her home in Maple Ridge, BC, with her husband and beloved Labrador dogs. *The Corpse with the Silver Tongue* is her first novel.